SAVAGE GAMES

BASTARDS OF BOULDER COVE: *BOOK ONE*

USA TODAY BESTSELLING AUTHOR
RACHEL LEIGH

"There is no trap so deadly as the trap you set for yourself."
— **Raymond Chandler**

THE BASTARDS OF BOULDER COVE SERIES IS A REVERSE HAREM ROMANCE WHERE THE MAIN CHARACTER GAINS MULTIPLE LOVE INTERESTS OVER THE COURSE OF THREE BOOKS. PLEASE ADVISE THIS IS A DARK ROMANCE WITH BULLY ELEMENTS.

For permissions contact: rachelleighauthor@gmail.com

ISBN: 978-1-956764-16-1

Cover Design by The Pretty Little Design Co.

Editing by Fairest Reviews and Editing Services

Proofreading by Rumi Khan

www.rachelleighauthor.com

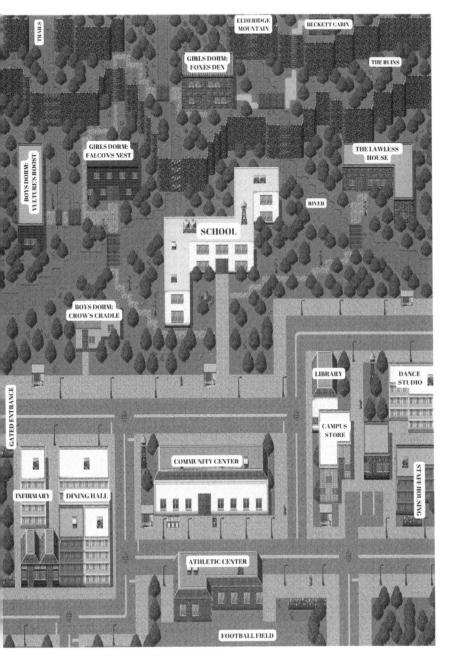

BLUE BLOODS

THE ELDERS

SAMSON CROSS	MIKAH SAINT	GERALD COLE	HENRY VANCE	ABBOTT SUNDER
NEL CROSS (ANNA JAVIS)	SEBASTION SAINT (CARIAN LUMURE)	CAIN COLE (BRIDGETTE TALVIN)	ASPEN VANCE (HARPER JETT)	NIKOLAI SUNDER (LUNA NYX)
RILEY CROSS				SCARLETT SUNDER

THE LAWLESS

NEO SAINT	JAGGER COLE	CREW VANCE

ORDER OF HEIRARCHY

THE ELDERS
THE LAWLESS
ACE
PUNK
ROOK

PLAYLIST

Listen on Spotify
Prologue: Bad Blood by Taylor Swift
1: Bittersweet Symphony by The Verve
2: Lovely by Billie Eilish
3: Guys My Age by Hey Violet
4: Push by Matchbox 20
5: You Broke Me First by Tate McRae
6: Without Me by Halsey
7: High by The Chainsmokers
8: She hates Me by Puddle of Mud
9: Monsters by Shinedown
10: Broken by Evanescence
11: I hate You by Three Days Grace
12: Bad at Love Halsey
13: It's Been Awhile by Staind
14: How's it gonna be by Third Eye Blind
15: Love Hate Relationship by Trapt
16: Comedown by Bush
17: Graveyard by Halsey
18: Therefore I am by Billie Eilish
19: Outside by Stained
20: Drift and Die by Puddle of Mud

21: Torn to Pieces by Pop Evil
22: Thing For You by Hinder
23: Shimmer by Fuel
24: Light it up by Fall Out Boy
25: Far Behind by Candlebox
26: The Reason by Hoobastank
27: If you could only see by Tonic
Epilogue: Shiver by Coldplay

CHECK OUT THE PINTEREST BOARD

PROLOGUE
SCARLETT

TEN YEARS Old

"Ready or not, here I come." Crew's voice carries down the hall, and as soon as it hits my ears, a mixture of excitement and nervousness swims in my belly.

I cover my mouth, trying not to laugh, but spurts of the concealed sound spit into my palm.

"Caught ya," I hear him say, and Jagger grumbles in defeat.

One down. Three to go.

The last to be found gets to pick our next game. Of all the years playing hide-and-seek at the Aima Hall—a place where all our Society meetings are held—I've never won.

There are so many times they'd find Maddie first and pretend they didn't see her, just so I didn't win. Being the good friend she is, Maddie's forfeited the loss more times than I can count, but it's not the same. I want the win because I earned it, not because someone gave it to me.

These jerks will never let me have it, though. Especially if it came down to me or Maddie winning—they'd always choose her.

With my legs hugged to my chest, I scoot deeper into the closet, hiding myself among janitor buckets and mopheads.

Shadows of footprints dance through the light, shining under the door, and my heart beats superfast. I place my hand over my chest, hoping no one can hear it.

I feel like I'm going to pee myself, but suddenly, the guys hearing me laugh is the least of my worries.

"Scar," Crew sings, "where are you?"

"Bet she's in the basement," Jagger says.

"No way. She's too much of a scaredy-cat to go down there by herself," Neo tells him. I didn't even know they found Neo already. Maybe he gave up, just to help them find me.

No surprise there.

More footprints graze the light. Coming and going. Stopping and moving. When their movements stop directly in front of the closet door, my stomach tightens.

I should just give myself up now.

"I bet she's in here," Neo says while the others urge him to open the door.

Before I can move—be it to scoot farther back or to come out of hiding—the closet door flies open and a beam of light shines in.

My heart is racing and I'm clenching my muscles to stop what's coming, but it's no use. I gasp when warmth trickles down my leg.

Oh no.

My entire body flushes with heat and I'd love nothing more than to disappear through the side wall and never return.

"Found ya," Crew beams eagerly, "you lose again."

What do I do? What do I do?

"Yep. I lost. You can go find Maddie now."

Crew comes deeper into the closet, then reaches over and

flips the light switch. His eyes immediately land on the puddle beneath me.

I shiver and shake and internally scream as a single tear rolls down my face. I can't even look at him. Instead, I tuck my chin to my chest, hugging my knees, and pinch my eyes closed.

The clicking of the light switch has my eyes shooting back open, noticing the closet is now dark, only the light from the hall shining into my hiding place.

"Yeah. Let's go find Maddie," Crew tells them.

My heart swells and I crack a smile, though he doesn't see it because he's already out the door.

That smile instantly drops when Neo barges in all broody and flips the light on again. Crew tries to grab his arm, rambling words about finding Maddie, but it's no use.

Neo knows.

"You guys have to see this." He laughs. "Scar peed herself."

"Just leave her alone," Crew tells him, but Neo doesn't let up as he stands there pointing and laughing.

More tears fall and I wish I could run out of here and never look at their faces again, but I can't move because it'll only make things worse.

"I didn't pee!" I shout. "The mop bucket tipped over." Neo sees right through my lies; I can tell by the way he's looking at me.

"Liar," Neo says, "you peed your pants and now you're trying to hide it."

Jagger stands off to the side with his head down. Not that I expect him to help me. I didn't even expect Crew to try. Standing up to Neo is something neither of them does often, if ever.

"Gimme your phone," Neo says to Jagger, holding his hand out to his side.

"I don't have it. I'm grounded from it for a week, remember?"

Neo looks at Crew. "Do you have yours?"

Crew hesitates, looking at me, and I shake my head. *Please don't do it.*

"Dude. Give me your phone. I gotta take a picture of this." He hesitates some more, warranting a shout from Neo. "Now!"

Looking at me, Crew reaches into the pocket of his jeans.

All I can do is sit there while Neo flashes the phone camera in my face, laughing his butt off. Because Neo gets whatever he wants.

But he's the only one laughing. Jagger doesn't make a sound while Crew looks at me and mouths the words, "I'm sorry."

If I wasn't so choked up right now, I'd tell Crew I don't forgive him. Because even if he tried to help me, he always cowers to Neo—they both do—no matter who gets hurt in the process.

CHAPTER
ONE
SCARLETT

Eighteen Years Old

My stomach twists in tiny knots as I pull open one of the glass double doors to the upscale long-term care facility where my best friend lives. I've been coming here twice a week for over a year, but it never gets easier.

The reflection from the sun hitting the crystal chandelier overhead has me blinking away the bright beams of light.

"Good Morning, Scarlett," Tammy, one of Maddie's nurses, says as the door closes behind me.

With my coffee in hand, I approach her. "How's she doing today?"

Tammy presses her lips together firmly and shakes her head. "Not great. Her blood pressure's been pretty high."

"Oh, no." After my last visit, I was hopeful she was taking small steps in the right direction, but it seems like every time she does, she takes two steps back.

"Hopefully, your visit will calm her down a bit."

"If only," I say, gripping my coffee and focusing on the

warmth in the palm of my hand. "I'm here to say goodbye for a bit. I'm leaving for school three hours away this evening."

Guilt has been gnawing at my insides since my parents decided for me. I hate that I have to do this. I shouldn't be leaving Essex. I shouldn't be leaving my best friend. If she could talk, she'd give me a massive amount of shit for not fighting my parents on my attendance at Boulder Cove Academy. Maddie and I always swore we'd stay in public school together, and we never swayed from our decision. Until I had no choice.

Tammy's eyes widen in surprise. "Three hours away? Wow! Hopefully, you'll be able to get away from time to time to visit."

Chewing on my bottom lip, I shake my head. "Not until Christmas. They're pretty strict over there."

"Well, make the most of today, then. She'll be here when you return."

A smile parts my lips. "Thanks, Tammy."

I continue walking, passing by the kitchen that smells delicious, like cinnamon rolls and sugar cookies. This place isn't your typical nursing home—it's a mansion-sized home in a gated community with high-paid staff who treat the residents like family. Maddie, being in a coma, doesn't require much care, but she's comfortable here.

I knock my knuckles on the open door, putting on my cheerful face as I enter Maddie's room. "Good morning, beautiful."

She can't hear me or see me, but I see her.

Leaning down, I kiss her cheek, then set my coffee on the bedside table. "I heard you had a rough night."

If she could talk, I know she'd tell me all about it. Just like she used to. We talked to each other about everything.

I reach into my pocket and pull out my phone to open our playlist. "Are you ready?"

I tap Play on the screen and "Bitter Sweet Symphony" by The Verve plays through the Bluetooth speaker I put in her window when she moved in over a year ago. It's one of our favorite songs from a movie we used to watch weekly.

"What do you think? Side braids today?"

She doesn't respond, but sometimes I pretend she does. In this case, I imagine she's beaming with excitement and screaming *yes*.

I grab a brush from my bag and pull the hair ties off my wrist.

My hand sweeps under her head gently and I part a chunk of her hair to the right side. It won't be perfect, but it's not about perfection. It's about spending time with my best friend.

"So, I have some news," I begin. "You remember how I told you they expelled me from Clearwater the last week of school? It was so bad, Maddie. There was no way in hell I could have talked my way out of that one. Someone parked my car in Principal Gunther's driveway with a gas can in the trunk. Anyway, I ran into his stuck-up daughter last week and she got all up in my face. She was all, *you tried to burn my house down. Blah. Blah. Blah.* Which you and I both know I didn't do. They did this to hurt me. A girl can only take so much, so I head-butted the bitch and broke her nose." I laugh, but it's not at all funny. The whole situation is beyond fucked up.

I feel like an ass for even rehashing this story, but it's necessary to explain why I'm leaving. Still weaving the braid, I get to the point of the story. "Anyway. Two school expulsions in one school year, topped with all the other things they did to make me out to be an insurgent, and my parents are sending me off to BCA." I hold my breath as the words leave my mouth,

7

hands held still with the wispy ends of Maddie's brunette hair wrapped around my fingers.

One of her monitors goes haywire and I see that her blood pressure is up again. When it doesn't stop, I drop the braid and rest my head on her shoulder, trying to calm her. "It's okay, Maddie. Everything is okay."

We've known for a while that Maddie's brain is still functioning, and on the off chance she can hear me when I talk to her, I keep doing it. I tell her everything as if she's my own personal diary. Moments like this, I'm certain she hears what I tell her, though we can't be sure.

The machine continues to beep as her heart rate spikes, too. "Calm down, babe." I walk around to the other side of the bed, peeking my head out to see if one of the nurses is coming, but I don't see anyone.

I panic, but not because I'm worried about leaving—because I'm worried about *her*.

Tears prick at the corners of my eyes as I watch my best friend lie there without a voice.

Why? Why her? Why this sweet girl who had a bright future ahead of her? Why not me?

The next thing I know, Tammy and another staff member rush into the room. "You'll need to leave."

"I can calm her down. Please, just let me talk to her."

"I'm sorry, hun. You can return tomorrow and hope for a better day.

"But..."

Tomorrow I'll be gone.

I take a step back, watching as they adjust the monitors and the cuff on Maddie's arm. Tears slide down my cheeks and I die a little inside, just like I do each time I have to leave her here alone.

CHAPTER

TWO

SCARLETT

"You're sure you can't change his mind?" I whisper to my mom. My eyes stay pinned to the back of the driver's seat, where my dad sits with his fingers locked around the steering wheel.

Her hand squeezes mine from where she sits beside me in the back seat, thumb grazing my knuckles. "It's only eight months until you graduate, then the future is yours."

"Yeah, right," I mumble under my breath. The future has never been mine. It's always belonged to the Blue Bloods.

Mom drops my hand and tucks my hair behind my ear. "You're going to do great here, honey."

"I'm not so sure about that." My voice is soft, as it always is with her. No matter how many mistakes I make, my mom is always in my corner. Dad is, too, but it's different with my mom. She's warm and gentle in a way that makes me feel safe and content.

"You'll check in on Maddie, right? Make sure she's doing okay?"

"Of course. You know how much we love Maddie. She'll be fine, as will you."

Dad shifts the car into park, rests his hand on the back of the passenger seat, and turns to face me. "Are you ready for this?"

"No," I spit out on impulse, "but it seems I have to be."

"Well, honey. You made your choices, and this is where they brought you. Can't say I'm sorry about it. You were meant to be here. The Academy is going to reshape you, and when you leave, you'll have a newfound appreciation about your place in The Society."

Maybe I want to reshape myself without this place. Instead of saying the words, I nod in response. My fate is sealed. I'll be getting out of this car, along with my bags, and staying here, no matter how much I don't want to.

Dad turns back around and pulls the lever to pop open the trunk. Once he's out, he pulls out my bags and sets them down on the sidewalk beside the car. Mom squeezes my leg and gives me a comforting smile before opening her door and getting out, so I do the same.

I'm looking up at the massive building, then to the smaller ones surrounding it when Mom holds out her hand. "Phone, Scarlett."

I look down at her open palm, moping. "Seriously, Mom?"

"Rules are rules. We've told you many times they're not allowed."

Reaching into the back pocket of my jeans, I pull it out and plant it in her hand. "Who made the stupid no phone rule? How's anyone in this day and age supposed to survive without a phone or the internet?" Not that it matters. I snuck my own untraceable phone for emergencies in one of my bags. There's no way in hell I was coming to this desolate place without one.

"That changed shortly after my and your mom's attendance here." Mom and Dad look at each other and it feels like the air has thickened—almost as if they're sharing an unspoken secret. "It's best to avoid outside communication during your stay." His tone shifts abruptly as he waves his arms out toward campus. "I mean, look at this natural beauty. You don't need the internet when you have this in your backyard."

He's right there; it is an impressive view. Rolling hills and sharp peaks that kiss the sky. A mix of greens, while autumn colors of fire red and burnt orange manifest in the distance. It's something straight off a postcard, but the Academy itself is nothing I want to write home about. Therefore, I grumble at his words.

A guy interrupts Dad's spiel about this outlandish place, joining us with a broad smile on his face. He's about the same height as Crew and Jagger—roughly six-foot—with a smaller frame. Not skin and bones, but also not muscled and toned. He looks young, and I assume he's a student here since he's wearing a teal polo shirt with the Boulder Cove Academy logo stitched on the pocket. "Good evening," he says, extending a hand to my dad, "I'm Elias, and I'll be Scarlett's tour guide."

My head immediately shakes no while Mom gives me a 'knock it off' look. "I appreciate that, but I'll be fine."

"Scarlett," Dad scoffs, "you really should have someone show you around. It's easy to get lost here."

"Dad," I say with contempt in my tone, "I'll be perfectly fine. Besides, I have a roommate, and I'm sure she'll show me the ropes."

Dad blows out a heavy breath. "Have it your way."

Elias nods in response, eyebrows raised. "Okay, then. I guess I'll just load up the cart and leave your things outside your dorm room."

"Thank you very much, Elias," I say, kindly.

11

Hugging myself, I look around and take it all in. It's much colder than I expected. I credit the chill in the air to the abundance of trees and mountains hiding the sun. It's dark here, almost eerily so.

Chills shimmy down my spine as soon as the car door latches shut. With them comes a weight on my chest that's suffocating.

I never intended to attend Boulder Cove Academy, let alone enroll for my final year of high school. Most of the kids who come here do so during their junior year. I've always done things ass-backward, though, so why should that change now?

"This is where we say goodbye." Mom pulls me in for a hug, a tear falling down her cheek and onto the shoulder of my black Led Zeppelin tee shirt.

I'd love more than anything for them to come up to my room and help me settle in, but it's against the rules—no communication with anyone outside of the Academy during our stay here. That's just one on a long list of ridiculous rules. I'm sure I'll break a few of them during my time here. Who am I kidding? I'll end up breaking them all and getting me and my family abolished from the whole damn Society.

Now, there's an idea.

Mom steps back, and I place my hands on her shoulders, looking her in the eye. "I'll be fine." I'm not sure who I'm trying to convince, her or myself.

Her head lifts, and she nods, wiping away the moisture from her eyes. "You will. And like your dad said, this is a good thing. You're going to come out of this stronger than ever." Her eyes slide over to my dad, who's helping Elias load my bags onto a luggage cart. Nodding to the left, she takes my hand and pulls me around the car. "Listen, Scarlett." Her hushed tone is unnerving. "Find your person. Stick with them. Never leave the dorms alone at night. Respect the staff and..." She stops, lips pursed.

The contempt in her tone, along with her worrisome expression, has me on edge. "And what?"

"Be wary of The Lawless. It doesn't matter that you know them outside of the Academy, they will not be the same people here. Times have changed since your dad and I attended, but the Lawless know their power and they use it to their advantage."

I almost laugh. *Times have changed?* No, Dear Mother, times have not changed as much as you'd like to think. The new Lawless—aka Crew, Jagger, and Neo—have always known they'd take the throne at BCA, considering their parents were also at the top of the Society's hierarchy, along with my dad. All of our dads grew up together, the same way Crew, Jagger, and Neo have. I've always been the girl in their way. Even Maddie was accepted by them—then again, she is part of the Saint family—but for some reason, they've always viewed me as a threat.

Over the years, their egos have only inflated. They're also the reason I fought to avoid this place. That is until they did everything in their power to get me here. Unfortunately, they got what they wanted.

"Don't worry about me, Mom. I can handle the Lawless."

A smile parts her lips. "I don't doubt that for a minute. You're one of the strongest girls I know, Scarlett, and you're destined for great things."

If only that were true. When you're made out to be something you're not and everyone believes it, you start to believe it, too.

Crew, Jagger, and Neo are the reason for my demise. They had this diabolical plan to get me to the Academy, so they could toy with me. They've never liked me because of their jealousy of my friendship with Maddie—even when we were kids, they'd find ways to prove I was beneath them, especially Neo. Maddie's loyalty lay with me, and he hated it. After her accident, his hatred for me spread and grew like an invasive weed, making itself comfortable in every crack and crevice of my life.

Even miles apart, Neo tried to screw with me, while using his minions to do his dirty work. The worst of it started with a cheat sheet for our exams they shared to my social media sophomore year. When my punishment for that wasn't good enough, they hit harder. A couple weeks later, three thousand dollars' worth of stolen school property was found in my locker. That was my first high school, the one I attended with them and Maddie. I was expelled the next day. As for punishment by law enforcement, my parents handled it.

In a matter of days, I went from being a socialite to a shrinking violet. The thing is, I sort of like dead flowers, and no one will ever change who I am or what I intend to become.

My second expulsion, at the end of my junior year, was the fire, which brought me here.

Dad returns and reaches into the trunk of the car, pulling out my snowboarding bag. "Take this."

My head immediately shakes no. "I won't be needing that."

He tries again. "Just take it. You never know when you might need it. The mountains here are a dream for someone with your skills on the slopes."

My gaze is lost on the mountains over his shoulder. They might be a dream, but they aren't my dream. Not anymore.

Dad drops the bag to his side and blows out a heavy breath before disappearing behind me.

"I'll miss you," Mom says, wrapping her arms around my neck for one last goodbye.

"I'll miss you, too."

Dad and I say our goodbyes, and he apologizes again for not getting me into a better dorm room. Apparently, since I'm coming in late, the rooms were full and no matter how big of a donation he made, my accommodations couldn't be upgraded. I'll be staying in a simple dorm, much like a college one, with a communal bathroom and kitchen.

Before I know it, I'm standing there alone, in front of the massive building, feeling like the ground could swallow me up and no one would even know I was gone.

I'M LOST. I've been here twenty minutes and I'm already fucking lost.

Pinching the map in both hands, I try to pinpoint my location, but it's useless. I don't know what this means. The Foxes' Den is the girls' dormitory I'll be staying in, which I should have run into at least a quarter mile back.

A drop of wetness hits my cheek, and I curse Mother Nature. "Dammit!" I dig the toe of my black Converse shoe into the dirt path, kicking up soggy leaves and rocks while throwing a little hissy fit.

Everything is fine. I've got this.

Okay. I passed Falcons' Nest, which is the other girls' dorm, and it looks like a luxurious mansion.

I stayed on the path as the map instructed me to do.

Then I took a left.

"Son of a bitch." I walk forward a few steps until I see another dorm. Only the wooden plaque out front does not say Foxes' Den. Instead, it says Vultures' Roost, which is one of the boys' dorms.

I was never supposed to go left. I should have gone right. Dammit, I should have just accepted Elias's help.

Stupid, stupid maze of a campus!

Spinning around to backtrack and try this again, I come face to face with a couple of girls wearing teal plaid skirts with matching polos and knee-high socks.

"Lost already?" the tall blonde says as she pops open an umbrella. She's like something straight out of a Cosmo magazine. At least three inches taller than me, tan legs, and flawless skin surrounding her bright blue eyes.

"I...yeah, I think I am." I squint at her. "Do I know you?"

"No. But we know you. Everyone does. You're Scarlett Sunder. Forgive me for my lack of manners." She extends her hand. "I'm Melody, and this is my best friend, Hannah."

I give her hand a subtle shake while my eyes skate from Melody to Hannah. The two girls are like night and day. One tall and blonde, the other short and brunette, but both are wearing the same cringey uniform that I'll soon be wearing myself. "How do you know my name?"

"Everyone's been expecting you, Scarlett. When word got around that a newbie from the Aima Chapter was coming in late, we were all beside ourselves. A girl who knows the Lawless, up close and personal." She claps her hands together excitedly. "We're all expecting some juicy secrets."

"Oh. I don't know them well, so there's nothing to tell." It's a lie. The truth is, I know them far more than I care to admit. How could I not? We grew up in the same chapter and attended all the same functions.

I know Jagger is an adrenaline junkie and always seeks out a thrill, whether it's climbing the tallest mountain or hooking up with the girl who shot him down—not that it happens often. He's a catch in the eyes of the female population.

Crew is the one that everyone gravitates toward because he's witty and cute—at least, that's what he wants everyone to believe. I used to think he was one of the good ones, but he proved me wrong there.

Then we have Neo—dark, mysterious, and the biggest asshole of the bunch.

Our Society is comprised of over a hundred chapters all over the nation. Each chapter has anywhere from a dozen to three dozen families. Our chapter, Aima, is on the smaller scale, but one of the more well known, considering the founder of The Society was an Aima.

Melody gives me a look, as if I'm holding back pertinent information. "Oh, I'm sure you've got some stories to tell." She adjusts her bag on her shoulder while holding tight to the umbrella she doesn't bother offering to her friend. "We have to get going, but we'll see you tonight?"

I sweep away the rain dropping on my arms. "Tonight?"

"The Gathering." She says the words like I'm supposed to know what the hell she's talking about. When I shake my head, she continues, "The annual kickoff to the school year party at the Ruins. Everyone attends."

"Oh," I click my tongue on the roof of my mouth, "hard pass. Large crowds aren't really my thing."

"Scarlett," she drags out my name with a big smile on her face, "you just have to come. It's the perfect chance to get to know your tribe. After all, that's what this place is all about." Her eyes dance around the forest. "Embracing our privileges as Blue Bloods. Learning the ins and outs in order to lead the next generation."

Embracing our privileges? More like being pushed into a pit of flames. I didn't ask for this. I'm here because my parents forced me to attend. I know my future rests in the hands of the Society, but it doesn't mean I'm ready to embrace it—or that I ever will be.

Giving up the fight, I tell the girl what she wants to hear.

All I want to do is find my room, make my bed, and lie in it for the next eight months. "I guess I'll see you later, then."

"Wonderful." She turns to walk away, Hannah following. "Oh," she hollers over her shoulder, "Foxes' Den is that way." She points a finger in the opposite direction I was heading.

Folding up the map in my hand, I say, "Thanks."

She seemed nice. The brunette, that is. Quiet is my type. The blonde was as fake as the smile I put on my face. Now let's hope my new roommate is also on the anti-social side and the school year will be smooth sailing.

CHAPTER
THREE

SCARLETT

I'M BREATHING a sigh of relief when I see a large building, similar to the main one where my parents dropped me off. It resembles more of a Roman cathedral than a campus dormitory, but I dig the vibe. Ivy vines climb up the sides of the five-story building and there are stained-glass windows scattered all over, each one etched with its own design. A wooden plaque out front has the words *Foxes' Den* engraved on it.

Home sweet home.

I walk up the four brick steps to the large wooden door and pull the U-shaped handle. It's a heavy door and I'm grateful I didn't have to lug my bags here myself.

Once inside, I look around, taking in the wide-open space. From the wall of stainless-steel mailboxes on the left, to the large stairwell in front of me, all the way up to the five indoor balconies. The vaulted ceilings occupy a stained-glass skylight that lets in only a hint of dim lighting due to the branches that hang over the building.

I'm making my way up to the second floor, when a few girls come jogging down the stairs. They're all wearing the same

BCA uniforms Melody and Hannah had on. Those skirts will definitely take some getting used to. I don't think I've worn a dress or skirt since I was like seven years old.

The girls all stop simultaneously and look at me like I'm an alien invading their space. I stop, too, lifting a brow and silently asking if they have something to say.

Yet, they say nothing at all. That is until I keep jogging up the stairs and the whispers begin. I hear them loud and clear, though.

"That's her. The new girl."

"Did you see what she's wearing?"

"Maybe she's a lesbian."

Cackle. Cackle. Cackle.

I loudly blow out a hefty hee-haw, mocking them without even turning to look at their expressions. It immediately shuts them up.

Screw what they think. I have my own sense of style and I like it. I prefer worn shoes and holey jeans. Garbage band tee shirts and no makeup. I'm not afraid to get my hands dirty or run down the sidewalk with bare feet. My point is, I'm not a girly girl and I never will be. No amount of insults will ever change that.

Once I'm at the second level, I step off the staircase. As I walk down the hall, I search for my bags that should be outside my door.

The rooms are spread out, which leads me to believe they are spacious. Some of the doors are decorated with cutesy little doormats outside them. I can already pinpoint which rooms belong to cheerleaders because of the paper-cut pom-poms taped to the door.

I come up to a door that is decked out in pink. Like, a lot of pink. It looks like a unicorn had a massive case of diarrhea in the room and it exploded all over the door. There's a dozen little pink flamingos spread from top to bottom, glittery cut-out hearts, and...lips. I run my finger over one of them, wiping up a waxy residue. No shit. Someone actually kissed their door like twenty times with hot pink lipstick. That's demented.

I wipe my fingers on my jeans and keep walking, observing the numbers. This is 211. I'm in...210. But my bags aren't there. I turn around and my insides freeze.

Fuck.

I'm in the unicorn shit room.

My stomach twists into knots. I don't do sweet. Maybe I can switch rooms. There is just no way I can...

My train of thought is interrupted when the door of room 210 flies open.

"Heyyyy," a cute girl with bouncy, blonde curls, wearing a pink dress with a jean jacket, comes barging out of the room. In two seconds flat, she's in front of me. "You must be Scarlett." Cotton candy floods my senses, and I feel light-headed. "I'm Riley. Your new roommate."

"Yay," I drawl. "So...nice to meet you." I take a step back, offering her my hand.

She looks down at my offering and snickers. "Silly girl. We're practically besties now." She throws herself into my arms while I throw up a little in my mouth.

Still wrapped in her arms, as if we're old friends, I pat my hands gently on her back. "Okay." I attempt to break free from her hold on me, but she only hugs me tighter. "All right then. Yup. This is nice."

Pat. Pat. Pat.

Finally, Riley takes a step back but keeps her hands on my shoulders. "What is the name of your perfume? I have to try it."

"Umm." I swallow down the saliva pooling in my mouth. "Dove bar soap."

Her head tilts slightly to the left, and she lifts a smile. "Well, it smells magnificent."

This has to be a joke. Punishment over. I've learned my lesson. No more cigarettes, no more pot, and no more fights.

"Let's get you settled in, roomie. I brought your stuff inside for you." Riley takes my hand in hers and tugs me toward the dorm room—*our room*—that we will share for the next eight months. "We have so much to talk about. Do you have a boyfriend? A girlfriend? Because I'm totally cool with either."

"Umm, no. No boyfriend or girlfriend. No friends at all, for that matter."

Her eyebrows pinch together as she searches me for humor. "You're funny. We're going to get along just fine."

Oh, joy!

She keeps tugging me along until we're inside the room. It's a nice size, which is good. Half of the room is decked out in the same color as Riley's personality—pink. Her twin-size bed is clad in a shaggy pink comforter that matches the square rug beside it. Her walls are decorated with flamingos, which I take to be her favorite. There's a large corkboard hanging on the wall overtop a desk with pictures of her and what appears to be some of her friends. The entire space looks super happy.

Then there's my side. A white, wood-framed twin bed with a gray sheet. On top of it are my neatly-pressed school uniforms. Aside from the bed, there's only a four-drawer dresser and a simple, white study desk. Unfortunately, it will not get much better because my belongings are minimal.

Bending at the waist, I pick up my larger bag and fling it onto the bed then pull out some of the mundane items I brought with me. A black-and-white skull tapestry to iron out and hang on the wall over my bed. A retro tabletop moon lamp. And some white string lights.

"Once we get you settled in, I'll give you a tour and show

you where the bathroom and common room is. There's a little kitchenette down the hall with a microwave and refrigerator. Put your name on *everything*," she enunciates. "A few of the girls in this dormitory are royal bitches."

Well, she swears so there's that.

"So, where are you from?" Riley asks, as I pull my bedding out of one of my bags and fluff the black comforter on my bed, letting it drop flat.

"Essex, here in Colorado. It's about three hours away. You?"

She pops a piece of gum in her mouth and rolls the wrapper with her fingers. "Really? I'm in Verdemont—Osto Chapter. About three hours from Essex."

"Small world."

"Very small." Riley crisscrosses her legs and rests her hands in her lap. "Why'd you come during the final year? Why not junior year like everyone else?"

I smooth my hand over my satin comforter before tossing my *Nightmare Before Christmas* throw pillows at the head of the bed. "It's a long story. I never planned to come at all, but my parents were persistent."

"Why didn't you plan to attend? This place helps to build who we will become. How could you willingly miss out on such a fundamental part of our future?"

Don't comment. Don't react. Just keep your mouth shut.

"I guess that's why I'm here now. To embrace all that the Academy offers for my future as a Blue Blood." I turn back around and throw up in my mouth for the second time since I arrived.

"You're about to get the full experience here. The grounds are breathtaking. Mountains, the river, endless trails. The only thing that could make it better is if we were in Falcons' Nest. Their dorm rooms are much better than ours. Private bathrooms and an in-room kitchenette. But beggars can't be choosers."

My parents mentioned not being able to get me better accommodations due to my late enrollment, but I'm perfectly fine without the added luxuries. One thing I swore I'd never become is an entitled brat.

"Speaking of embracing. There's a party tonight to kick off the new school year. You totes have to come."

Did she really just say totes?

"So I've heard. Unfortunately, I already have plans tonight that involve me and my new book boyfriend." I hold up my closed Kindle Paperwhite, then drop onto my freshly made bed.

She frowns. "It wasn't a question, really. Everyone attends."

I reach into my suitcase and pull out a family photo of me, Mom, and Dad at a ski resort in Aspen. That was a good day.

"Which is exactly why I won't." I turn around to face her, feeling a tad guilty for being such a downer. "Look, Riley. You seem like a sweet girl and I think we'll get along great, but I'm sort of a loner. Don't take it personally. I'm awkward as fuck and put my foot in my mouth far too often. It's best this way. I promise."

I leave out the fact that socializing with me in any way will only put a target on her back.

"You're still here, though. Which says a lot, considering last year I went through four roommates before they even unpacked...in one day."

My eyes pop wide open. "One day?"

"Mmhmm. Apparently, I'm too much. Crazy, right? I mean, I like loud colors and have a high-pitched squeal, but that's who I've always been. I've tried to change, but in the end, I decided to just be me."

That's it. I'm officially a bitch.

Bent over my bag of clothes, I exhale a heavy breath before I straighten my back. Slow steps lead me across the room to Riley's bed, where I take a seat beside her. "I don't like loud noises, large groups, or bright colors, but don't change for anyone. Especially me."

Her mouth curls upward as she fidgets with the gum wrapper. "I hate the quiet, ripped jeans, the color black, and," she glances at my side of the room, "freaky skulls. But I don't think you should change either."

I smile back at her. "I think we'll be just fine."

Her arms fly around my neck before I can react and I'm squeezed so hard, all the air expels from my lungs. "We're going to be perfect." She squeezes harder, and I could only be so lucky to pass out.

"Okay. That's enough." I gasp for air. "That's a big hug. Okay. You can let go now."

Riley releases her hold on me and we both laugh until the awkward moment is interrupted by a knock on the door.

I jump off Riley's bed and head back over to my side to finish unpacking my clothes, placing them in the drawers of my dresser.

Riley peeps out the hole in the door, and mumbles, "Oh no."

"Who is it?" I ask, folding my black Seascape Snow-boarding Club shirt and tucking it into the second drawer.

I'm grabbing another shirt from my bag when Riley backs away from the door slowly. "Okay. Remain calm. Everything is fine."

I chuckle. "What are you going on about? Just open the door."

"Scarlett." Her tone is fretful. "It's them. Or him. One of them. They've never come to my room. Why is he here?"

She's in full-blown panic mode and now clutching my arm as if I'm expected to save her from the monster in the hall.

"Anyone here?" A masculine voice hovers outside the door. *Knock. Knock. Knock.*

"What is the matter with you?" I chuckle again. "It's just a boy." I take a step toward the door, but Riley grabs my arm.

"Not just any boy. It's one of them—the Lawless."

Ah. Now I get it. One of the chosen ones everyone must fear. *Screw that.* I jerk my arm away from her, grinning as I cross the room and rip the door open.

Face to face with one of my three enemies, I press my hand to the doorframe, not allowing him to enter, if that was his plan. "What the hell do you want?"

"Scarlett!" Riley bellows, shuffling to my side. Her fingers are back to being wrapped around my arm as she smiles nervously at our guest. "Ignore her. She's new."

Once again, I jerk my arm away from her and hold my stance, not intimidated whatsoever by this asshole's presence.

Standing in front of me is the infamous Jagger Cole. Drop-dead gorgeous, sun-kissed skin, and the lightest brown eyes I've ever seen. Seems he's gotten some ink since I last saw him. He's now sporting a full sleeve with various designs, all black with some red shading. He looks good. But he's also one of the biggest douchebags in existence. He's the type of guy who will suck you in with his good looks and charm, then spit you out and watch as everyone stomps all over you.

"Well, well, well, I see you've found me."

"Good to see you again, Scar."

"It's Scarlett. And I wish I could say the same, but I'd prefer a root canal over whatever conversation is about to be had."

Riley takes a step back, analyzing the situation.

"Just came to welcome an old friend to the Academy. As a

member of the Lawless, it's my sworn obligation to befriend all that enter."

I spit out a laugh. "As if you even know what a friend is."

"I do. In fact, I happen to have two of the best. You remember them, right? Crew and Neo."

"Oh, I remember them all right. How could I forget? After all, you three jackasses are the reason I'm at this hellhole."

"Come on, babe." His fingers brush across my cheek, but I swat his hand away, still bracing my right hand on the doorframe.

"Don't touch me!" I grit out. "And *never* call me be 'babe' again."

"Isn't it time we put the past in the past? It's a new day and I'm here with a peace offering." His honey eyes slide down my body, landing on my chest. The corner of his lip lifts in a smirk, causing my stomach to stew with heat.

I instantly drop my hand from the door and cross my arms over my chest, knowing that the hand-ripped V in my tee shirt shows more skin than I'd like him to see. "Thanks, but no thanks. Any offering from you comes with a price I'm not willing to pay."

"Do you two know each other?" Riley points between us, standing off to the side while taking all of this in.

"No," I spit out at the same time Jagger says, "Yes."

"They don't know me at all. Not anymore." I go to close the door, but Jagger presses his hand to it, stopping me from shutting it any farther.

His fingers rake through his light-brown hair. "There's a party tonight and your presence is required."

I swallow hard, trying to hold myself together. I will not let any of these boys get the best of me. "Oh yeah? By whom? You?"

27

"By all the Lawless. Keep in mind, you're on our turf now and what we want, we get."

Laughter climbs up my throat, spilling out more violently than I intended. "Well, you can tell the rest of the Lawless I said to suck my dick."

Jagger puffs out a breath, his eyes locked on mine. "You have a dick?"

"Yes, I do." I smirk. "Wanna see it?"

He laughs menacingly. "Nah. I'll just ask my good friend Crew to confirm. He should know."

My cheeks immediately flush with heat and a rage consumes me that I fear I won't be able to control. "Get out!" I shove him from the doorway, causing him to stumble into the hall. "And don't come back unless you want said dick shoved up your ass."

"Oooh. That sounds fun. We'll have to try it. Only, I'm a giver, not a receiver."

"Fuck you, Jagger. And tell your friends I said the same."

"I sure will, Scar." His voice rises to a near shout. "I've got no doubt they'll happily accept the *fucking* invitation."

"Ugh," I huff, slamming the door shut as my blood reaches its boiling point, "God, he's so infuriating." My back presses against the wall and I close my eyes, willing myself to get a grip.

I will not let them get the best of me.

"Oh. My. God." Riley drags out the words. My eyes open as she says, "We have so much to talk about."

I push myself off the wall and walk over to my bed, picking up my bathroom bag. I need to change the subject, and fast. "How about that tour?"

"Are you sure you don't need a minute to cool down and figure out how you're going to get yourself out of this? Talking to a member of the Lawless like that..." She halts. "I'm afraid you just put a target on your back, Scarlett."

She seems genuinely worried, which is cute, considering she has no idea that these guys don't scare me one bit.

I straighten my back and place a forced smile on my face. "I'm not the least bit concerned. Bathroom? Please?"

It's obvious my downplay of the situation has her on edge. Regardless, she pulls the door back open slowly. Her head pops out first and she looks both ways before saying, "He's gone."

"Ya know," I begin as our feet pad down the hardwood of the hallway, "you shouldn't be concerned either. They aren't as badass as they want people to think they are. I mean, anyone can pull cruel pranks and treat people like shit. Doesn't make them superior."

"No. But their position does. Prior to my attendance here, I may not have been *as* intimidated. But being a Rook during junior year was brutal."

"A Rook?" *What the fuck is a Rook?*

Riley looks at me like I should know exactly what she's talking about. "Come on. You have to know what junior year is like here. We all assumed maybe that's why you skipped out and came in late."

My neck twists, brows squeezed together. "I've heard about the hierarchy ladder, but I didn't think it was a big deal."

The hierarchy ladder is supposedly this secret thing among students that the Lawless enacts. Basically, they create cliques for the juniors and the seniors and are assholes to the newcomers. I never paid much attention because I wasn't here for the first year.

"Um. Yeah," Riley drawls. "It's absolutely real. The Ladder Games are savage, which is why most students forgo them. There are a few who choose to play because the stuff they made us do as Rooks was deplorable. For those who do, you play the games for a week, then get moved up to Punk status. It's not much better, but it's definitely not as bad as being a Rook. As long as you don't massively screw up, you enter senior year as an Ace."

"Wait. What does that mean for me? I'm an Ace, right?"

Riley shrugs her shoulders, her attention shifting to the girls' showers as she points them out. There are a dozen small spaces, each separated by a white vinyl curtain. "Hot water doesn't last long, so you'll want to make your showers quick. And always wear shower shoes. I prefer Crocs, but it's your choice."

Ignoring everything she says, I return to the topic of the ranks. "Tell me about these ranks. What exactly do Rooks, Punks, and Aces do?"

Riley reaches into the pocket of her jean jacket and pulls out a bag of Skittles. Ripping off the top, she dumps a few in her hand, then pops them in her mouth. "Well," she says, chomping on her candy, "Rooks are like slaves. It's brutal. We cleaned up after all the parties. I'm talking vomit, feces, dirty condoms. Basically, whatever we're told to do, we do it. It's only for a month, though. As long as you don't screw up, you're automatically promoted to the next rank. Punks also cannot approach Aces and we're pretty much the Lawless's bitches. Whatever they want, we make it happen. Neo makes the smart Punks do all his schoolwork. Pretty sure the guy has never done a single assignment himself."

Riley offers me some Skittles, but I shake my head. "What a douchebag. This isn't school. It's a fucking prison."

"It sucks, but it doesn't last forever. Senior year, we all started out as Aces, as long as we didn't have any strikes against us the prior year. We have it made compared to the juniors."

"So, when do these ranks all take hold?"

"Tonight. It's the reason *everyone* must attend the Gathering. Including you."

"And what about you? Did you play the games?"

Riley winces. "No way! I'd rather be someone's bitch for a month than subject myself to that level of cruelty. People have literally died playing those games. Two, to be exact. Possibly three. One guy went missing, like, eighteen years ago, and was deemed dead, even though they never found a body."

"I have never heard of a more ridiculous thing in my life. Yet, I'm not surprised in the least. Those guys will do anything to empower themselves—even if it involves putting others' lives at risk."

These aren't just accidental deaths. If people died during the Ladder Games, that's straight-up murder. the Lawless from all years here should be held responsible for putting on this horror-fest.

"In their defense, it's not just them. The games and ranks have been around for years. If I remember right, Neo's great-grandfather set them in place."

"Of course he did, with all his sovereign bullshit." Neo's dad is the former mayor of Essex, and currently the state governor.

Riley nods, dropping more Skittles into her hand before going into a bathroom stall. She closes the door, but I continue to talk while she pees.

"Why didn't my parents warn me about this?"

Her voice rises, so I can hear her over the flushing toilet. "At the party tonight, the Lawless will do their welcome ceremony, at which they'll explain the rules. They'll also clarify that the ranks are not to be discussed outside of the Academy. The concern is that it will deter students from attending. They'll give some bullshit story about how hierarchy is necessary to prepare us for our futures as Blue Bloods."

She comes out of the stall and washes her hands in one of the row of sinks.

"Fucking A," I spit out, "if I could go back in time and slap some sense into our ancestors, I'd smack them hard."

"It's the price we pay for the safety net of our future."

"Screw that. I'd be perfectly content controlling my own damn future."

"Would you, though? Think about it, Scarlett. Not just the stability, but the protection. We have privileges that outsiders only dream of. A full ride to an accredited private university. No outside law enforcement. Financial stability. With the connections made from the Elders, we are untouchable. *Our kids* will be untouchable. I mean, do you really think Neo's dad would have the position he does now without cushioning from the Society?"

"Absolutely not. But there are other jobs. Normal people struggle for their success. *This* isn't normal."

"Normal or not, it's the way it is."

Jesus, they've corrupted Riley just like every other student in this place. If we're so safe, we wouldn't have to worry about what the Lawless has planned for us. We wouldn't be cleaning up their messes and doing their schoolwork for them. We are touchable—but only by them.

CHAPTER
FOUR
CREW

"How'd it go?" I ask, straddling the seat of my bike with my helmet dangling from my hand.

Jagger shakes his head, teeth clenched. "She said to suck her dick." He snatches his helmet off the handle of his Yamaha.

"Sounds like something she'd say."

Gripping the handles, I speed up and burn out behind Jagger. He leads the way down the trail to our house. One of the many perks of being one of the Lawless is the privacy that comes with having our own place. A two-story house with a massive, finished basement, a gym, a big-ass kitchen, and our own bedrooms. Not to mention, our own rules.

It's good to be a king. The downside: it won't last forever. Once we graduate, we're just your average Blue Bloods. Responsibility will kick in and we'll have to earn our place as an Elder, just like every other family before us. Until then, I'll sit on my throne alongside my boys while the students at Boulder Cove Academy earn their right to exist in our world.

We park our bikes in front of the house, right beside Neo's.

33

It won't be long and we'll be pulling out the sleds and storing our bikes for the winter.

I pull my helmet off and tuck it under my arm, following behind Jagger. "So that's all she had to say, huh? Suck her dick?"

"Pretty much. You know how unreasonable she is."

I laugh, because it's true. Scarlett Sunder is something else, that's for sure.

"Well, her mouth might be dirty, but I have no problem making her eat her own words while she wraps her lips around my dick."

"I hear ya there. The girl is fucking hot." Jagger pushes open the front door. "Let me know when you're done with her and I'll dirty her up even more before passing her to Neo to finish her off."

"Neo'd fuck her lifeless corpse before he'd ever fuck her alive."

"Eh. That's debatable. Pretty sure he'd fuck the life out of her, given the chance."

Once we're inside, I kick off my shoes. I'm not surprised to find Neo sleeping on the couch with a pillow over his head. "Wake up, fucker." I grab the pillow and chuck it at his face.

"Eat shit," he grumbles, rolling onto his side with his eyes still closed.

Jagger reemerges from the kitchen with three bottles of beer. He passes me one and I twist the cap off, tossing it on the coffee table in front of the couch.

"Wake up," Jagger yells to Neo. "We need to talk."

Neo curses under his breath but scoots himself into a sitting position.

I tip my head toward Jagger while sipping my beer. "So I have to eat shit, but you listen to him?"

"Aww," Jagger mocks me with a baby voice, "are someone's feelings hurt?"

Taking another swig of my beer, I flip him my middle finger and drop down beside Neo, who's sporting the homeless look with his scruffy face and unkempt hair, only wearing a pair of gym shorts.

"Shouldn't you be at practice?" Neo asks me as he runs his finger down the moisture of his cold bottle.

"Skipped. We had more important things to do while you were here getting your beauty rest."

Jagger takes a seat on the floor in front of us, legs bent at the knees. "It seems the little ray of sunshine has no intention of making an appearance tonight."

Neo doesn't even lift his tired eyes as he continues to trail lines down his bottle. "She'll be there."

"I don't know, man. She seemed pretty—"

"She'll be there," Neo raises his voice, kicking his feet out and getting off the couch. He sets the unopened beer on the table and disappears up the stairs. "What the hell is his problem?" I ask.

Jagger shrugs. "Might be the update on Maddie. Apparently, she's had some issues with her blood pressure and heart rate."

"Shit, man," I run my fingers through my hair, "that really sucks."

"Yeah. I'm sure she'll bounce back. Maddie's got a rebel soul, even if she can't dance to the tune in her head."

It's been five months since I saw Maddie, and the guilt of not visiting eats me up inside. I just can't bring myself to look at her like that. All our lives, Maddie was the light in a room full of darkness. The one everyone flocked to. She cracked jokes and made us laugh. I had genuine love for the girl, even if I didn't love her the same way she loved me. Back then, it was Scar I had eyes for, but I knew we could never be together. Not with how much my friends despised her. Maddie was the safe choice, and I think that's why I was with her for so long. But even after a year together, my feelings for her never blossomed into more. Which is exactly why I planned to end things with her that day—the day our lives forever changed.

"Well," I drawl, slapping a hand to my thigh, "I've got a present waiting for me upstairs that needs to be unwrapped." I finish my beer in one swallow, then slam the bottle on the table.

"If your present purrs like a kitten, I'm pretty sure it's been opened."

Craning my neck, I hold my breath and listen to the silence. Silence that is broken by a girl's flirtatious laughter. "Mother-fucker." I jump up and make a beeline for the stairs. "Neo," I holler, "you better not be in my fucking room."

I bust through the open door of *my* bedroom, hands in the air. "What the hell?"

Neo winks at me with his palm pressed to the back of the girl's head. "That's right. Wrap your lips around my cock and suck it like a lollipop."

"Dude. I'm all for sharing, but she was supposed to be mine first."

His fingers knot in her hair, forcing his dick down her throat.

Now standing behind her, I put pressure on the back of her head with my hand, causing her to gulp Neo's cock. "Your lack of patience pisses me off, Emily. Had you waited a couple more minutes, you'd be sucking me off right now."

Neo smirks, rolling his hips faster. Emily picks up her pace, struggling to keep up with Neo's full length in her mouth, thanks to me.

She gags some more, but he doesn't let up. There's no way

in hell she'll quit and face humiliation. It's an honor to be in this position, and she knows it.

Neo drops his head back and closes his eyes. "Open your throat, so I can fill it up."

With my help, he rams himself so deep in her mouth that she gurgles, choking on his cum. When he pulls out, she slaps a hand over her mouth.

My lip twitches with humor. "She's gonna blow." *Just like I knew she would.*

"Swallow it down," Neo demands of her. "Don't you dare hurl on this floor."

He takes a step back, while I do the same. Emily opens her mouth, still heaving.

"In the bathroom," Neo shouts, but before she can even get off her knees, she begins vomiting all over the floor.

Some of it hits his barefoot, and I burst out in laughter. Neo curses and kicks his foot, trying to get the vomit off. "Are you fucking kidding me?" he bellows. "Clean your ass up and get the hell out of my house."

I laugh because it's fucking hilarious. "Should've just waited for me, Emily."

She climbs to her feet, eyes downcast, as she wipes the back of her hand across her mouth. "It's Emma." She disappears out the open door, and I laugh some more.

"You can have her now," Neo says, lip curled in disgust.

"Fuck that. I don't want her sloppy mouth anywhere near my dick. I was supposed to be her first, until you ruined her for all of us."

He grabs a shirt off the floor and begins wiping his foot off. "For her sake, let's hope it's her last time."

I shrug my shoulders. "Beggars can't be choosers."

Neo raises his hand and chucks the vomit-infested shirt at

me. I dodge it by leaning to the left. "Hey, that's my fucking shirt."

"And you're the reason it's covered in vomit. Thanks a lot for that, asshole." He tugs up his shorts, snapping the elastic on his waistband. "And for the record, I've never in my life begged. They beg and can only be so lucky to be eye level with my cock."

"Sure. Sure," I say, though I know it to be true.

Neo is one of the most sought-after guys on campus. He's quiet and mysterious, with dark hair and olive green eyes that soak all the girls' panties. A little taller than me and Jagger and packing more muscle. The guy is fucking ripped. He's never had a girlfriend and doesn't want one. Which works well for him because with his sour-ass attitude, I doubt he ever will.

Then there's Jagger. Light brown hair that matches his eyes. He's packing muscle, too, but not as much as Neo.

I'm a combination of the two, which makes for a hell of a good time—when I'm up for it. Anger and anxiety often get the best of me, but I take out all my emotions on the football field. As long as I don't screw things up this year and do well at college, I've got a chance at going pro. One of the many perks of the Society are the connections and, given my skills on the field, I'm sure it's in the bag. Which is exactly why I can't let this girl get under my skin.

Neo presses his fist to his jaw, popping his neck. "I've gotta shower. I'll meet you guys at The Ruins."

"Whoa, whoa, whoa. You're not leaving your spewed jizz all over my floor. Clean that shit up."

Neo keeps walking, speaking as he exits my room, "I'll send someone up to take care of it."

Of course he will. Why would he do anything for himself when he has minions to do it for him?

Stepping around the small puddle on my floor, I pull open

my dresser drawer and retrieve a solid white tee shirt. I'm taking off my uniform that consists of a teal polo and navy blue twill pants when something catches my eye outside my window.

I lean closer, palms pressed to the windowsill. My jaw locks the minute I see her. "What the fuck is she doing here?"

FIVE
SCARLETT

AFTER RILEY FINISHED GIVING me the grand tour, she stayed in the kitchen and made herself something to eat. While she was busy, I snuck out of the dorm.

I might live to regret this decision, but I have to put my foot down. Jagger came to *my* room and tried crawling under *my* skin. They might be the leaders of this place, but that room will become my sanctuary, my safe space. They have no business going there. We are not friends and we never will be.

Instead of bowing at their feet, I'm coming to their turf to make my presence known—to all three of them.

The torment ends here.

I'm actually pretty damn proud of myself for not getting lost, though the house is massive and hard to miss. Don't even get me started on the arresting view. It's walled with mountains and a river passing through the side of the property.

Before I even make it to the door, it flies open.

I'm taken aback when I see Crew. I'm not sure who I was expecting, but it wasn't him. It's been months since we've been face to face, and I'm unsure how I feel about seeing him.

The thudding of my heart is confusing the rage in my head. He hasn't changed much, aside from the brown stubble on his face. It looks like he was getting dressed, considering his shirt is hung around his neck and his pants are unbuttoned. Probably just finished up with a girl. The thought knots my stomach.

Reaching behind him, never breaking my stare, he pulls the door closed then aggressively stalks toward me.

I head his way, but he holds up a hand to stop me as he continues in my direction. I'm not sure why I do as he asked, but I stop moving. In a swift motion, he grabs me by my arm, jerking me close to him. His fiery breath hits my face.

"Let go of me!" I snap my hand out of his. "You have no right to touch me."

"You've got some nerve coming here."

"You all left me no choice. They kicked me out of yet another school because of your juvenile games."

"I didn't mean the Academy. Our house is what I meant. What the hell are you even doing here?"

"I came to set the record straight."

Crew tosses his hands in the air before smacking them to his sides. "Okay. Set things straight with me. Say what you need to fucking say."

"Not just you. All three of you assholes. So," I push myself up on the toes of my canvas shoes, looking over his shoulder, "where are they?"

I know they're here. If they weren't, Crew wouldn't be trying to hide me. *Some things never change.*

"Inside."

"Go get them."

"No can do. They're busy getting ready for the party. I assume Jagger invited you."

"No, Crew!" I spit out. "An invitation gives you the option.

41

He demanded I attend."

"As he should. You're a student at BCA and all students must attend."

He's just as infuriating as he ever was. "Cut the bullshit, Crew. You and I both know I will not do a damn thing you assholes ask of me. If anything, I won't attend just *because* you've demanded it."

His lip curls. "I can see your stubbornness hasn't faded."

"This has nothing to do with being stubborn and everything to do with you all trying to destroy me."

"We did what we had to do."

I can feel the rage climbing through my body and filling my cheeks with insatiable heat. "Oh yeah? You just had to make it look like I was cheating on our exams? Or that I stole school property?" My voice rises to an uncontrollable shout. "Of course, let's not forget setting my principal's fucking shed on fire."

His arrogance is trying. "You're here, aren't you?"

"Yeah, Crew. I'm here. So what are you fucktards going to do now that I am?"

"Don't you worry your pretty little head." He smirks. "We have a plan. We *always* have a plan."

I despise the way his presence makes my chest heave and my head dizzy. My heart wants so badly to dig for the memories of us before everything went to hell, but my head tells me not to go there. He's not the same guy. Or maybe this is who he always was and I just hoped I was enough to change him.

"You know what? Screw this. Just relay the message to your idiot friends. I will not be pushed around anymore. If you three think you're going to ruin this school year for me by pulling the shit you did when I was home, you've got another thing coming. I'm here now and I will fight back."

"Message received and I'll be sure to relay it."

Why is he giving me that mischievous grin? My eyebrows pinch together. "This isn't funny, Crew."

"Never said it was. In fact, I agree. Nothing about this is funny at all."

"I'm dead serious. Enough is enough. I get it, you guys hate me. The feeling is mutual, so let's just get through these next eight months and we can go back to only seeing each other at the quarterly meetings."

His thumb grazes his chin and he snickers. "I wish it were that easy, Scar."

"Of course it's that easy. It's a simple choice to be nice."

"You seem to forget that you being here means you belong to us now."

I grind my teeth, nostrils flaring. "I belong to no one."

"Oh, but you do. Before long, you'll be reaching for my hand, begging me to help you." He wears his smugness proudly with drawn-back shoulders and a dominating stance.

"I'd die before I ever asked you for help—any of you."

"Well, we can't have that, can we? We need you alive in order to torture the fuck out of you."

He's even worse than he was back then, but his words don't cut as deep as they used to. Now, they barely skim the surface of my thick skin. "I can't believe we were ever friends."

"We weren't. I just let you believe we were. Keep your friends close and your enemies closer. Everything I did and said was to earn your trust, so I could yank the rug out from under you."

"You're unbelievable."

Okay. That one stung a little. Wasn't expecting that. My head shakes during the moment of silence before I blow out a breath, feeling like I was just kicked in the gut. "You know what, screw you."

"Nah. I'll pass. My dick already spread you wide enough."

He did not just say that! "I fucking hate you, Crew Vance." I flip him my middle finger before spinning on my heels.

I don't make it far before his arms fly around me from behind, squeezing my back to his chest. "Flip me off again and I'll break that finger of yours and use it to get you off. Would you like that, Scar? Your dismembered finger fucking your pussy?"

His hold on me drops and I refuse to give him another second of my time. My feet don't stop moving as I make an escape, his vile words on repeat in my mind.

"Stupid. So fucking stupid." I snap a branch from the tree as I make my way down the trail. *Why did I ever think I could reason with any of those idiots?* The dry bark digs into the skin of my palm as I smack it against a tree.

Out of nowhere, Riley jumps out from behind a bush, startling me. In a knee-jerk reaction, I swing the stick, missing her face by a centimeter. "Jesus, Riley. Are you trying to get yourself killed?"

"That's hardly a deadly weapon, but I could ask you the same thing. What were you doing at the Lawless house? Don't you know you need an invitation to step foot on their property? Unless..." She smirks, her eyes quizzical. "Were you invited? Holy shit, Scarlett. If you've got a foot in that door, you have to tell me."

"What? No," I stammer, tossing the stick in front of me and continuing down the path. "They didn't invite me. It was stupid. Should've never gone."

Regret eats at me. If only I were the type to sit back and let things happen, I might actually be able to slide through this year unscathed. Instead, by showing up there, I'm sure I just made everything so much worse for myself. All this time I thought Neo was the worst of them all, but Crew just proved me wrong.

Riley walks in step with me down the trail and I'm still not sure why she's here. I don't even look at her as I talk out of fear she'll see how worked up I am. "Did you follow me?"

She shrugs a shoulder. "I saw you sneaking down the hall and curiosity got the best of me. I had a feeling you were going there, and I wanted to make sure you were okay when you left. I know how cruel those boys are."

"I appreciate your concern, but I can take care of myself."

"Can you, though? I mean, it's obvious you have some sort of history with those guys, and if there's bad blood, I need to know."

"Why does it matter?"

Riley goes quiet for a second, and by the time I glance over at her, I've already answered the question for myself. "Because you think being my roommate puts a target on your back?"

"Well...yeah. Sort of. You might be new here, but you're not new to the rules. You know the pull those guys have, and if you know them as well as I think you do, you also know what they're capable of. No one wants to be on their bad side. Especially someone who's just trying to blend in and survive another year here."

The last thing I want is to drag Riley into my mess. I think the best way to avoid doing so is by keeping my relationship with Crew, Jagger, and Neo to myself—much like I've done my entire life.

"Don't worry. We're all from the same chapter, so I've known them for, like, ever. There's no bad blood."

Before I know it, we've reached the Foxes' Den. The sun is setting and there's a chill in the air that has me hugging myself.

"About that party tonight," Riley begins. "I think you should reconsider. It'll be fun."

"Oh, I'm going."

Riley's smile is so big, her cheekbones practically touch her eyes. "Really?"

"Yeah. I think you're right. It's time to embrace everything this school has to offer."

Will I live to regret another rash decision? Probably. Do I care? Nope. My life is heavy with regret, but it's some of those regretful decisions that gave me the backbone I have today. I need them to know I'm unaffected by their cruelty. Once they see that tormenting me isn't as fun as they hoped it would be, they'll stop.

If I can stay two steps ahead of the Lawless, I'll be just fine. After all, in order for them to beat me, they have to catch me.

Riley's excitement is apparent. "Then I guess we better go find you something cute to wear."

"I don't know about cute, but I think I have just the right outfit for tonight's festivities."

When we get back to the room, Riley and I both stop, sharing a look as we approach the door. "Did you leave the door open when you left?"

Riley shakes her head in a subtle no. "I didn't lock it because I wasn't sure if you had your key, but I most definitely closed it."

"Hmm. Weird." I push the door open, and we both look around before entering. I shrug my shoulders and push down the strange feeling inside me. "No one's here."

"It was probably Melody. She's the den leader and nosey as hell. I have no doubt she'd enter an unlocked door just to snoop."

"I can't believe there are no cameras here," I say to her as I walk briskly to the one bag I have yet to unpack. I flip it onto my bed and pull the zipper. Once opened, I analyze my belongings and make sure my phone is still hidden. Everything is in place as it should be.

"Trust me, students and some parents have tried, but the Elders believe cameras ruin alibis, should we ever need one."

"That's the dumbest thing I've ever heard." I toss my bag down on the floor, and as I do, something catches my eye. Dropping to my knees, I get a better look. When I see the resort tag peeking out from under my bed, my heart splinters. My fingers caress the paper that was put on my bag the last time I went boarding. Remorse consumes me. But more than that, anger rattles my bones. How dare my dad have this bag put in my room when he knew how badly I didn't want it.

"You okay?" Riley startles me as she comes up behind me, looking over my shoulder.

"Ugh. Yeah. I'm fine." I push my snowboard bag farther under my bed and slap my hands to my mattress. "Do you know what you're wearing?"

Riley holds up a finger. "I might need your help." Her expression twists. "If you're up for it. I know your style isn't..."

I laugh it off before she makes the situation any weirder. "It's fine. I might not dress up, but I do have an eye for fashion and hair. Show me what you got."

Riley opens the doors to her armoire closet she must have brought from home and pulls down two dresses. One, a very short, bubblegum pink dress with a floral overlay. The second, a navy blue satin dress with braided spaghetti straps. I don't even have to give it a second thought before I blurt out, "The blue one."

"I knew you'd say that, which is why I have a third option." She lays the dresses on her bed and walks over to her dresser. Pulling out a drawer, she retrieves a jean miniskirt. "Or this with a cutesy tank top."

My finger taps to my chin as I assess all the outfits. "Navy dress with the jean jacket you have on and a pair of flats. If this party is as epic as it's made out to be, you don't want to be in heels."

Riley flashes her eyes. "Impressive. You do have a sense of style."

I rest my arm on my stomach and curl over, bowing gracefully. "Why, thank you."

Riley goes to the bathroom to wash her face while I get changed. I decide on a pair of baggy jeans, a solid black tank top that rests just above my pierced belly button and my black slip-on Chucks. Bending over and flipping my head, I bunch my long, black hair together, then flip my head forward to tie a ponytail holder around my messy bun.

When Riley returns, she takes one look at me and palms her face. "That's the perfect outfit?"

"Hey now, I didn't ridicule you for dressing like you're going to a dance club."

"Dance club, party. Tomayto, tomahto."

"This is me. Take it or leave it."

Riley scans my body before a smile parts her lips. "I'll take it. Only if you'll help me curl the back of my hair."

"Your hair is already curly?"

Her shoulders do a little dance. "I want more. Big, bouncy curls with loads of body."

Taking a seat on the vanity stool beside her bed, she applies her makeup while I tap my finger to the curling iron to make sure it's hot enough. When it burns the tip of my index finger, I know it's ready.

My fingers slide under a thin chunk of her hair and I press the lever on the curling iron. My chest splinters as I clamp the iron down and wrap it around her hair.

"Will you do my hair before we go?"

"Maddie," I laugh, *"we're snowboarding, not going to a dance."*

"I know, but I still wanna look cute. Crew will be there."

"Of course. How can I forget? Maybe I need to invite him every time, just to get you on the slopes. You'll be an avid snowboarder before you know it."

"Not likely. I can barely stand on my own two feet, let alone with them both together as one. I am excited for today, though. I won't pretend I'm eager to be on those cold mountains, but if Crew's around, every part of my body is warm." She winks at me in the mirror and we both start laughing.

"Okay. How do you want it?"

"Hmm. How about curls? They can bounce around as I fly down the hill."

"Curls it is."

"Scarlett? Hey. You okay?"

I quickly snap out of the trance. "Oh shit?" I unclasp the iron and let Riley's steaming curl fall to her back. "We're good. It's not burnt."

"Better not be." Riley pins me with a glare through her reflection in the mirror.

"It's fine. A perfect curl." I brush it off like nothing ever happened as I look down at the blonde strands stuck and sizzling on the iron.

Once I'm finished, Riley looks like a homecoming queen. A homecoming queen wearing a skimpy dress that barely covers her ass with a V-cut so low, her tits pop out, but she's stunning nonetheless.

"All right," she beams, crossing her pink purse over her chest, "let's party."

I internally scream. The idea of socializing with strangers has me more on edge than being questioned about arson on the principal's shed. In that situation, I was hushed by my attorney, who had the case dismissed. This time, I can only save myself.

CHAPTER
SIX

SCARLETT

My heart is in my throat as we near the end of the trail where the Ruins are. There are so many terms used here, and I'm not sure how I'll ever keep track of them all. I guess it goes hand in hand with the rules, which I'll also be struggling to remember.

As much as I've dreaded my attendance at BCA, I have to admit, the atmosphere is intriguing. I'm really digging this whole dark academia vibe. Although, I'd prefer to dig it from inside my dorm, in solitude.

"You ready for this?" Riley asks, the powerful stench of her perfume filling the space between us.

"You're the second person who's asked me that today and my response is the same: I have to be."

There are people everywhere. Shuffling and moving through the dim beams of light casting over a chunk of the area. Pillars are set around the property, about two stories high, with fluorescent lights shining down. "High" by The Chainsmokers is pounding out of the speakers that surround us.

My eyes skim the crowd as I look for the guys. Crew said it himself, keep your friends close and your enemies closer.

"Let's get a drink." Riley tugs at my arm eagerly, whisking me over to a keg that sits beside a tree. There's a crowd surrounding it, and she wastes no time planting us right in the middle of it.

"Actually," I speak loudly over the music and chatter, "I'm good on the beer." I point a thumb over my shoulder at a cluster of large rocks. "I'll be over there."

"Okay. But don't go far. We need to stick together."

I'm reminded of what my mom said as I backtrack to the rocks. *Find your person. Stick with them. Do not go out alone at night.*

I'm settled on a rock, twiddling my thumbs and watching people drink their beverages while carrying on and having the time of their lives. Sometimes I wish I could be carefree and enjoy the simplicity of a good party. I hate that my anxiety gets the best of me in social situations and I feel the need to make an escape before I even say hello to anyone.

Speaking of saying hello. Here comes Melody and her side-kick, heading straight for me.

"I'm so glad you made it, Scarlett. Not that you had a choice in the matter."

"So I've heard." My tone is flat and I'm hopeful she gets the hint that I'm not in the mood to chitchat.

"Well, if you need anything at all, let me know. Be it liquor, cigarettes, happy candy, dust, bud. I'm your girl."

My eyebrows hit my forehead because I was not expecting that. Melody most definitely does not come off as the dealing type. "Thanks. I'll keep that in mind."

What is this place?

While dusting off my legs, I get up. This is much too awkward for my liking. "You two have a good night."

Melody's eyes follow me. "You, too, hun."

I see familiar faces and a couple people I've interacted with from our chapter, but I never really got to know anyone on a personal level. It's safe to say, I'm the outcast here. The one and only person I trust and want by my side during this phase of my life can't be here, and it kills me.

Maddie and I made a promise to live our lives outside of Society standards, yet here I am doing exactly what I swore I'd never do, not like I had much of a choice in the matter.

I'm pushing through the crowd while "Without Me" by Halsey vibrates my eardrums. Memories of my last ride out to Coy Mountain infiltrate my mind.

"Turn it up. I love Halsey," Maddie hollers over the already blaring music.

She stands up in the back seat and the upper half of her body disappears out the moonroof of Crew's car.

"Are you fucking crazy?" I tug at her snow pants, trying to pull her back down. "Do you see how low those branches are?"

Maddie drops back down in the seat, and at the same time, my eyes catch Crew's in the rearview mirror. His eyes crinkle at the corners with his sly smirk. Warmth swarms my belly while I push away the guilt brewing behind it.

You can't have him, Scarlett. He's already spoken for.

Fuck it. I make a beeline for the keg, pushing my way to the front of the line, while getting cussed at and shamed for cutting. Bending down, I grab the bag of red plastic cups off the ground while stray ones are scattered all over.

"Listen, noob. You can wait in line just like everyone else."

"Yeah. What he said."

"Did you hear me, bitch? Get in the back of the fucking line."

Ignoring them, I focus solely on filling my cup. I need to drink away the irrational thoughts taking over. It might be temporary, but at least the open wounds will close for a little while.

I go to grab the hose connected to the keg when the guy before me drops it, but someone else snatches it up. His dark eyes bore into mine. "I said, get in the back of the line, you entitled cunt."

"Aww," I clasp my chest, still holding my empty cup, "are your words supposed to make me obey?" My eyes roll and I try to grab the hose from him. Before I can, I'm being doused in keg beer. It trickles down my face, sliding into my shirt and soaking my clothes.

Everyone around me starts laughing, but all I see is red. "You asshole." I charge at him, bumping my knee really hard into the keg. Jumping up, I wrap my legs around him, trying to get the hose from his hands, but he continues to spray it in my face, soaking every inch of my upper body.

My neck twists and turns to dodge the sprays while my ankles lock behind his back so tight, a lion couldn't break my hold.

"You fucking whore."

"Oh, now I'm a whore, too?" I open my mouth wide, letting some of the beer spray into it. "Keep it coming. I am pretty thirsty."

The next thing I know, I'm being pried off him. It's not by a lion, though. It's worse.

Neo's arms wrap around my waist and I'm lifted away. The stream of beer immediately stops, and the guy spraying me now wears a look of panic.

"She cut the line," the guy says softly, an ample shift from his roaring insults just seconds ago.

Neo sets me down, and I catch my feet.

"In the tunnels," Neo remarks to the guy with a stern finger pointed toward the trail.

Everyone surrounding the keg is quiet. The guy's chest rises and falls breathlessly as he speaks, "Just because she's new doesn't mean—"

"Now!" Neo shouts. The rumble in his voice vibrates against my back and I'm hesitant to make a move out of here.

"I can explain..." the guy begins, but is immediately cut off by Neo.

"You've been demoted. We'll discuss your punishment at The Gathering."

I tuck my chin to my chest, unable to even look at the guy. Sure, he's an asshole, and I'd love nothing more than to shove the keg tap down his throat, but does he really deserve to be demoted? If what Riley says is true, he's in for a year of hell. We could've eventually handled this situation without Lawless interference. I'd probably punch him a few times and he'd continue down his list of vile female insults. In the end, I'd leave with a cup of beer and he'd gracefully bow out with a bloody lip.

"Come with me," Neo says sternly, grabbing my arm and pulling me away, as if he has the right to do so.

"Excuse me?" I jerk my arm, trying to free it from his clutches to no avail. "No hey, hi, hello?"

"I don't have time for small talk, especially not with you."

"Gee, thanks." Sarcasm drips from my words. "Nice to see you, too."

"It's never nice to see you, Scarlett. In fact, it's downright torturous to be in your presence."

"Torturous, huh?" I tease, using humor as my scapegoat. "Is that because my hot body tortures your mind?"

He winces. "If only. Maybe then I wouldn't have the dire urge to chain your hot body to a tree and leave you there just to watch you suffer."

"So, you're saying I'm hot?"

His eyes narrow and he keeps jerking me along, getting annoyed by my unpleasantries.

Once there's some distance between us and the party attendees, Neo gives me a forceful shove and releases his hold on me.

"You've been here six hours and you're already causing trouble."

"I didn't do anything. That guy was a grade-A asshole."

"Maybe so but you walked up to that keg like an entitled *bitch*, which you are not."

"You're right," I mumble. "I'm not a bitch."

"I meant you're not entitled. As for you being a bitch, we both know that to be true."

"I can say the same about you, *Neopolo*." I emphasize his legal name, knowing he hates it.

His jaw tics. "Don't you ever call me that again!"

"Or what?" I pop a hip, placing my hand firmly on it.

"Do it again and you'll see what happens."

"Am I supposed to be scared? Because I'm not. If anything, I'd like for you to try and hurt me, just so I can piss on your plans to ruin my entire year. In case you haven't heard, I refuse to be your doormat."

"Oh, I heard. Crew relayed your little message after I saw you two talking outside of *my* house. You wasted your time going there. Nothing you do or say is going to change the fact that we own you this year. Now be a good girl and go to the tunnels with the rest of your classmates."

We could stand here and argue all day, but I'm already bored with this back and forth conversation. Snuffing him, I step past where he stands like a domineering statue. "Fine, I'll go, but don't expect my compliance anymore this year. You won't get it."

He throws an arm out, stopping me. "Don't fuck with me, Scar. You'll live to regret it."

I shove his arm away and keep on my way.

Neo disappears back into the crowd and I skim the area for Riley. *Where the hell did she go?*

Everyone heads in the same direction, so I follow them, hoping to get to the right place. I'm not sure what the tunnels are, but it sounds creepy. In that case, sign me up—I love scary shit.

My parents always tell me I need to be more fearful because, without it, I have no protection. I always remind them that I'm not fearless, I'm just spiteful. Our fears set boundaries for us and I'll be damned if any human emotion is going to dictate my life.

"Excuse me," I say to a lanky boy walking alone. *Wait. I know that guy.*

He pushes his glasses up and acknowledges me with raised brows. "Hello, again."

I offer him a smile. "Umm. Hi. Elias, right?"

His eyes light up, pleased with my memory. "You're correct."

"Hi, Elias," I say again. "Have you seen a girl, about five-foot-five?" I estimate a measure of her height with my hand, holding it up to my nose. "Bubbly and loud. Goes by the name of Riley."

"Sorry. Wish I could help."

Well, dammit.

The distant sound of a revved-up engine grabs everyone's attention. I follow the direction of their stares, looking over my shoulder.

What the hell?

Directly in front of me is a dirt bike coming at full speed. The driver is wearing a helmet, so I'm not able to see his face, but he's got a passenger behind him with hands wrapped snug around his waist.

"Watch out!" Elias shouts. I'm pulled back at the same time the bike comes flying past me. The wind from its high speed causes my hair to whip against my face. My heart leaves my body as I fall back on Elias and we both hit the ground.

"Is that..." *Riley?*

I'm still on the ground, watching as the crowd parts for the driver and what appears to be my roommate. I push myself up and wipe the dirt from my jeans. "Asshole!" I shout.

"Get used to it. They ride wherever they want and pay no regard to anyone in their way. On another note, I think I found your friend."

"Yeah." I lean to the right, trying to see where they went, but all I see is a cloud of dust as the students come together again and continue toward the tunnels. "I think she's officially lost her mind."

Elias gets off the ground and offers me his hand, which I accept.

We're standing under one of the overhead lights, and I get a better look at him. He pushes his glasses up his slender nose and I note his blue eyes. They're as bright as mine, but with tiny specks of black on his irises. He's actually a pretty good-looking guy, if you're into the preppy, nerdy type.

Elias nods toward the open space in front of us and I realize we've fallen behind the group. "You should probably get going. They like to humiliate anyone who's late."

"Of course," I say, sarcasm apparent, "wouldn't want to keep the leaders waiting."

"Or your friend."

"Shit. You're right. I should make sure she's okay." I pick up my pace, hurrying to catch up with everyone.

Before long, I'm mixed in with the group as we step under a

cement overhang. Pushing myself up on my tiptoes, I try to see where they're all disappearing to, but it's too crowded to see anything but more people.

Like flies, they drop one by one, and that's when I realize everyone is descending through a hole in the ground.

It's so loud that the chatter in my ears helps to drown out the questions racing through my mind.

When it's my turn to go down, I hesitate.

"Go!" someone shouts.

Without another thought, I step down into the black hole, the chatter following. Someone bumps into me and I stumble into the person in front of me. They say nothing, nor do I.

Finally, I see light. Lined along the walls are old torch sconces with sharp metal teeth. Inside each one is a lit pillar candle. Flames dance around the walls and the ceiling, the shadows fading and reappearing as people walk by.

We're in some sort of a dungeon, and when we come to a four-way, I continue following the crowd straight ahead. There are so many turns that it'd be easy for anyone to get lost down here. The thought has the tiny hairs on the back of my neck standing.

I've done well by not asking questions, but curiosity is getting the best of me. "What are we doing down here?" I ask some girl walking by my side.

"At the start of every school year, the Lawless holds the Gathering to welcome the junior class."

"What sort of gathering?"

Her eyebrows rise, and she smirks, leading me to believe it can't be that bad. "You'll see, new girl."

Why is it so damn important that I'm a new girl? So what! All the juniors are new and no one gives a damn. It's almost as if everyone from this Academy got together and had an in-depth conversation about me coming in late. I mean, I can't be the only one to enroll during senior year, can I?

Minutes later, we're walking through a large doorway to an open space with vaulted ceilings. It's not dirty like I thought it would be. It's old, but the area is well kept. Stone walls surround us with the wall-mounted sconces as our only source of light. That is, until I step deeper into the room and look at the front where the Lawless stand in black-hooded robes. On each side of them is a burning torch set in metal stands.

The slamming of the doors behind us startles me. As they latch shut, the crowd immediately silences.

"Welcome to the Blue Bloods' seventy-ninth Gathering to kick-off the school year," Neo begins, speaking through a microphone clipped to his robe, his voice carrying through the wide space.

"I'm Neo Saint, one of your Lawless members. It is my honor to present to you your other student leaders at Boulder Cove Academy." Jagger steps forward, his expression void of any emotion. "Jagger Cole." He steps back in place while Crew comes forward, wearing the same desensitized expression. "Crew Vance."

Everyone claps, while I just observe. It doesn't seem right to applaud these assholes. They're no leaders; they're devils in disguise.

Neo continues, "Decades ago, an empire stood where your feet are now. During a time when some locals were battling the Blue Bloods over this property, a bulldozer crashed into the stone wall, taking it down, along with a structural building that was set right behind it. This is all that remains. Many of our events are held above ground, but a few stragglers like to sneak off and try to get themselves lost down here. I advise you not to be one of those idiots. Rumor has it, a group came down here about twenty years ago and never came back up. A few years ago, a girl was lost in the tunnels and she came across remains that were claimed to be the missing students. Needless to say, this is not your playground."

"Hey." Riley bumps her shoulder to mine. I glower at her while she stares ahead at the guys with a coy look.

"Hey yourself," I whisper back. "Jagger? Really?"

Her shoulders shrug causally, but there is nothing casual about this situation. "He's no Crew Vance, but he'll do."

"Crew?" I laugh. "Please don't tell me you have a crush on that guy."

Riley's cheeks tinge pink. "I wouldn't call it a crush as much as an extreme infatuation."

"Same thing." I shake my head. "I'd be careful if I were you. Crew, Jagger, Neo—they're all trouble."

"It was just a ride on a bike. What's the big deal?"

Neo goes on to discuss the ranks and games, which I was already filled-in on, while me and Riley exchange words.

"The big deal is that Jagger Cole isn't a nice person."

She waggles her brows. "He was nice to me."

Who is this girl?

Jagger takes his place in the limelight and talks about the Society's motto and the urgency to protect our secrets. "We will now begin the initiation for the junior class."

It isn't until Crew comes forward and begins talking that my ears perk up.

"Junior members, please see yourself at the front of the group." His eyes immediately land on mine, as if he knew exactly where I was in this crowd of over a hundred people.

My chest tightens, pulse pounding.

"As most of you know, we have a new student," he continues, still watching me. "Scarlett Sunder, could you please join the junior class in the front?"

My eyebrows cave in while my cheeks flush with heat from the unwanted attention.

When I don't move, he uses an authoritative tone. "Now, Scarlett."

What the hell is he doing? He knows I'm not a junior.

"Go." Riley nudges me.

"No. I'm not going up there. I'm a senior. I have the credits to prove it."

"We're all waiting for you, Scar."

Oh no, he didn't. He knows how much I hate when they call me that in public. A nickname entails some sort of friendship or bond, and we most definitely have neither.

Everyone is looking at me. Not a single person in this crowded room has their eyes set anywhere but on me.

Riley bumps me again. "Ask questions later. Just *go*." She drags out the word, making her demand clear.

Seems I've got no choice, unless I want all these people mad at me for wasting their time. Against my better judgment, I make my way to the front. People step aside, allowing me through while watching me intently as I pass by them.

I don't let them see my unease. My beer-drenched head is held high, hands stuffed in the pockets of my jeans, and I walk through the parted crowd like a fucking rock star. All the while, there is a torrential downpour coming from my armpits.

Once I reach the front, I stop directly in front of the Lawless. "What's this all about?"

Crew's gaze drags up and down my body before landing on my eyes. "You're new here and the initiation is required for all students. Can we trust you, *Scar?*"

I'm convinced he's fucking with me, but I won't let him see how agitated I am right now. "Fine." My shoulders slouch and I roll my eyes toward the junior class. Muttering under my breath, I say, "I'll do your stupid initiation."

"What's that?" Neo pipes up. "We couldn't hear you?"

I raise my voice. "I said, I'll do the initiation."

"That's what I thought."

He's an even bigger dick than I remember.

I join the juniors, feeling extremely out of place. Everyone's attention is still on me, and I downright hate it.

"Our initiation process is simple. By taking the oath, you agree to the following rules: to protect the secrets of the Society. To not discuss anything that happens at Boulder Cove Academy with outsiders. You will respect and follow all rules set forth by the Lawless. As per the Society's rules, we maintain that outside relationships are forbidden. If you're caught fucking around with anyone who is not a Blue Blood, you risk expulsion from the Society.

"Lastly, you are committing to a complete school year and will not be dismissed until the final Gathering at the end of the year, at which we will release you from your obligation to attend in the future." Crew pins me with a hard stare. "Some choose to never return." I bite my tongue so hard, a metallic flavor coats my taste buds. "If everyone agrees, please say *I do* as we make our way down the line. Scarlett, we'll start with you."

They sure are hell-bent on making a mockery of me. No time to think. No time to go over my options. Well, I'm not going anywhere. I made it this far, and if they want to push me, I'll just have to push them back. My arms cross over my chest and I look Crew dead in the eye. "I do."

I swear he breathes a sigh of relief as the words leave my mouth. As if he wasn't expecting my compliance.

Everyone in line agrees to the rules. Once we're all "initiated," everyone claps, and this time, I join in just so I'm not standing out.

After a moment of *celebration*, Crew waves his hands down,

silencing everyone. "As Neo explained, the games are a week-long event that test not only your physical endurance, but your mental stability. Those who choose to play and complete the games, advance on the ladder of hierarchy before the next Gathering.

As you all know, Scarlett Sunder is entering as a second-year student at Boulder Cove Academy. It's not common that we have students enter as seniors, but it has happened before. After speaking with the Elders, they have informed us that Scarlett's placement on the ladder is to be left to our discretion. Being the transparent leaders we are, we let the senior class voice their opinions on the matter."

My smoldering glare burns into him as my chest heaves with a fury I'm fighting hard to contain.

With a smirk on his face, Crew looks at me. "We're glad to have you here, Scar. Now it's time to earn your place."

Is he serious? I can't tell. I don't need to earn my place. I was born into this damn Society. "Yeah, right." I chuckle nervously.

Neo steps up next to Crew. There is no smirk or glint of empathy on his face. Not that Neo has ever had an ounce of empathy toward another human being. "If you want to reap the benefits of being a Blue Blood, you will earn your place just like everyone else."

"Yeah," the crowd chants in unison.

"She has to earn it."

"Make her play the games."

"That girl's not entitled to anything here."

"Who cares if she's a Sunder?"

Those are some of the hasty remarks being made by my classmates.

"You can't be serious," I grit out.

Neo looks at Crew, then Jagger. Their expressions are saturated with smugness. They're loving every second of this.

"Being the generous leaders we are, we're giving you the option to play the games and advance early, or you're welcome to fulfill the duties of a Rook until our next ceremony."

I gulp. "You're really making me a Rook?"

Everyone goes silent. Not a sound to be heard other than the pounding of my heart in my chest.

"Unless you'd like to play," Jagger says before his gaze shifts elsewhere. "Hammond, get your ass up here."

Everyone looks to the left, where I assume *Hammond* is. Whoever that is. From the crowd emerges a guy with beer-soaked clothes, matching my own. *It's that asshole.*

"Earlier today, I demoted Victor Hammond from his seat as an Ace. We're giving him a chance to redeem himself." Neo looks at Victor. "Take your clothes off, Victor. You smell like stale beer."

Victor's Adam's apple bobs as he swallows. "My clothes?"

"Did I fucking stutter?" Neo spits. "You wanna behave like your dick is bigger than everyone else's. Let's see it."

With shaky hands, Victor strips down. First his beer-stained tee shirt. When he undoes his belt buckle, I turn my head, not wanting to see what he's about to expose.

When his belt clanks against the cement floor and everyone giggles, I'm inclined to look. I can't help myself. I have to.

Oh my god! I cover my mouth, choking down my laughter. It's not big at all. In fact, it's the smallest penis I've ever seen in my life.

"You'll remain naked in front of your fellow students for the duration of the ceremony."

Victor folds his hands in front of him, cupping his penis with his chin to his chest.

"Now that we all know Victor's cock is smaller than his ego, we can move on. Victor," Neo says sternly, "you have a choice. Play the games and move up upon completion or remain a Rook for the rest of the month until the next Gathering."

"I'll pass, sir. I'll fulfill my duties as a Rook," Victor responds timidly.

"Okay," I cut in, "can someone please tell me what the hell—"

"Excuse me," Neo interrupts, his voice thick with distaste. "Did we say you could speak?"

My eyes practically bug out of their sockets. "Ugh, no. But the First Amendment did."

Get a grip, Scarlett. Do not let them get to you.

"Keep your mouth shut until I ask you to speak."

Nope. Can't do it. I'm gonna fucking kill him.

"Now. Would you like to play, Scarlett?"

"No. Hell no. I'm not playing any games that you jerks make the rules to."

The next thing I know, Neo is stalking toward me with a death glare. He grabs my arm, pulls me close, and seethes, "We're not in Kansas anymore, princess. You wanna stay in this school, then you'll do what we ask of you. Now, you become a Rook and earn your place, just like everyone else, or you earn it by playing."

For the first time, Neo has instilled fear inside me. It's a strange feeling, but one I don't care to explore any further. "What exactly do these *games* consist of?"

"Whatever we want."

Neo pinches the skin on my upper arm before shoving it away and retaking his place in front of the crowd.

I rub the spot on my arm where his fingers were tightly clenched. "How long do they last?"

"They're held over the course of one week." Neo says, speaking to the crowd. "Could be in the middle of the night when you're sleeping. Could be at a party when you least expect it." He returns his attention to me. "This is a generous offer, considering first-year students work their way up for an entire month just to be Punks. We're giving you the opportunity to join the Aces after only a week, Scar. I'd accept the offer."

So it's not even really a competition, just games we have to complete. It's almost a simple choice. One week of some games over one month of pure hell at their hands...

Fuck it. If they wanna play, I'll play. Nothing they do can hurt me any more than they already have. I certainly won't be their little bitch, waiting on them hand and foot. "Fine. I'll do it."

The guys all share a look, pleased with my response.

"Juniors who would like to take part, please step forward and Jagger will be around to collect your information and get waivers signed."

Everyone watches, including me, as a handful of students step forward. Some who do, then step back. Some hesitate and finally move into line. After a minute, eighteen juniors are in line to play, three of which are girls. Only eighteen people want to forgo being a Rook for an entire month. It has me wondering if I made the wrong choice here tonight.

"There we have it," Neo says, waving his hand toward the juniors, "your next players in the Ladder Games." He steps down and leans close, whispering in my ear, "We've got something special planned just for you."

CHAPTER
SEVEN
SCARLETT

WE'VE BEEN DISMISSED from the tunnels, but I make no effort to hurry out. I was hoping to have a civil conversation with one of the guys to find out about these games I agreed to, but they were the first to leave.

There are still a few students lingering when I step out of the room we were in. I look both ways to assess the area and opt for straight ahead. I've always been fascinated with history and the nostalgic feeling of puzzling pieces of the past together. Everyone thinks I'm a pessimist when it comes to our Society. In some ways, I am. I don't like being told what I have to do or how I should live my life. If I could get over those prideful feelings, I might be able to embrace what I was born into. As for the antiquity of the Blue Bloods, I'm very knowl-edgeable, but I also know there is so much more to learn.

My fingers trail along the stone, hitting each groove as I walk through the larger tunnel. It's probably stupid of me to explore down here after the stories I've heard, but the aged beauty tempts me further.

The mechanically lit sconces on the wall become few and

far between, but there is still enough light to see where I'm going.

I'm still sliding my fingers down, walking at a leisurely pace, when I feel something slither over my hand. I jerk my arm and shake it, unable to see what was crawling on me. Not many things scare me, but I don't do spiders or the dark. I have to see everything around me; I even sleep with a nightlight beside my bed.

Once the creepy-crawly on my skin stops and I'm sure I got it off, I continue on my path.

I come to a T and have to choose left or right. I should just turn around before I really get myself lost, but I don't. Instead, I choose left, since right is pitch black.

I keep walking, noticing some sort of engraving on the wall ahead. The light beside it flickers and chills skate down my spine.

A strange feeling washes over me that has my head snapping around. "Hello," I say in a hushed tone. "Is someone there?" I hold my breath, listening intently. When there is nothing but silence, I keep on. Once I see what the engraving is, I'll turn around and go back up to the party.

My slow steps become quicker until I'm standing under the light, looking at what seems to be a map carved into the stone.

I run my finger through the dips and trails, following each turn. The light above me flickers again, but I pay it little attention as I observe the precise details of the map. I keep walking, trailing the grooves that continue farther and farther down the tunnel. There are different turns, corners, and dips in the stone that run up to the ceiling and down to the ground.

I stop, finger held in place. *That's the river.* I look up and see the etching of the mountains above ground. This is a map of the entirety of Boulder Cove Academy. Sure enough, the tunnels run beneath the entire property owned by the Blue Bloods.

Suddenly, the flickering light dims. My heart jumps into my throat. My head shifts to the left. "Hello."

I press my trembling body to the wall and hold my breath again to listen. *Nothing.*

Seconds later, I'm standing in complete darkness as the light goes out. Since I can't see anything, the silence is more deafening than ever.

"This isn't funny." My words get lodged in my throat. Unease rippling through me.

With my hands pressed firmly to the wall behind me, I shuffle my feet in the direction I came, hoping for the light to come back on.

An ear-splitting thud has my heart racing. It sounded like a boulder crashing into a cement wall. "Who's there? Show your damn face, you coward." The shake in my voice makes my fear well known.

I'm slipping around the corner, still bracing the wall, when I see that all the lights are out. If I move my hands, I'm sure to get lost. My sense of direction is one of my many weaknesses, yet here I am wandering through ancient tunnels. What the hell was I thinking? And why do I want to explore more once I have light?

My heavy breaths are the only sound as I shimmy back the way I came. The scent of wet cement floods my senses, and it's not something I remember on my way down. I inhale deeply, letting it flood my mind, hoping to revive a memory, so I know it was there before.

When my shoulder crashes into something against the wall, my entire body freezes. Stomach clenched; breath held. I'm positive even my heart has stopped beating. The scent of spice and bourbon now overpowers the wet-cement odor.

There is most definitely a guy standing beside me. I can smell him, hear him, feel his presence.

Fear has me grasping at the wall, hoping to find something to hold on to in case I'm pulled away.

"Who's there?" I ask feebly. "It's you, isn't it, Neo?" It has to be. Neo is a different level of cruel and I wouldn't put it past him to put me in a vulnerable state, then fuck with me.

I don't try to run. I just stand there, shoulder to shoulder with the prowler. My fear is that if I let go of this wall and try to go around him, he'll grab me. If I could see his face, I wouldn't care. I'd fight to the death, if that's what it takes. But fear of the unknown keeps my feet cemented.

"I can hear you breathing. Smell your cologne. Say some—"

In a swift motion, a hand claps over my mouth, shutting me up. He tugs me to his chest, venomous breath spilling down my spine.

With one of his arms bracing mine against my sides, I squirm and pull, trying to get away, but his fingertips dig deeper into the skin of my cheeks, parting my jaw.

"Let me go!" My words hit the palm of his hand. "You're gonna regret this." I lift my leg, bend it at the knee, and kick backward, missing him and kicking the wall.

When I give up the fight, knowing I'm not going anywhere until he lets me, he pulls me closer, with one arm wrapped around my waist and the other held firmly over my mouth.

"Shut the fuck up," he grinds out, his tone thick and gravelly.

"Crew?"

"I said shut your mouth."

My head shakes, trying to get his hand off my mouth. "No! I won't shut up. Get off me!"

Finally, he frees his hand from my mouth, crossing his arm over the one still wrapped snugly around me.

"You're really grating on my nerves, Scar." His voice is a whisper against my bare shoulder.

I, on the other hand, do not whisper at all. "You're lucky I didn't bite a chunk off your hand, asshole!'

"That'd be more desirable than listening to you run your mouth."

I laugh sarcastically. "Oh, would it? Cover my mouth again. We'll see how desirable it is."

"You never shut up, do you?"

"If holding me in place is in any way an attempt to calm me down, you're failing miserably. As soon as you let me go, your face will meet my fist."

"In that case, I better hold you here all night. This face is too pretty for those knuckles."

He's chipping at my patience and trying to get a rise out of me. *How the hell did I ever find this guy charming?*

Getting bored with this entire waste of time, I humor him. "What do you want, Crew?"

"To talk to you." He's still whispering for reasons unbeknownst to me. "Come with me." He slides his feet, carrying me right along with him.

My body convulses as I try to fight him off. There is no way in hell I'm going farther into the dark tunnels with him. "No! You wanna talk, then we can do it above ground with witnesses."

My feet leave the ground as Crew tosses me over his shoulder, hauling me away as if I'm weightless. I can't see where we're going, but we're moving quickly, and I hope like hell he's memorized these tunnels.

"You're hiding from them, aren't you?"

His only response is a blown-out breath.

"I knew it. You don't want Neo or Jagger to know you're

associating with me at all. So why do it? Why not just leave me the hell alone?"

"Shut up!"

His outburst jolts me and I say nothing as he pulls something out of his pocket that turns the lights back on. He was the one who shut them off in the first place. *Jerk!*

I stay quiet for the rest of the walk and Crew does the same. I focus solely on every turn, instilling it to memory, in case I need to retrieve it later.

We turn left. The map continues down the wall.

Another left and the map ends. There's two wooden doors. One on each side and each with their own unique design etched in them. The only light is at the very end of this row and I'm grateful we're headed toward it.

Right. Passing by another door.

Minutes have passed. Ten, maybe?

What's behind these doors?

Left again.

Dammit. I give up. There is no way I can remember all this.

It isn't until we reach another door that he finally sets me down. There's a light directly above it, which I'm grateful for.

"You can try to run, but you'll be doing yourself more harm—"

I shut him up with my fist in his face, just like I promised.

"Bitch!" he howls, cupping his left cheek.

"Next time you wanna manhandle me, remember what a bitch I am." I shake my hand, working out the kink in my knuckles. That hurt worse than I thought it would, but it was more than worth it. I spent so many nights wishing I could pop this asshole in the face.

Crew gnashes his teeth and hurls toward me. His fingers web and he reaches out, grabbing me by the neck. I swallow hard, feeling the lump in my throat grate against his palm as he squeezes.

"I could kill you right now and make it so no one ever found your body, Scar." His lips curl in a smile at his deranged thought. "Then again, I always dreamt of fucking you one last time before you expire."

My air intake is restricted, and while I'd like to think Crew would never hurt me, I'm not so sure anymore. "Please stop."

"Oh," he laughs, "*now* we're using our manners?" He gives my throat one more forceful pinch before letting go.

Rubbing the soreness from my neck, I fight back tears. "Who are you anymore?" My words crack and break while crushing my heart at the same time. Because the truth is, I don't know this stranger in front of me.

"Someone neither you nor I know."

Ignoring his cruelty, I look at the door, observing the carved BCA emblem. The map from earlier comes into play. I run my fingers over the carving and take in the etching. This must lead to one of the buildings at the Academy?

I lift my chin. "Are we going in here?"

He digs into the pocket of his pressed khakis and pulls out a set of keys. Dangling them in the air, smugly. "I am."

"Wait. You're not leaving me down here, are you?"

The devious look on his face tells me all I need to know. "Good luck finding your way back."

"This is one of those games, isn't it?"

"Maybe it is. Maybe it isn't. Your games are extra special, Scar. Instead of group competitions, like the others, you're our own little lapdog. One we can play with and pet whenever we want. And now that you took an oath, there isn't a damn thing you can do about it."

"Like hell I can't." I lunge for the keys, missing them on my first attempt. "You seriously dragged me through the tunnels just to leave me?"

"I seriously did. You see, these doors all lock automatically and the only way in, or out, is with a master key."

I'm angry. No, I'm furious. Yet, really fucking hurt. I hate what he's become. The guy who I once thought was nothing like the others is earning his place as the most ruthless member in our generation of Blue Bloods.

Crew sticks the key in the hole, turns the handle and looks at me before pushing the door open. With his eyes locked on mine and that sinister smirk back on his lips, he clicks the remote in his other hand, turning the lights off.

Panic sets in, my chest heavy with anxiety. "No. God, no. Please, Crew. Don't leave me down here." *I can't breathe. I can't see, and I can't breathe!*

Irrational thoughts flood my mind. I'm going to get lost and die down here. Either that, or someone else is going to find me, rape me, and dismember by body. My bones will become dust on the ground.

Suddenly, my thoughts elude me. It's as if I'm no longer in control of my own body as I reach out and grab Crew by the shirt. Once I know where he is, I move my hands up to his shoulders.

"What the hell are you doing?"

"Don't do this, Crew. Please. It doesn't have to be this way."

Reverse psychology. Manipulation. Whatever it takes, I'm getting the hell out of here.

I move my hands to his cheeks, cupping them in my hands. "We were so good together. Don't you remember how good things were?" My voice is shaky, but I don't stop trying to sway his decision to leave me. "We can be good again. If you'll let us."

It makes me sick to even say the words, but I have to try.

Crew grips my hips and I'm hopeful the key is still in the door. "*We* were never good. The sex was good, and that's the only reason I kept coming back."

I. Hate. Him.

My chin rests on his shoulder, and I whisper in his ear, while reaching behind him, "I miss the way you used to touch me. You made me feel so good." My neck cranes. I can't see him, but I feel like I'm looking into his eyes. "Touch me again before I'm lost for days in these tunnels?"

"You're fucking with me, Scar, and I don't like to be fucked with." He gives me a shove backward.

"Wait." I reach out and grab his arm, dragging my nails down as hard, and for as long as I can, before I'm shoved to the side. His thunderous footsteps come closer, but I duck and move, trying like hell to stay away from him while luring him farther from the door.

I have to get the hell out of here.

"You fucking slut!" he shouts, causing a ripple in my chest. "Fuck the plans. Fuck everything. I will destroy you, Scar!"

My hands swat and pat, until finally, I find the door. In a swift motion, I pull the keys from the lock and quickly slam the door shut.

"You fucking bitch!"

Pound. Pound. Pound.

They wanna play games, then all four of us are playing.

"Unlock this door now or you'll live to regret it."

Pound. Pound. Pound.

"No, Crew," I shout, anger ripping through my vocal cords, "the only thing I regret is you."

It's completely dark, but I don't even care. Feeling on top of the world after fighting off Crew, I walk straight ahead, up another flight of stairs, and find another door. I keep my head held high, even though I feel like I'm going to lose the contents of my stomach.

Once I'm on the other side, I collapse onto the floor, inside a building I've never been in. There is light, though dim, and for that, I'm grateful.

My eyes dance around the room and that's when I realize I'm inside the library.

Crew has likely alerted the guys already, so I need to get the hell out of here while I have the chance.

EIGHT

CREW

"WELL, boys, we did it. She's all ours. Mission accomplished. She's playing the game. Which I must add was a fucking genius idea." Generally speaking, the games are played as a group, but not for Scar. Neo has organized a mental mind-fuck solely for her participation.

I drop down on the black leather couch, swinging my feet around and kicking them up.

Neo continues pacing in the center of the room, his phone clutched in his hand. "That's where you're wrong. You didn't do shit. *We* did it." He points from himself to Jagger, keeping his eyes down.

I spring up defensively. "What the hell are you talking about? I was just as much a part of this as you two."

"No, you weren't," Jagger chimes in. "You argued that we should let her join the seniors but gave up your fight when you knew you'd lose. You're still soft for the girl."

"Soft for her?" I chuckle. "I don't even want her here." I look between them. "Wait. Are you guys fucking serious? What more can I do to prove to you that my loyalty lies with the two of you?"

Neo tips his chin. "Where'd you get the black eye?"

"And what the fuck happened to your arm?" Jagger leans in, looking at the bandage that runs from my bicep to the crease of my arm.

"Hell if I know. I was so wasted last night. Probably some chick who I pissed off."

"Some chick?" Jagger asks, now standing directly in front me.

Neo joins his side. "Pretty crazy how you went down to take her deep in the tunnels, but you're the one who disappeared."

My shoulders shrug casually. "Couldn't find her."

I didn't wanna have to tell them that I got my ass kicked by Scar and she stole my keys. Really don't need that level of humiliation, when I'm already trying like hell to prove myself to these guys.

Neo gets in my face. "You fucking helped her, didn't you?"

"Dude! Are we really gonna let that girl come between us? It's *us*. We've been best friends since we were in diapers. Chill the fuck out."

"You didn't answer the question," Jagger says directly.

"All right." My shoulders drop in defeat. "She was in the tunnels when I found her. I planned on taking her deeper into them and leaving her for the night like we planned, but..."

Neo shakes his head, teeth grinding as he continuous to pace. "But what?"

"Didn't exactly work out the way I planned, considering she shoved me back through the door and slammed it shut with my keys in her hand."

Jagger's voice rises. "She has your fucking keys?"

Neo's steps become thunderous. "This is great. Really

fucking great, Crew. Ya know, she's the enemy for a reason. That bitch will manipulate the fuck out of you if you let her. Just like she did Maddie."

My head drops forward, and I run my fingers through my hair. "She's not manipulating me. Not the least bit."

Neo stops walking, glaring at me. "You've gotta toughen up and get over this girl. She's not who you think she is."

"I'm fucking over her!" I shout. "Jesus! Just let it go!"

He steps around me and goes toward the stairs, making it halfway up before saying, "Get your damn keys back by tomorrow's sunset or I'll take matters into my own hands. We can't have her snooping around where she doesn't belong."

I look at Jagger, who's scratching his neck. "Come on, man," I say, you know I'm on your side, right?"

He doesn't even look at me. Just shrugs his shoulders and walks in Neo's footsteps. "I believe you're on our side, but I think you're still on hers, too."

With a heavy sigh, I drop back onto the couch. "Fuck!"

Neo's in my fucking head too much. I wish for once I could be who I want to be without him trying to dictate our fucking lives.

"Go away," Scar hisses as I join her side on the trail.

"No can do. You've got something I'm gonna need back."

"Aren't your feet tired from walking back through the tunnels last night?"

"Ha," I mock her, "very funny. And for your information, these legs just pressed a hundred and fifty pounds for a solid forty minutes."

She doesn't even look at me as she walks, just keeps on

with her textbooks clutched to her chest. "How did you even find me out here?"

"Followed you. Saw you leaving the library while I was coming off the football field."

"Well, now you can unfollow me. I have things to do."

"You've got some guts doing what you did last night. Stealing my keys, fucking up my throwing arm."

"And your eye," she adds, pleased with herself.

She stops, her eyes smoldering when she looks at me. "Are you really going to give me shit for what I did after everything you assholes did to me?"

"Is that what we're doing now? An eye for an eye? If that's the case, we'll both be blind before we see this through to the end."

"Why are you still here?"

"I thought I made that clear. You have something that belongs to me." I hold out my hand. "Gimme my keys back."

Glancing at my open palm, she smirks. "I lost 'em."

"What?" I huff. "It's been fourteen hours. How the hell did you lose them?"

Her shoulders shrug. "Threw them on my walk back to my dorm last night. You can go look around, but I doubt you'll find 'em." The casualness of her voice is unnerving.

"Fucking A, Scar." My fingers weave through my sweat-soaked hair before I lift my eyes. "You better be joking."

I don't know if she's fucking with me right now or what, but for her sake, I hope it's a joke.

"Gimme my damn keys or I will make it my mission to torture you the entire school year."

"School hasn't even started yet and you're already well on your way." She keeps walking, grinning. "Tell me what it is you want from me and maybe I'll consider giving them back."

She wants the truth. I'll give it to her. "Easy. I want you miserably eating out of the palm of my hand."

"Point made. You'll torture the hell out of me all year, whether I hand them over or not. Now that I know you want me to be miserable, I guess I have to force myself to be the exact opposite." Her feet stop moving, books tucked in her arms as she turns to face me. "You can expect smiles and laughter from me for the rest of the year."

"Bullshit. You enjoy being miserable too much. You love nothing more than to hide in your room and wallow in your own self-pity because your life is so damn bad."

I know this girl better than she knows herself. Even when I was dating Maddie, I watched Scar from across the room, memorized every quirk, every facial expression, every blank stare. I know when she's annoyed, when she's angry, when she's nervous.

Things changed, though. We've changed. Sure, Scar and I fucked—multiple times—but we got caught. Our relationship was exposed like an open wound that caused nothing but pain for both of us. That same day, more than one truth was revealed.

We reach the end of the trail to Foxes' Den. Scar stops walking and turns to face me. "Maybe I wallow in my own self-pity, but at least I don't drag others down with me."

I smirk. "Misery loves company, baby."

"I'd rather lie in an open grave with a dead body than be stuck in your company." With her books held to her chest with one hand, she stuffs her other hand in the pocket of her baggy, shit-colored corduroy pants, and I hear the jingle of keys. She should only have one key to her room, not multiple ones that clank together.

"That mouth of yours is bound to get you into some serious

trouble." I look at her pocket and when my eyes slide up to hers, she's watching me.

Her expression twists. "Why are you looking at me like that?"

I take one step toward her, slow and steady. "I can think of one way to shut you up. Save you some trouble." And another step. She's watching me closely. Knows I'm up to something. "It wasn't long ago that you loved sucking my cock, Scar." I quickly swoop an arm around her waist and pull her close. "I think you could love it again."

Her hands come up between us, pushing on my chest. "Let go of me, asshole."

She jerks and wiggles her body, causing me to tighten my hold on her. I forgot what a feisty little thing she is. "Give me my keys and I will."

"You want them, then get them."

There's no way I can reach her pocket at this angle, so I take her down to the ground. Her textbooks fly out of her arms. My body cloaks hers, but she doesn't give up the fight. She's as stubborn as she's always been. Never the type to give in or give up. She's always doing the opposite of what she's told to do, just to show everyone she can.

When we were eight years old and at a charity gala with our parents, she was told to sit at the kids' table, even after arguing that she wasn't a kid—clearly, she was. Scar forced crocodile tears down her cheeks and convinced full-grown adults to give up their seats, so she and Maddie could have them.

"Ya know, I kinda like it when you fight back. It'll make it all the more satisfying when I wreck your world."

"Not if I wreck yours first." She reaches her hand between us and presses her thumb into my wounded arm.

"Bitch!" I bellow. "You're gonna regret that."

"Oh yeah?" She snorts. "You said the same thing last night, and I still have no regrets. In fact, I think you're proving to be as weak as your performance in the bedroom."

"You wouldn't know because we never fucked in a bedroom. You were either riding me in the back seat of a car or I had you bent over a piece of furniture."

"It seems your memory has escaped you once again, because you spread my legs nice and wide and fucked me on the floor in a bedroom at the cabin. I still have a scar on my back from the rug burn."

Shit. She's right. I got the same burn on my knees. I still remember the way I bent her legs so far back, her feet touched the floor over her head. I exploded in her pussy that day. But that's beside the point. "You know damn well I'm a fucking athlete in the bedroom."

"See?" She quirks a brow, still squirming. "You do remember."

Hell yeah, I remember. And now that I'm thinking about it, my cock is twitching in my pants.

After a couple more rounds of fighting against each other, Scar drops her head back in defeat. I'm surprised, actually. Figured she'd make this a little harder for me.

With her hands pinned over her head, I know she's not going anywhere, so I take a second to catch my breath before getting the keys. "Don't sweat it, Scar. Those keys would only get you in trouble. You've got enough on your plate as it is."

She licks a bead of sweat from her top lip. "What do they all go to?"

"Places you don't need to be."

"Ah," she faintly nods, "another secret for the *Lawless*."

"Someone's jealous."

She winces. "Jealous is hardly the word I'd use."

"Admit it. You wish female members could form the Lawless and have all the control, don't you?"

"I don't think there should be any control. I believe in equality, not ranks."

Scar's a hothead and hates authority. Must be why she hates this place and the rules so damn much. No matter what you do or say here, those with supremacy always come out on top.

"Be the change then. For starters, suck it up, push down your pride, and do what you have to do to come out on top."

Her eyes close while I hold her in place. Watching her, waiting for the right moment to reach in her pocket and get my keys.

She's pretty relaxed right now. Almost makes me wonder what she's up to. "What the hell are you doing?" I ask, bringing her eyes back open.

"Listening."

"Okayyy," I drag out the word. "What are you listening to?"

Her eyes find mine, expression stoic. "Your heart."

I hold my gaze on hers, head tilted slightly to the left.

Scar places a hand on my chest, mouth curled in a smile. "Oh my god, Crew. Your heart is beating so fast."

"You do that to me, Scar." I place my hand over hers, leaning in for a kiss. My words are a whisper against her lips. "My heart beats faster. My knees go weak. Sometimes I forget to even breathe when you're around."

Her fingers wrap around mine and she takes my hand, moving it from my chest. Leaning closer, she rests her ear against my heart. "It's singing to me." Her eyes land on mine. "Mine sings for you, too, Crew. It shouldn't, but it does."

Don't go there, Crew.

You have to do this. Make her hate you. Hate her back.

I shake away the thoughts, pinch both her wrists together under one of my hands and reach into her pocket.

"Sorry, Scar. It has to be this way." I pull out the keys, and the next thing I know, her forehead is meeting my nose. Hard, painful, and so quick, I can't even wrap my head around what just happened.

I drop to the side, feeling dizzy as hell. Blinking my eyes rapidly to refocus, I don't even notice as Scar grabs the keys from my hand.

"No, *I'm sorry*, Crew. Because I'm a firm believer in karma and it's about to bite you in the ass."

Holding my head, I watch as she scoops up her books and runs to her dorm—my keys in hand.

If the girl wouldn't fight me so damn much, I might be able to treat her with a little more decency. She's the only girl in the world who makes me wanna slap her and fuck her at the same time.

CHAPTER
NINE
SCARLETT

I'M RUNNING AS FAST as I can, feeling like a goddamn queen for pulling that off. *Listening to your heart.* I knew that one would push his guard down.

At one time, I thought Crew had a heart. Actually, I knew he did. I saw it—raw, beautiful, and vulnerable. At the same time, he saw mine. We turned to each other for comfort, knowing how wrong it was. But the minute our secret was brought to light, he joined Neo and Jagger in the darkness. I wouldn't even call him a bully. He's nothing but a coward.

I walk through the front door and spot Riley. "There you are." She comes skipping down the stairs, wearing a pair of black spandex shorts and a cutoff tee shirt. "Did you get your books?"

I lift my shoulder, showing the books clutched under my arm. "Got 'em."

"Oh my god, Scarlett. What happened?" Riley runs her fingers over my forehead. "Did someone punch you?"

I rub the sore spot on my forehead where I hit Crew. "No. It was dumb. I was running down the trail and, *smack*, right into a tree."

"Damn, girl. You need to be more careful."

"It'll be fine. I'll grab some ice. Where are you headed?"

"Cheer practice. We're working on our dance routine."

"Whoa. You never mentioned you're a cheerleader?"

"Sure am." She sticks both arms up. "Go Panthers!"

I shouldn't be surprised, but I am.

"How's that work, anyway? Do other teams come here to play?" I could go for some hot, forbidden football players outside of the Society. Lord knows none of the ones here have caught my eye. Not yet, anyway.

"Nope. Juniors against seniors. Best of five games wins. It's really more about the experience and preparation for those who want to play next year at BCU."

"I see." I continue up the stairs. "Well, you have fun with that dance routine."

"Hey," Riley stops me, "me and a couple of other girls are having dinner in the dining hall tonight. Join us?"

My shoulders rise and fall laggardly. "Sure. Why not."

Riley blows me a kiss before heading out the door.

It's only noon, and I already feel like I could crash for the night. I roll my shoulders as I make my way to my room. Crew really took me down hard and I think I pulled a muscle.

As I take out my key, a rapid movement near the staircase catches my eye. I drop it back in my pocket and go over to the banister. Leaning over, I look down and see someone with a black hood over their head running. In an instant, they're gone and a shadow of the person drifts across the wall before fading into nothingness. They didn't go out the front door, though. Whoever it is, went behind the stairs.

An ominous feeling flows over me. "I know it's you, Crew," I shout loudly over the banister.

It has to be him. If not, then it's Neo or Jagger. They were wearing the same robes last night.

Hurrying over to my door, I set my books in front of it then bolt back down the stairs, taking two at a time.

"This again? Really?" I say loud enough for him to hear me. "Haven't you learned your lesson about sneaking up on me?"

When I reach the bottom, I round the staircase. I don't know what's back here since I haven't ventured this way yet. There's a crawl space under the stairs. A few doors that look like janitor closets, a mop setting in a bucket leaned against the wall. It isn't until I look straight down the stretch of hallway that I see him standing in front of a wooden door with a stained-glass insert.

He's standing there in a black robe with his chin down. The hood over his head hangs low, so I'm not able to make out his face, but I don't need to. I know it's Crew.

"You want 'em. Come and get 'em, fucker." I reach into my pocket and pull out his keys, dangling them in the air.

He doesn't make a move for me. His feet remain planted to the hardwood floor beneath him while he watches me.

My shoulders tighten, and my heart palpitates. *Why is he looking at me like that?* "Crew?" I say, tone low.

Something feels off and I have the sudden urge to flee. I take a few steps backward, never letting my eyes leave him.

Crew, or whoever it is, reaches into the pocket of his robe. I'm a deer in headlights: unable to move, think, react.

In slow motion, he pulls something out. I adjust my eyes, trying to see what he's holding.

A phone. It's definitely a phone.

That's proof enough that it's one of the guys. They're the only ones with enough guts to show their phones on Academy grounds.

I take another step back as he raises it. A light on the back of it flickers a few times. *What the hell!*

"Are you taking pictures of me?"

One. Two. Three. He keeps snapping them repeatedly, even as I cover my face.

I go around the corner of the staircase, setting my foot on the first step, still unable to take my eyes off him out of fear that he'll come up behind me.

Suddenly, he swings around and escapes out the door behind him.

My feet carry me up the stairs quickly. I stumble, catching myself with my hands on the step above me. When I look down, I see blood running down my shin. I don't even feel the pain as I continue moving, not stopping until I'm at my door, scooping my books off the floor.

Once I unlock the door and I'm inside, I go straight to bed and empty my hands and pockets, tossing my books and both sets of keys on it.

I stand there, staring at Crew's keys. Maybe I should just give them back. Right now he's after me for them, but what happens when he sics the others on me? I can handle Crew. Maybe even Jagger. But I'm positive I don't want to get any further on Neo's bad side.

The door suddenly flies open, and I gasp before ruffling my blankets and covering Crew's keys.

"Riley!" I clutch my chest. "You scared the hell out of me."

She comes skipping into the room, her curls bouncing with each leap. "Since when do you get scared? I assumed you were fearless." She snatches a bag off her bed, holding it up. "Forgot my bag. I'm gonna get ready in the locker room after practice and I'll see you for dinner."

I nod in response, my insides still trembling. "Hey, Riley," I blurt out, stopping her in the doorway. Her brows quirk in response. "Are the football players having practice right now?"

"Yep. Saw your old friend, Crew, there. He was looking mighty hot." She waggles her brows before closing the door behind her.

I pull the blanket off the keys and pick them up. If Crew was there, then who was here?

TEN

"PENNY FOR YOUR THOUGHTS?" Elias asks, pressing his hands to the table I'm at in the library.

"Hey," I say through a cracked smile. Ever since Riley confirmed Crew was at practice today, I've been in a weird headspace.

Elias swings his black backpack off his shoulder and drops it to the floor. "Everything okay?"

The last thing I want is to be a downer, and there's no way in hell I'm spilling my guts to a guy I hardly know, so I say, "I'm fine."

From the expression on his face, I'm guessing he's not buying it. Elias nods toward the chair. "Do you mind?"

I remove my hand from where it's pressed to my forehead and wave it over the chair beside me. "Have a seat."

Biting back a smile, he sits down.

"What?" I ask, wondering why he's on the verge of laughter.

His eyes pin to my forehead and he grazes his fingers across his own. "Your...forehead. It's really red."

"Oh," I laugh, rubbing the spot where I headbutted Crew, "I'm a klutz. Ran right into a tree."

He laughs with me then his expression goes stoic. "So what's really going on? When a girl says she's fine, it usually means she's anything but fine."

"Just adjusting to this place, is all."

He looks around the library, as if I'm talking about this place specifically. Though, he knows exactly what I mean. "Yeah. It definitely requires some adjusting. You're tough, though. You'll be fine."

"Hey," I say to him, feeling bored with this place and the conversation, "wanna get out of here?"

"Sure. What do you have in mind?"

"Food." I chuckle. I'm supposed to eat dinner with Riley, but that's not for another hour and the rumble in my stomach tells me I can't wait that long.

"The buffet in the dining hall opens in twenty-minutes. We could hit that up."

"Actually, I already have dinner plans. Isn't there some sort of snack store around here?"

"The campus convenience store? Yes. They definitely have snacks and anything else you might need." He suddenly frowns. "Unfortunately, they close at five. But the vending corner is open. They've got pretty much anything you could want that's processed and packaged."

Grinning, I slide my chair back. "Processed and packaged it is."

Elias puts on his backpack and I stuff my books in my messenger bag and hook it on my shoulder. We weave through the tables filled with other students, then leave the library.

"What do you think of BCA so far?" he asks as soon as the fresh air hits our faces.

"Breaking the ice with a big question, I see." It's an attempt at humor, but I often fail miserably, much like this moment.

Elias gives me a questioning look. "That bad?"

Gripping the strap of my bag crossed over my chest, I follow his lead, since I have no idea where this vending corner is. "I can't say it's bad, but I will say it's exactly what I expected. Entitled assholes, stuck-up girls, and the best view our state has to offer."

"Well, at least we've got the view going for us."

"That is true. That is true."

Elias and I look at each other, both opening our mouths to speak at the same time, and at the same time, we both say, "Go ahead."

I smile through the awkwardness. "No. You first. I insist."

"I was about to tell you to hang in there because it always gets worse before it gets better."

"It does get better, though, is what you're saying?"

His shoulders rise, both hands holding tight to the straps of his backpack. "Depends on who you ask, I guess."

We take a left, still on the sidewalk we stepped on outside of the library. It's pretty cool how this place is like a little town of its own. A very vintage, dystopian town run by pompous Society members and the kids they put in charge of us all.

"I'm asking you." I glance at him as we keep on our path. "Has it gotten better?"

"Truthfully. No. I'm not impressed with anything the Society has to offer me. And eventually, I won't partake in any of the privileges. I'm only here because I have to be."

I smile broadly, stop walking, and turn to face him. "Hi, I'm Scarlett, and I think we're going to be great friends." I offer him my hand and he laughs at the gesture, though he returns it with a shake.

"Elias. And I could really use a friend around here."

RACHEL LEIGH

We start walking again, talking about our favorite foods and books. It turns out, Elias and I have a lot in common. He loves classic novels, although I prefer romance and he's more into thrillers. We both prefer tacos over pizza, and beer over wine. I told him a list of the books I love that I couldn't find in the library, and he told me he knows of a small bookstore in town that carries all the classics. If only we could get away and go there.

After we load our arms with snacks, we end up on the large cement steps in front of the library and begin stuffing our faces.

"Cheese curls next?" Elias asks, handing me the bag.

I graciously accept and squeeze the bag until the bottom of it pops open.

"That's an easy way to have all your snacks in your lap."

I flip the bag over and pull one out, tossing it in my mouth. "Not if you do it right."

Minutes of laughter and conversation turn to an hour, then another, and before I know it, the sun has set. "Oh no!" I jump up, dusting cheese powder and pretzel salt off my jeans. "What time is it?" I ask the question at the same time I look at my wristwatch. "Shit. Shit. Shit. I was supposed to meet Riley an hour ago."

"Go," he says, "I'll take care of the trash and I'll catch you later."

"Thanks, Elias. This was a lot of fun and just the distraction I needed today."

He smiles in response before I turn around and head briskly toward the dining hall with my bag on my shoulder.

I'm almost there when someone jumps out of nowhere, grabbing me.

I try to scream, but my sounds are muffled by the cloth pressed to my mouth.

Everything is quiet.

Everything disappears.

Until all I see is black.

"Dude. She's awake."

"Do it now and take the damn picture, so we can get the hell out of here."

"I'm not doing it. You do it."

My eyes open, and I blink a few times, trying to adjust them, but I can't see. Panic settles in my stomach when I go to speak, but my mouth doesn't open.

"Fuck no. Did you hear what she did to Crew Vance? He's one of the Lawless, and she still slapped him."

If I could talk, I'd set them straight on the fact that I did not slap Crew, I punched him. I continue listening, hoping to recognize one of the voices, but so far, I don't.

"You untie her, Steven can push her in, and I'll take the picture."

"Dude. You said my name. He told us not to say our names."

Three voices, all arguing about a picture. *A picture of what?*

I save the name Steven to memory, so I can use it later when I hunt the fucker down and beat his ass.

In an attempt to move my hands, so I can remove the cover over my eyes and my mouth, I realize I'm bound. Lying on my side, on the ground, tied up. I flip over, feeling the grainy dirt between my fingers. *Definitely on the ground.*

"Whoa!" one of the guys bellows. "She's moving, she's moving."

"Hurry up and do it, you fucking pussy."

Ignoring them, I try using my senses to get out of this

mess. There's definitely some moisture in the air, which leads me to believe we're by the water—likely the river. One of them told Steven to push me in. *Oh god!* Did he mean into the river?

I flip over again, now on my back. I can feel my flannel bunched beneath me, so it's still tied around my waist. That could come in handy if I need to choke them with it.

"We're wasting time. We've only got six more minutes or we lose the game."

The game?

If this is a game, then whose game is it? Theirs, mine, or all of ours.

"Five minutes, guys."

Someone touches my shoulder, and I jolt. My legs kick together, and I swing my arms up, trying to hit whoever is near me. "Get off me," I try to say, but my words come out as gibberish against the sticky plastic substance covering my mouth.

"All right. All right. I'll untie her." His loud voice drops to a whisper and I can't make out what he's saying.

That's right. Untie me, fuckers. Give me a free hand or a free foot, so I can shove either up your asses.

Seconds later, I'm being lifted to my bound feet while someone holds my waist from behind.

"Go."

The tight hold on my legs loosens, but it's replaced by strong hands holding them in place. Same with my arms. I squirm endlessly, trying to free them, but I can't do it.

Suddenly, I'm shoved from behind, my feet leave the ground, and before I can think or react, I'm dropping into freezing cold water. It streams up my shirt, cuts through my nostrils, and chokes me. But I can't cough. Anxiety rips through my body like a sharp knife, leaving me debilitated and unable to think logically.

You can do this. You will not be another casualty in their fucked-up games.

I remember my hands are freed and I use them to swim up as I push my feet off a rock, giving me the surge I need to get my head above water.

"Got it," I hear one of the guys say. "Leave the note and let's get the hell out of here."

Two fingers pinch the side of the tape on my mouth and I rip it off, immediately coughing up the water that went straight to my lungs. I sputter and flap my hands, still unable to see.

The blindfold is hanging now, only covering one eye, and I pull it over my head. I blink my eyes a few times. It's dark. No. It's pitch black. My heart pounds in my chest as I swim through the ice-cold water, unsure where I'm going or how I get out of here.

It's so cold I can barely feel my limbs as they move.

"When I find out who you..." I attempt to shout, but I start coughing up more water. Between my heart racing and my shortage of air, I can't get the words out. It's no use anyway. They're long gone by now.

I'm moving at a steady pace when I catch a glimpse of light up on the riverbank. It flickers, much like the ones in the tunnels. I head toward it, eventually finding an out.

It's a small, but slippery climb over the rocks. I'm thankful I didn't hit my head on these when I was pushed. My body would float down this river, never to be found. No one would look for me because the Elders would silence my disappearance.

Quit thinking like that, Scarlett. Just get the hell out of here before you catch hypothermia.

I manage to get over the rocks, and I breathe out a heavy sigh of relief when my feet are on solid ground. Wasting no time, I go straight for the lantern, thankful it's here to guide me out of this place.

Water drops in plentiful amounts from my clothes and I untie my flannel that's making the trek heavier, and I toss it to the side.

As I approach the lantern, I see an envelope with my name printed on it. Bending down, I pick it up and slide my finger along the seal.

I'm not surprised to see a note inside, considering I heard one of the guys mention it.

With bent knees, I crouch down, my soaked jeans straining against my skin. Using the light from the lantern, I open the note and read it out loud...

"What's harder to catch, the faster you run?"

I flip it over, expecting more. That's it? A stupid riddle?

I repeat it a few times while my entire body shivers. "What's harder to catch, the faster you run?"

The sound of a chainsaw nearby has my heart jumping in my throat as I grab the lantern handle. It gets louder and louder, as the handler comes closer and closer. It's not just one, it's two—maybe three. They close in on me. One from the back, and one on each side. Definitely three.

Do something, Scar. Think. Move. Run.

I move quickly, and the next thing I know, I'm dodging branches and jumping over rocks before my mind even processes what's happening.

No matter how far I get, the distance doesn't increase between me and the sound.

"Stop it!" I shout, feeling light-headed and off-balance.

I keep running, unsure where I'm going. My body shivers as chills prick my skin.

They're fucked up. No. They're beyond fucked up. They're

deranged. These guys are not human. They're soulless bastards.

My throat swells as I choke back the tears that beg to fall. This is what they want. They want me to crumble, so they can sweep up the pieces and mold me into whatever the hell they want.

Something, or someone rather, comes out of nowhere, and I crash right into him, or her. My body flies backward and my back hits the ground, knocking the air out of my lungs.

I grunt, trying to reach for the lantern that flew from my hand. I've almost got it, when a black boot stomps down on it, shattering the glass casing and extinguishing the flame.

Swallowing hard, I try to get a grip and stand, but my shaky limbs don't allow it.

"Take a minute, Scar," my offender says. It's a familiar voice—masculine and deep, sexy and mysterious.

"Neo?"

A shift in the air tells me he's near. I listen intently to the crunch of the leaves. The scent of worn leather and pine floods my senses and I'm assured it is, in fact, Neo.

My hand extends, needing to find out how close he is, and when I hit his leg, I quickly retreat.

If it were the light of day, I wouldn't be so feeble. But in the dark, I am weak. They know this. They know my fears and they indulge in them like they're their own personal drug. Getting high on my misery. Basking in my unease like it's warmth to their cold hearts.

"How are you enjoying the games so far?"

I spit at him, hoping I hit his face, but his lack of anger leads me to believe I missed. "Fuck you! You assholes could've killed me."

"Yet, here you are, alive and well."

I push myself up until I'm sitting on the ground. "Just lead me the hell out of here, so I can go back to my room and plot your demise."

I'm almost on my feet when I'm shoved back down. This time, I land on my ass. My fingertips dig into the soil as I bite down on the urge to claw this asshole's eyes out.

"Not so fast, Scar. You're not finished yet. You need to catch your breath. You were running pretty fast."

"Because you jerks were chasing me with chainsaws."

"Quit being so dramatic. They didn't have the chain in them. And you should be thanking me for that. Had we not brought them, you'd be running in the wrong direction."

"You expect me to thank you?" I laugh, fisting chunks of dirt in my hands. "I'd rather find my way out of here alone in the dark while risking hypothermia than be anywhere near you three."

"Now, that's not very nice. You don't even know the guys who helped me tonight." I can feel him getting closer again. This time, it's too close for comfort. His warm breath hits the nape of my neck and my entire body stills, all but my heart that's rapid-firing against my rib cage.

"As if it would be anyone other than Crew and Jagger."

"Oh, but it was." His fingers run along the hem of my short sleeves, fingertips grazing my skin. He exhales, this time the air spilling down the V of my drenched tee shirt. My nipples pucker on impact.

I raise my balled fists, ready to open them up and shove dirt in his face, but before I can, he grabs my wrists.

"Drop it."

When I don't, he squeezes harder. "Now, Scar."

Giving in, I slowly spread my palms, letting the dirt fall to my sides.

"Nice try but you have to be quicker than that. Now, answer the riddle and you move on. If you fail, you're out of the games and left out here all night to find your own way back. Although, you said yourself, it's what you wanted."

No. It's not what I want. I'd rather dig a hole and hide in it until the sun rises than walk through these woods alone.

Okay. The riddle. *What was it again?*

Something about running and catching.

"I...I can't remember what it was."

"What is harder to catch, the faster you run?" He goes silent as I think.

Shit. I don't know. I'm no good at riddles. Even Eloise, the little girl who comes to the quarterly Society meetings, gets me with her knock-knock jokes.

"Think about it, Scar. I'd hate to report a missing student on my watch so early in the year."

"Yeah, right," I sneer. "You'd love nothing more than for me to go missing. Never to be heard of again. I know you hate me, Neo."

"Wrong," he says. "I don't hate you. I loathe you. You are the bane of my existence. Everything I do that involves you is smothered in ill-intent. When I look at you, it pains me. When I touch you, it makes me sick."

My voice cracks and breaks and I push down the lump lodged in my throat. "Why? What is it you hate so much about me?" I choke out.

It shouldn't hurt like it does because I've always known everything he's telling me. It does hurt, though. It hurts because I don't know why. What did I ever do to make him hate me so much?

"Everything." The emptiness in his tone is disturbing, and I truly believe it when he says he hates everything about me.

I won't get any other answer. I've asked Neo countless times why he's never liked me and it's always the same simple response.

Maddie once told me he's jealous of my friendship with her. But back then, Neo tolerated me. Sure, he pulled little pranks and cracked jokes at my expense, but he was never this detestable. It's like, when Maddie left, he felt free to finally set my world on fire.

"You've got one minute."

"One minute?" I blurt out. "How am I supposed to solve that in one minute?"

"You're a smart girl. You'll figure it out."

I inhale deeply, filling my lungs while trying to clear my head.

"Forty seconds."

"Okay," I say, "I've got this. *What is harder to catch, the faster you run?*"

I speak out loud, hoping it helps me solve this riddle. "Harder to catch. Faster you run. When you run fast, you could be chasing something..." *No. That's not it.*

"What happens to your body when you run, Scar?" he asks, making me think harder.

"Fast legs?"

"No," he deadpans.

"Depth perception?"

"Yes. But no. Twenty seconds."

"A healthy heart. Strong lungs?"

"Headed in the right direction."

What is harder to catch the faster you run?

Breath!

"Your breath!" I spit out eagerly. "That's it. When you run fast, you lose your breath. The faster you run, the harder it is to catch."

"Well done," he says, tone flat. "Now get up. I've got better things to do than tail your ass in the woods."

102

I was expecting more congratulations on his part. Then again, this is Neo.

Feeling depleted, I push myself off the ground, dirt embedded in my nails and my clothes caked in earthy debris.

We're walking along in silence, Neo shining a flashlight in front of us, when I interrupt the quiet with a question that's heavy on my mind. "Did Crew and Jagger know about this?"

I can hear his tongue clicking on the roof of his mouth and I imagine a smug look on his face as he says, "Of course they did."

I always knew they disliked me because Neo made them turn their backs on me after Maddie's accident, but I didn't realize how much until now.

At the Gathering, Neo said these games will test not only your physical endurance, but also your mental stability. He never mentioned that they cause emotional damage. Walking out of these woods with Neo as my guide, I feel weak and belittled. I lost part of my dignity in the river and I'm choking on my pride as I follow behind Neo, knowing that, in his head, he's thinking he won. Because tonight, he did.

CHAPTER
ELEVEN
SCARLETT

SINCE I MISSED dinner with Riley last night, I agreed to hang out with her and a few other girls at the hot springs right outside Boulder Cove Academy grounds. Technically, we're not supposed to leave the property, but Riley claims students go there all the time. Normally, I wouldn't give rule breaking a second thought, but after yesterday, I've been on edge.

Who came to our dorm wearing that robe? Did they come for me? And why on earth would they take pictures of me?

I still have Crew's keys, but I have every intention of giving them back to him tomorrow during lunch. I'm not sure if we have any classes together, but Riley said all seniors eat lunch at the same time, and I damn well better be on that senior list. I don't care what games they make me play to earn a rank; I will not be pushed into junior schedules and activities.

"Ready?" Riley asks when she returns from the bathroom.

"Yep," I say as I pull a maize-and-blue Essex High hoodie over my head, covering my black, one-piece swimsuit. It's not exactly summer, even if the water is warm.

Riley tosses me a towel, and I drape it around my neck. She

looks all cutesy in a hot pink bikini with her hair in a high ponytail on top of her head. She covers herself up with a long-sleeved tee shirt, then we head out.

Following her through the door, I pull the scrunchie off my wrist and pile my hair in a messy bun on top of my head. "Who should I expect to see at this little swim party?"

"Just a few students. Mostly the girls from the senior cheer team."

I quirk a brow, looking at her as we turn down the stairs. "And guys?" I'm not asking because I have any interest in the guys here. My hope is that none of the Lawless will be there. I've never felt intimidated by any of them before coming here, but something about this place and their power leaves me with an empty feeling in my stomach. I knew being here under their authority would suck, but I didn't expect it to suck this bad. I'm torn between telling them to fuck off and abiding by their rules, so I can leave this place unscathed. My pride is a pesky little bitch.

"About that," Riley winces, stopping with her hand on the door. My head immediately shakes no. I'll go back up to my room right now if she's telling me they'll be there. "I sort of got us a ride."

My shoulders slump while my expression does the same. "You're kidding, right?"

She pushes open the door and, sure as shit, our rides are here.

Two guys with helmets and UV goggles sit on the seat of their dirt bikes, with extra helmets hanging from their hands. Both are wearing matching red-and-black riding gear. I don't even have to see their faces to know it's two of the three Lawless members. I'm just not sure which ones. My guess is Jagger and Crew. Regardless of who it is, I'm not going.

"Nope!" I pivot around and head back for the stairs.

"Scarlett, please!" Her whiney voice is like nails on a chalkboard. You'd do anything to stop it. "It's the last day before classes begin, and we need to have some fun. I can't have fun without my new bestie there."

I'm not sure how rooming together makes us best friends, but her offer of bestieship is not changing my mind.

The look on her face, however...

"You expect me to hop on the back of one of those dirt bikes—*in my bathing suit*—with someone I literally hate with every fiber of my being? Do you have any idea what those guys did to me last night?"

"What Neo did was awful and I hate him for that, but Crew and Jagger were just innocent bystanders. You said it yourself, they weren't there."

"They might not have made an appearance, but they were just as much a part of it as Neo was."

"Well, look at it this way. You getting on that bike and going to this get-together, where they are, shows them how strong you really are."

She's got a point. A really good point, actually. If I don't go, it'll give the impression that they scared me off.

"Besides, you told me that things were good with you guys."

I did say that but I lied. I hate them. I hate them so much.

"Come on, Scarlett. Try not to take the games or ranks personally. We all go through it."

It's hard not to take it personally when everything about what they're doing *is* personal.

"Can you just do this one thing for me? After all, you stood me up at dinner last night." She folds her hands in a plea and puffs out her bottom lip.

"Ugh!" I roll my neck, cracking it. "Fine! But I don't like this and I really think you need to reconsider befriending these guys."

"I'm not befriending. Just climbing the ladder to bigger and better things. Associating with them keeps targets off my back. Eat or be hungry, right?"

"No," I laugh, "I think the saying you're looking for is, eat or be eaten."

Riley hooks her arm around mine and pulls me through the door. "Then let's eat."

That sliver of cheerfulness dissipates almost immediately when I see them again.

Leaning against Riley, I whisper, "Are they really allowed to have those bikes here?"

Jagger points and curls his finger at Riley, calling her over.

She hops in place, all giddy and excited. "They're the Lawless. They can have whatever they want." Her arm leaves mine as she skips to his side, where he's leaning against his bike.

Standing halfway between the building and the guys, I chew on my bottom lip.

Jagger's sudden interest in Riley has me questioning his motives. He's not the type to commit to one girl, like ever. Even when we attended high school together, he was known as a player. All the girls would crawl on their knees for him, hoping they'd be the one to change his ways. It never happened.

When Jagger kick-starts his bike, Riley pulls on her helmet.

"Let's go," Crew calls out, though his voice is muffled behind the face mask on the helmet.

"Get on, Scarlett. It'll be fun," Riley hollers before Jagger takes off, stirring up dust behind him. Her arms fly up and she hoots as they burn out.

My heart is fucking pounding. I do not want to get on that bike. It gives them leverage and it does not make me look strong. Accepting the favor of a ride from any of them makes me look weak as hell. I told Riley I'd do it, though, and I always stick to my word.

Swallowing down the saliva pooling in my mouth, I walk over to him. He hands me a helmet and I pull it over my head with the towel still hung around my neck. "Just so you know, those junior boys could have done anything they wanted to my body when I was knocked out, and it would've been all your fault. You might not have been there, but I blame all three of you equally."

His body tenses up and his head rolls inside the helmet before he says, "We'd never let that happen. Now, you better hold on tight." Then he kick-starts the bike, and before I'm even fully seated, he takes off.

"What the hell?" I shriek, grabbing his sides and squeezing.

Oh my god, I'm going to die. This is how it ends.

Ignoring my outburst, he whips a one-eighty, which causes the bike to lean and almost touch the ground. I'm using all my strength and barely hanging on.

As quick as we *almost* went down, we're back up.

"Asshole!" I bang my fist hard on his shoulder. "Are you trying to kill us?" The bike is so loud, I'm not even sure he heard me, but at least he felt the wrath of my fury.

We're flying down the trail and I can't even look. My eyes pinch shut; head turned to the right. The next thing I know, my towel flies off my neck. I try to look to see where it went, but we're moving too fast.

I'm taken aback when Crew reaches behind him and grabs my hand on his side and pulls it farther around him. Then the other, until I'm hugging his waist.

My heart gallops a few times before settling down.

We turn down another trail and my nerves have gone from extremely high to just mildly annoyed.

It's not exactly warm out and riding on the back of this bike through the cool air has chills dancing down my body.

Still unable to look out of fear that I'll panic and fall off, I rest my head against his back and just hold on, hoping we get to where we're going safely. I've never ridden on a dirt bike and I have no interest in getting on one again. He's officially ruined it for me. *Thanks, Crew.*

After a few more turns, he slows his speed, but it still feels like we're riding in the wind. It's not as loud, which makes it less scary, so I lift my head. I don't have those funky goggles on like the guys, so the cool breeze nips at my cheeks.

My anxiety has dissipated, and though I'll never admit it to him, this is kinda nice.

"I decided to give you your keys back," I say, loud enough for him to hear me over the rumble of the bike.

Had I known I'd be riding with him, I would have brought them today. Those keys are nothing but a reason for Crew and the guys to fuck with me. Even if they can get me in and out of the tunnels and every other place on Academy grounds, I don't want 'em anymore.

He doesn't say anything.

Holding Crew like this, being so close to him, it feels strange. Almost like old times when I felt safe in his arms. Like nothing could touch me or hurt me. Warmth fills my belly and I find myself bringing our bodies closer.

What am I thinking? This guy orchestrated a game that involved me getting thrown into the river blindfolded and running through the woods, thinking my life was on the line.

I loosen my hold on him, straightening my back, so my chest isn't so close.

In the last forty-eight hours, I've had to punch him, scratch him, and headbutt him just to defend myself. I'd have to be completely losing my mind to ever catch feelings for Crew again. Although, inflicting pain on him does turn me on in some weird, sick way.

All I hear is the roar of the bike and the crunching of leaves beneath the tires, but my ears are ringing with my own internal thoughts.

When did everything go to hell?

Was it when the guys caught Crew and me together? When the guilt inside me was too much to bear that I ignored it and continued to chase waterfalls with Crew? Or when they relentlessly sabotaged my reputation, killing me slowly with each strong-arm tactic?

No. It wasn't any of that. I know exactly when my life flipped upside down. It was the day Maddie fell.

"Crew," I mumble. Much too quiet for him to hear. It's a good thing, because when I open my mouth to ask the question I intended, nothing comes out.

Does the guilt of what we did feast on your insides like it does mine?

How Crew feels is not my problem anymore. Therefore, I don't want the answer to my question.

I was too lost in my thoughts to even notice the beauty surrounding us. My shoulders draw up and I straighten my back, taking in the scenery. It's breathtaking.

Walls of rolling hills surround us. Behind them are the lofty peaks of the mountains. The leaves have faded in color while the evergreens are still vibrant and un-withered.

Looking to the left, I lean over a tad to peer down and I see the hole of the hot springs. There are around a dozen people prancing around in swimsuits. Laughing, drinking, and dancing. To what song, I'm not sure yet.

We come to a stop at the edge of a hill, at least two

hundred feet off the ground. I'm curious, and slightly nervous, as to how we're gonna get this bike down there without us spilling over the side of the hill.

Crew twists the handle over and over, keeping the bike running. My heart is racing again.

"Please tell me you're not going down that hill."

He revs the bike again and I find myself holding on to him like my life depends on it.

"Crew," I say his name in warning.

The next thing I know, my body is flying back and I'm squealing sounds I didn't know I could make. "You're insane!"

We tear up another trail that runs along the edge of the high hill, and dare I say, I'm smiling.

The adrenaline rush is unbelievable. Scary, but exhilarating at the same time. For the first time since I've arrived at BCA, I feel alive.

When the slope gets steeper, my chest falls into Crew's back. My chin rests on the flank of his shoulder, and I look straight ahead.

A minute later, we're whipping around again, making a grand entrance.

As my body dips to the side, I notice two bikes beside us— Neo's and Jagger's.

I pull my helmet off and inhale a breath of the fresh air, dampened by the moisture from the hot springs. It's much colder than I thought it would be, fortunately, the water should be nice.

Crew kills the engine and knocks the kickstand down. When he hops off the bike, it shakes from the weight shift.

Two hands plant on my sides, and he lifts me off. I'm not sure whether I should be thankful or embarrassed because everyone is watching us.

"I Hate Everything About You" by Three Days Grace is

pounding out of a portable speaker sitting on a rock. There are beer cans scattered all over, and a few coolers sitting around. Everyone resumes what they were doing before we arrived and I'm grateful their attention on us was short-lived.

I spot Riley, who's in the water, waving me over. Beside her is Hannah, who has a guy's arm wrapped around her neck. It isn't until my eyes slide to the left when I see whose arm it is...*Crew*. Submerged in water up to his chest, which is tattooed with a design that extends around his shoulder blade, is the guy I thought I came here with.

But if...

My gaze lands on the person who just drove me here. His hands set on the sides of his helmet and he lifts up, taking the goggles with it.

"Neo?"

He raises his brows, smirking. "Hope the ride wasn't too rough for you. Then again, I heard you like it rough." He leans in, invading my personal space. His lips ghost my ear as he whispers, "Is that true, Scar? Do you like it so rough it takes your breath away?"

I fight the urge to strangle the life out of him because I know how he is. He'll make a spectacle out of me in front of all these people, if I dare put my hands on him. Neo thrives off my humiliation.

My hands smooth down my swim cover and I take in a deep breath. On the exhale, I use sarcasm as my defense. "Yes, Neo. That is true." I give him a pat on the back. "Unfortunately, you weren't rough enough for me. You do owe me a towel, though." I loop around him and wave to Riley, who's engaged in a conversation with Hannah.

"Come join us," Riley says. "The water feels great."

Never in my wildest dreams—well, my wildest dreams in the last year and a half—did I ever think I'd be at such a small social gathering with these three guys. I'm insane for even agreeing to this.

The closer I walk to the water, the softer the ground becomes. It's a mixture of dry grass and mucky mud. There are rocks surrounding the reservoir. It looks well maintained, which has me curious if this is public property. When I see the solar lights around it, I realize it's probably not.

It's not large, by any means. In fact, it's so small that only a dozen people can fit comfortably. Any more than that would be body-to-body.

"Hop in, Scar," Jagger says from beside Crew, "got a seat right here for you." His arms stretch out on either side of him, resting on the edge of rocks. I take in the full sleeve of tattoos on his right arm. It's an array of designs that all flow together seamlessly.

My arms cross over my chest, shielding myself from the awkward stares set on me. Melody is sitting on a large rock with her feet in the water. From the way she's looking at me, I'd say she's jealous of the attention the Lawless is giving not only Riley, but me as well. After all, we did ride here with two of the three members.

"I'm good. I think I'll just hang out above water for a bit."

"Go ahead and freeze then." Jagger tips back the amber-colored bottle of beer in his hands.

Snarling at him, I sidestep around a large rock in front of me and take a seat on it.

I'm sharing a glance with Riley and I hope she's reading my raised brows and subtle head shakes. It's my way of telling her I disapprove of this whole situation.

From the corner of my eye, I watch Neo. With his backside facing me, I notice his full back tattoo. Detailed images of swords, skulls, and trees with delicate lines and shades of red that run into the black. When he turns around, his cut of abs on display, his eyes catch mine and I quickly look away.

Neo drops in the water beside Crew, making a splash and taking Jagger's spot. He leans in and whispers something in Crew's ear that has him scratching his head. When he reclaims his space, he catches me watching him again and my upper torso flushes with heat. I wasn't actually *watching* him, rather just glancing in his direction.

People get in and out, but I'm more focused on Crew, who is wooing Hannah. I'm not sure how I feel about it, but it's definitely stirring some sort of emotion inside me. When he flicks some water at her, she giggles sheepishly, causing me to roll my eyes away from them.

I shouldn't care. Crew and I were over before we started and our mutual hatred for each other has assured us we will never be anything more than enemies.

The hairs on my neck prick as a cool breeze brushes across my backside.

"Need a drink?"

I flinch.

Jagger.

His hand comes around me holding a bottle of beer, cap off.

"No, thanks."

"Come on, Scar. You screw one of my best friends and let the other between your legs on the way here and you won't even have a drink with me."

"You're an idiot. You know that, right?"

"An idiot who's trying really fucking hard to be nice."

"Nice, my ass." Licking my lips, I let my head fall back. "Fine. I'll take the drink, but only because I'm thirsty." I grab the beer, bring it straight to my lips and drink down a quarter of the contents. It carbonizes my esophagus, but the uncomfortable feeling quickly subsides.

"You're welcome."

If he thinks I'm going to thank him, he's wrong. He's lucky I don't give him hell for what happened last night, too. It doesn't matter, though. No matter what I say, it won't stop whatever they have planned for me.

"So. How was the ride here?"

Why is he still talking to me?

Giving him the silent treatment, in hopes he'll go away, I take another sip.

"Looks like Crew's found a new friend."

My eyebrows perk up and I look at him with the bottle still pressed to my lips. "Hmm?" I hum, pretending I didn't hear him acknowledge the flirtation going on between Hannah and Crew.

Jagger nods toward the water, and I follow his gaze.

"I really don't care what Crew does. I hate him as much as I hate you, remember?" Turning to face him, I shove the bottle of beer to his chest. When his arms fly out instead of catching it, it falls down, cracking on a flat rock.

Without even looking at the mess on the ground, I head to Riley. The last thing I want is to get in that water with Neo and Crew, but I also don't feel like conversing with Jagger.

"Clean it up." The demanding words don't come from behind me, but rather, in front of me.

I look at Neo. "Excuse me?"

"You heard me. Clean it up." Casually, he takes a drink of his beer. His stoic expression never faltering.

I'm taken aback but comprehend what he's telling me to do pretty quickly. "No!" I spit out on impulse. I refuse to be degraded in front of my classmates.

My eyes widen, stomach clenched as Neo jumps out of the

water in an angry form. In a swift motion, he tosses his own beer bottle against a rock, shattering it.

It looks like he took half the water with him as it drops in heaps off his soaked swim shorts. I take a step back when he comes at me full speed with an intense gaze burning into me.

Eyebrows caved in, his chest bumps mine. "Who do you think you are talking to me like that?" he grits out. "I told you to clean up the mess you made, now fucking do it."

I swallow hard and I'm sure my distress is widespread for everyone to see. I look over his shoulder at Riley, hoping she'll come to my defense, since she's been all chummy with these guys, but she won't even look at me. With downcast eyes, she just runs her fingers over the water as if this isn't even happening.

"I said no!" I shove Neo in the chest, causing him to step back. "What you're doing isn't leadership. This is straight-up bullying, and you three should know better than anyone that I don't cower to bullies."

"Everyone, back to what you were doing. We've got this under control," Jagger says loudly.

I laugh, bitterly. "Have what under control? There's nothing to control." My hand waves toward the broken bottle. "It's a cracked bottle, and much more put together than the one Neo just threw. I'll clean my mess up if you clean up yours."

Neo grabs me by the bicep, lifting as he pulls me away. Jagger doesn't bother following, heading back to the water instead.

"You realize how ridiculous you're being, right?" I laugh it off, but it's not funny at all. When I'm nervous, I laugh. It's something I've done since I was a kid.

"You're really testing my patience, Scarlett. You're lucky

you have the Sunder last name or you'd be facing expulsion from the Society."

"Is that supposed to scare me, Neo? Do you really think I care if me or my family are a part of this stupid cult?"

Neo blows out a blustery breath, squeezing my arm tighter before spinning me around to face him. He walks his body into me in rapid steps, and my back crushes against a tree. "You ever call this a cult again, and I'll remove your last name and make you a nobody. Got it?"

He's so close, I can feel the rage spilling from his pores. Sweat pools around his hairline. Of all the bad sides to get on, I just had to get on Neo's. *So fucking stupid.*

"Got it," I say, just to end this.

"No, you don't." His tone is sharp, like a knife. "You hate this Society. You hate who you are because of it. You hate everything about being a Blue Blood, don't you?"

I open my mouth to speak, but the words get lodged in my throat. Truth be told, I don't hate it all. I don't hate who I am or what I'll become. "No. What I hate is being told what to do. By you. By them. By anyone."

"Why is that, Scarlett? Think long and hard. Is it really about the Society's rules or the Academy's rules, or is it something more?"

What is he talking about and why is he calling me Scarlett? They always call me Scar.

Neo presses his palm to the tree behind me, his forearm blanketing my shoulder. "Perhaps it's because your grandparents, who were madly in love, had to divorce so your mom and dad could get married before she birthed a bastard child."

My eyes close, tears pricking at the corners. Not tears of sadness, but anger. I open them slowly, glowering. "How dare you? My family is none of your fucking business."

"Did I hit a nerve, *Scarlett?*"

My grandfather, Abbott Sunder, passed away shortly after I was born. Two weeks later, my grandmother took her own life. From what my parents told me, they were so in love that neither could live a life without the other. The Elders would have forced my parents to abort me or be abolished from the Society if they did not marry. They also couldn't marry until my mom's mom divorced my dad's dad. Apparently, stepsibling love affairs that result in pregnancy are frowned upon. *Who knew?*

Regardless, none of that is Neo's business, or anyone else's for that matter.

"Is it so wrong that I believe we should be able to love who we wish to love and live how we wish to live?"

"When you're a Blue Blood, this is your life, and unless you want to live in misery as an outcast, abolished by the Society, while knowing every member is breathing down your back and waiting for you to make a mistake they can use against you, then yes, you're wrong for fighting the rules."

"I'm not fighting the rules. I'm fighting the three of you. You waged this war and now we have to see it through."

"That's where you're wrong. A war was never waged. A declaration was made. If you want to reap the benefits, you have to put in the work. And you've reaped those benefits more than any student at this Academy."

"Bullshit! The only benefit I've ever taken advantage of is getting out of the trouble you all put me in. I didn't do all that stuff and you know it."

"That's not what I'm talking about."

"Then what the hell are you talking about? Because if this is all just a case of miscommunication, then let's clear the air. Say it. What do you think I've benefited from that you haven't?"

He says nothing. Just assesses me.

"Just say it, Neo. And while you're at it, apologize for the hell you put me through to get me here."

He sucks in his bottom lip, eyes peering at the tree behind me. "Forget it." Dropping his hands, he shuffles back a few steps. "Just drop your holier-than-thou attitude and follow the rules, Scar. And speaking of rules, go clean up the fucking glass before I make you walk in it."

"Oh. Now I'm Scar again?"

While rubbing the back of his neck, unwilling to make eye contact with me, he slaps the tree with a guttural growl then heads back to the party.

Once he's gone, I slide down the trunk of the tree and drop my ass to the ground. Neo brought up my grandparents and mentioned them being the reason I'm so rebellious with the rules. In some ways, I think he's right. Two people who were so in love were torn apart, so it could bring together two others, all so they could give me life.

Maybe my problem isn't this place or the Society, after all. Maybe the weight of guilt inside me just forces me to pretend it's everyone else and not me.

I have a choice to make: to eat my pride and comply, so I can come out stronger than ever, or refuse and slowly break.

TWELVE

I CHOSE STRENGTH. Which is exactly why I'm soaking in this hot pond, or pool, whatever the hell it is, drinking my third and fourth drink of the night. Or day. But I think it's night.

The sun is setting behind the mountains and the solar lights outside the spring have come on.

A few people have left, leaving only me, Riley, the three jerks, Melody, and Hannah. I'm not even sure why Melody is still here, considering no matter how much attention she gives to Neo, he doesn't give any back to her. She looks desperate, if you ask me. But no one did ask me, so I'll just finish my drink and keep my mouth shut.

Ever since I've cleaned up the glass—both mine and Neo's —it's been a chill night. The guys haven't given me any more shit. Crew is still flirting with Hannah, and I've determined he's doing it to try to get a rise out of me, which he will not. Not publicly, anyway.

I don't care. I really don't. I don't even know Hannah, so who am I to tell her that Crew will fuck her three ways to

Sunday then throw her away like she's Monday morning's cold coffee?

Coffee sounds fantastic, though. I wonder if they have any on campus. "Hey," I say to Jagger, who somehow wound up right next to me, "do they have coffee at this place?" I slap a hand over my mouth, sputtering, "I'm sorry. Am I allowed to talk to you, almighty Lawless member?"

"I'll allow it tonight. And yes, there is coffee back at the dorms and in the dining hall. Why? You want coffee?" He laughs, noticing my double-fisted drinks.

"Oooh," Riley chimes in. "Coffee sounds so good. Let's drink some and stay up all night."

I laugh at her enthusiasm. "We have school tomorrow, babe."

"Oh, shit. That's right." She sulks, sinking back down in the water. I might be drunk, but Riley is worse off.

"Maybe," I say, answering Jagger's question. "Maybe later, I might want some."

Jagger raises an eyebrow. "Then coffee you shall get."

"Why are you being nice to me? Aren't you supposed to be mean to me, too? Aren't those the," I air quote, "'*rules?*'"

"Being mean to you isn't a rule. Your obedience is. As far as I'm concerned, you're obeying everyone just fine."

Hannah laughs hysterically when Crew pulls her onto his lap. My forehead crinkles as I glare at them.

Crew. Complete and utter asshole. An asshole that I want to strangle with my bare hands while shaking some sense into him. Or at least, shaking him back to a time when he was a decent human being.

"Does that bother you?" Jagger asks, catching my stare across the pool.

"Them?" I chuckle. "Not. At. All." I tip back one of my

drinks, the fruity one, and finish it off. Instead of throwing it, because it's glass and I don't want to break another one and have to clean up the mess, I push my body up and lean over some rocks outside the water to settle it between them.

A hand slaps, hard, on my ass, and I jump. "What the hell?" I spin around and notice Riley settling back into her spot in the water.

I turn off my defense mode and laugh it off. "Oh. It was you."

Riley throws her hands up. "Wasn't me?"

Biting my lip, I glower at Crew. "Better not have been you. Especially when you're over there getting handsy with another girl."

Did I really just say that out loud? What the fuck is wrong with me?

"Hate to break it to ya, babe," Crew begins. "But the only ass I plan on tapping is the one sitting on my dick right now."

My mouth drops open to speak, but no words come out. I think I'm in shock, really. The old Crew would have never been so cruel. I'm not sure if I should be angry, jealous, or hurt. Regardless, I choose violence. "In that case, Hannah, you might wanna drink until you get double vision in hopes that it'll double the size of his penis." I click my tongue on the roof of my mouth, pinching my fingers together in the air. "It's pretty small."

"Okay," Jagger says, grabbing one of my drinks from my hand, "I think it's time to cut you off."

"What? No! I was only kidding. Like I'd know how big Crew's penis is." Once again, I've put my foot in my mouth. This is exactly why I'm not social.

"Come on, Hannah." Crew takes her hand and pulls her until she's standing in the water. He steps out, leading the way. "You, too, Riley. Come with us."

"Me?" She slaps a hand to her chest, splashing water on her own face. She and I share a look before she glances back at Crew. "Why me?"

He winks at her. "Because two's better than one."

Riley hesitates, but when Crew says, "Lawless rules." She sighs and gets up. "Are you good?" she asks me before getting out.

"I'm great."

Once she's out of the water and has her towel wrapped around her waist, she comes over to me and whispers, "I'm sorry. Seems I have to go, though."

"Just be careful. Okay?"

Riley nods before padding her feet through the muck to a still flirting Hannah and Crew. I know Riley won't partake in their festivities. She doesn't really strike me as the orgy type. But I've got no doubt Crew and Hannah will be hooking up.

I look around at the rest of the people here and everyone is quiet. Neo's puffing on a joint with Melody. His eyes are blood-shot and glossed over and he looks bored as fuck.

"Hey," Jagger says quietly, "you're not still into him, are you?"

"Fuuuuuck no." I take a drink of the one I'm still holding, this one a beer. It's warm and disgusting, but I drink it anyway. "For the record, I was never into Crew. We were both going through shit, the same shit we all went through, and we had comfort sex. Nothing more, nothing less."

I'm not sure why I'm feeding Jagger these unnecessary lies. We aren't friends. He's one third of the reason my plans went to hell.

"Good. So him hooking up with ninety percent of the girls at BCA won't bother you one bit."

"Is that a question? Because no, I don't care who Crew

hooks up with. The only person I'd be concerned about is Riley. So far, she's the only decent girl I've met."

Jagger takes a drink, laughing into the mouth of his bottle.

"Why is that funny?"

"Riley's a nice person, but so are most of the students at BCA. Just remember, people aren't always what they seem. You're proof of that."

"Me?" I clap a hand to my chest. "What did I do?"

"Come on, Scar. You've changed just as much as the rest of us. What once was a quiet girl with her face in a book is now a girl who says fuck like it's a sentence and drinks like a fish. Lest we not forget, you did beat Crew's ass."

Neo starts laughing, and it's an odd sound coming from him.

"Crew deserved everything he got, and let it be known, I have no problem kicking both your asses if you continue to fuck with me. I don't care how civil you're being at this moment. My guard is not down. Not even a little."

"Duly noted."

Neo laughs again. This time it's followed by the hefty laughter of Melody.

"Is she always like this?" I hear Melody ask, regarding me.

"Yup," Neo responds.

"How annoying."

My body shifts as agitation gets the better of me. "Do you have a problem?" I spit out.

"Don't," Jagger says, pressing his hand to my thigh under the water.

"Don't what, defend myself?"

"Just sit down, relax, and enjoy a night of peace before the chaos of classes begins tomorrow."

I sink deeper into the water, trying to heed his advice. "I almost forgot classes start tomorrow." I look at Jagger. "Hey.

When do these games start for the juniors?" According to Neo, my games are separate, and it's safe to assume last night was the kickoff, but I'm curious about the others.

"They've already begun."

My expression drops, neck craned. "They have?"

"Mmhmm. That's the thing about the games, you never know when you're gonna be playing." Jagger's fingers drum against my thigh and I forgot his hand was even there.

I clear my throat and stretch my neck, pretending to ignore what's happening under the water. "Where's Riley and those other two? They've been gone a long time."

"Probably left. Why do you care?"

Is he closer now? I think he is.

"I don't care."

"You keep saying that."

His hand slides farther up my leg and tingles spread upward from his touch.

Jagger grabs the beer from my hand and chucks it behind him.

"Hey," I scoff, "I was drinking that."

"You've been drinking it for over an hour. You're done with it now."

My head turns to look over my shoulder for my drink, which is out of sight, but movement in the distance catches my eye. I push myself up a few inches to get a better look, and see the shadow of someone, or something, moving steadfastly on the edge of the trees. Seconds later, they're gone.

Not thinking any more about it, I sink back down into the water. When I do, Jagger curls his body closer to mine, his back to Neo and Melody. Fingertips rim the edge of my swimsuit and my body shivers.

"Jagger, what are you doing?"

"Shh," he whispers as his lips trail down my neck, sucking

125

and kissing. Goosebumps erupt on my skin, even in this hot water.

Slowly, he peels back the layer of fabric and slides his hand underneath, cupping my crotch.

"Jagger," I say his name again, this time in warning.

"Don't talk. Just relax."

The pad of his thumb presses to my clit, and my body jolts. One finger slides inside me and I clench around it, unsure if I want to force it out or hold it in.

An audible breath slips out of my mouth when he adds another finger, this time pushing deeper with his thumb still rubbing my clit.

I arch my back, inhaling the scent of malt beer and cedarwood rolling off his wet skin.

I shouldn't want this. I should push him back and make a mockery of him right now. But I don't because my head is in a fog and I'm under the spell of his touch.

Resting my head against the bed of rocks behind me, I close my eyes, pretending that this is okay. This is normal. That it's not Jagger. I'm not sure who I want it to be, but it's not him.

He picks up his pace, pushing deeper and faster, causing the water to ripple where his inked arm is submerged.

"Does that feel good, Scar?"

I don't respond, but if I did, I'd ask him not to talk because his voice will only ruin this for me.

He adds another finger and hums against my ear. "Do you like how my fingers are spreading apart your tight pussy?"

Okay. He can talk a little because his dirty words are making this all the more satisfying.

I open my eyes to see him watching me. Licking my lips, I nod.

I wanna touch him and see how big he is, but I'm also battling to keep this just about me.

When my eyes close again, he shoves his fingers so far inside me that my body shoots upright and my eyes pop back open. "Look at me, Scar. I wanna watch your eyes when I make you come."

The way he says my name so authoritatively does wild things to my insides.

"You pretend to hate us because we're in control, but I think you like being told what to do. It turns you on, doesn't it?"

It's like he's reading my mind and it's creepy as hell. Maybe part of me is turned on by their power, just not their power over me.

Jagger curls his fingers, pumping them steadfastly inside me. His thumb laps at my clit, forcefully, and I buck my hips, gaining friction. A subtle moan parts my lips and my eyes slide past his, over his shoulder.

Melody is gone now, and it's only Neo sitting there, watching us—watching me. He's got one arm stretched out at his side, resting on the rocks, and the other immersed. Water swashes around him, and I realize he's stroking himself. Our eyes lock and my body swelters.

I bite on the corner of my lip, hard, trying not to cry out. It's impossible, though, as moans tear through my vocal cords with Neo's lustful eyes fixed on mine. The surrounding water sloshes faster and his mouth falls agape before he grunts with a heavy chest. I catch myself breathing in sync with him, and as fast it started, it stops.

Jagger slides his fingers out and returns them to his lap.

Regret consumes me, followed by humiliation. Fortunately, I'm still pretty buzzed, so I'll deal with the fallout tomorrow.

Neo stands up, smirking as water drops in abundance from his shorts. "See. The games aren't so bad, are they?"

Jagger stretches his arms out on either side of him, and he laughs. He actually fucking laughs.

My heart drops into my stomach. "What did he just say?"

Jagger doesn't even look at me, just stares straight ahead with a shit-eating grin on his face. "You heard him. Now go pick up your bottle I threw out and head back to your dorm. It's getting late and you have school tomorrow."

No.

I swallow down the bile rising up my throat.

I'm speechless. Can't even think. "What?"

"Did he sputter, Scar?" Neo gripes. "Get your ass out of the water and get back to campus. Now."

With an open palm, I slap Jagger across his face. "You fucking asshole."

He doesn't even flinch, just grinds his molars and rolls his neck to look at me. "Just for that, you can pick up all the bottles and cans." He stands up, flings one leg over the rocks, and steps out.

"No!" I shout, now thigh-deep in the water. "You can't just leave me out here. I don't even know where to go."

An animal could eat me. I could get lost and never find my way back. It's dark. It's fucking scary.

"Please, you guys," I beg, "I'll do anything."

My body freezes while Jagger and Neo share some unspoken words. Neo finally looks at me, his eyes glistening with mischief. "Anything?"

I'm desperate, so I say, "Yes."

CHAPTER
THIRTEEN
CREW

I swear to all that is holy if Scar doesn't give me my damn keys before class, I will tie her to her bed and tear her room apart until I find them.

"Open up." I pound my fist repeatedly on her door.

"One sec." I hear Riley's voice on the other side.

I drop my hand, my lack of patience getting the best of me. "Hurry your ass up."

Seconds later, the door swings open and I'm face to face with Riley. Her dripping blonde hair and pink robe tied around her lead me to believe she just got back from the showers.

Without a hello, I push the door open farther and torpedo into the room. "Where the hell is she?" My eyes skim the space, but she's not here.

"She was still in the shower when I left the bathrooms. Do you want me to go..."

I don't even give her a chance to finish talking as I spin on my heels and leave the room, walking hastily down the hall.

My palms press to both revolving doors, and I burst into

the bathroom. A couple of girls wrapped in towels scurry away quickly.

"It's Crew Vance."

"He's in our bathroom."

"Cover your tatas, ladies. Boy in the room."

Ignoring the hushed comments, I cup my hands around my mouth and holler, "Scarlett," as I walk farther into the girls' private space.

Melody emerges from one of the bathroom stalls wrapped in a white towel, a vampish grin on her face. She stretches her arm up, pressing it to the frame, and lets her towel drop from her body, but it does absolutely nothing for me.

"Now, what are you doing in the ladies' bathroom, Crew?" Her attempt at flirting is embarrassing for both of us. I now see she was a one and done fuck.

"Where's Scar?"

Melody's expression twists as she bends over and grabs her towel, shielding herself now that she knows I'm not interested in what she's putting out. "Who?"

"Scarlett. Where the hell is Scarlett?" I don't have time for this shit. Had Scar not been such an uncompromising little shit, we could have avoided this altogether.

"Forget it." I head for the showers. "I'll find her my-damn-self."

I tear open curtain by curtain. The first three are empty.

The second holds a cute little redhead with freckles sprinkled on her nose. She squeals a high-pitched sound and attempts to cover herself with her hands as water spills down her body. I wink at her before tugging the curtain closed.

Finally, I find her. Stark naked under the running water.

"Oh my god, Crew. Are you fucking insane?" She jabs a stern finger in the air. "Get the hell out of here."

It's odd to me that Scar makes no attempt to hide her body.

Not that she should. It's a perfect body. My eyes drink in the sight. Milky, flawless skin. An innie belly button with a small brown mole beside it. Auburn-colored areolas surrounding her budded nipples. Perky breasts that aren't too big and not too small. Then I see it. Something I wish I could unsee because it shouldn't even be there.

"What the fuck is this?" I barge into the shower, submerging myself in the water. My hand flies to her neck, grabbing it and tilting it to the side. "Who the hell did this to you?"

Scar slaps a hand over her neck, covering the hickey. It's faint, but it's most definitely there.

"None of your damn business," she seethes. "Now get off me and get out of my shower."

Water sprays from the showerhead, drenching my uniform and the fresh bandage on my arm, but I don't even fucking care. I grab her hand and peel it away from her neck, squeezing the tips of her fingers tightly in my hand. "It was Jagger, wasn't it? He did this?"

"Stop it! That fucking hurts, you idiot. Besides, what do you care? You were all over Hannah anyway."

It's true, I was. Because I was trying to prove to the guys I was over Scar. They've been breathing down my neck and I figured if they saw me flirting with someone else in front of her, they'd let go of this nonsense that I'm still into her.

"Fuck Hannah. This is about you and that hickey on your neck." I squeeze her fingers tighter, demanding the truth. "Now tell me who did it, dammit!"

"Yes! Okay," she spits out. "Jagger did it. As if you didn't already know."

Dropping both hands, my fists clench at my sides while water continues to stream down my body.

I do know what happened because I watched it all. When

those fuckers told me to take the girls and leave, I knew they were up to something. So I sent them on their way with Melody, when she chased us down, and I sat back and watched.

At first, I thought she'd stop him. After all, this is Scar. She doesn't do anything unless she wants to. When she didn't push him away, I knew she wanted what he was about to give her.

Last night, from behind a tree, I watched Jagger's hands all over her body. Saw her face when she came. Even witnessed Neo getting off on her pleasure. I saw every fucking second of it.

My cock twitched every time her mouth formed an O. I imagined her juices squirting into the water as she orgasmed —but around my fingers, not his.

Watching her was sadistic, but it was satisfying.

When I got home and my head hit my pillow, I laid alone with my thoughts, paralyzed by the memory.

Now, standing here in front of her, I see proof of what he did on her fucking neck. A rage is induced inside me, one I fear I can't control. Until that mark is gone, it's all I'll see. A constant reminder that Jagger was the last one to taste her skin.

Him—not me. And we can't have that.

My hands fly out and grab Scar by the head, fingers braiding through her drenched black hair. With her blue eyes on mine, I pull her face closer.

"What the hell are you doing?" She pushes and tries to fight me off, but I don't let her go.

Our lips crush together while she curses into my mouth. I tug her closer, parting her lips with my tongue and sliding it in, taking her own hostage. My head tilts and I coerce hers to do the same.

I mutter into her mouth, not slackening my hold on her. "You let him dip his fingers inside your cunt, but you can't kiss an old friend?"

She turns her head, spitting on the shower wall. "You're not my friend, Crew. Never were." She spits some more, treating my bodily fluids like poison in her precious mouth.

"Am I that appalling, Scar? So much so that you can't even swallow down my taste?"

Her hand flies across my cheek. "Yes. You really are."

Ignoring the sting she left behind, I grab her hands and pin them over her head against the shower wall. "Too fucking bad." My lips go straight for her neck, the same spot Jagger sucked last night. She squirms, but once I have a good amount of suction, she surrenders. I suck in, marking her, claiming her.

"You jerk! Quit it!"

Once I know I've covered the spot he left, I retreat.

"What the hell did you do? Did you just give me another hickey?"

"Does it matter? It just covered the one you already had."

"Yes, it matters! I don't want your lips anywhere near me. Especially after the *game* you had me play the other night at the river."

"You're being a little dramatic, Scar. It was a simple scare tactic."

"A scare tactic?" She laughs. "Is that what it's called when you have someone's mouth taped shut while blindfolded and tossed into the river?"

"Tossed in the river? What the hell are you talking about?"

"Don't play dumb. You know damn well what Neo set up the other night."

No. I didn't know that, and now that I do, I'm pretty fucking pissed because that wasn't our plan.

The water has run cold and Scar begins shivering, so I reach behind her and turn the handle, shutting the water off.

"Everything okay in there?" a voice comes from outside the stall. Hannah's voice.

I look up, speaking into the air, "We're fine."

Her soft footsteps pad away, and I return my attention to Scar, ignoring her question. "I'm sorry for what Neo did. I seriously had no idea, and I'm sure Jagger didn't either, but why the fuck would you let Jagger touch you like that?"

Her eyes burn into mine, mirrored with the same indignation I'm feeling. "Why do you care?"

"Answer the fucking question."

Her eyes roll but come back to mine as she lifts a smirk. "Because it felt good. Is that a good enough answer for you, Crew? It felt really fucking good."

Is she trying to piss me off? Sure as hell feels like it, but it's not working. In fact, I'm suddenly turned on all over again.

My eyes slide down to her breasts, peppered with beads of water, then back up to her mouth. "Describe what it felt like?"

"I told you it felt good." I watch her mouth as she speaks. The way her pink lips slightly part, every now and then the tip of her tongue surfacing.

"In detail. Tell me how it felt."

"You're deranged, you know that?"

With her wrists in the palm of my hand, I pull forward then slam them against the shower wall. "I'm a glutton for punishment. Now tell me!"

"Have you ever eaten shrooms, Crew?"

"No," I respond, honestly. "But I assume you have?"

"Once. That's what it was like. Like all of my senses were hypersensitive. The smell of the water I was submerged in was suddenly a bath full of liquid, seeping into my skin and heating my insides." Her tone is provocative and I'm suddenly hanging on every word. "Jagger's touch pricked every nerve inside me and my core sizzled with ecstasy."

My lips press together firmly and I close my eyes momentarily, haunted by her admission.

When she continues, I watch her again. The lust in her eyes as she recalls her height of pleasure.

"The sound of the water moving each time his fingers slid in and out of me. Fast, then slow, deep, then shallow."

"Okay, stop!" I blurt out. I can't take any more of this. "Just stop."

This is downright torturous, but I must relish in torturing my mind because my cock is fucking throbbing.

"Why?" She forces a pout, mockingly. "Does it bother you that someone else had their fingers inside me?"

"Shut up!"

Scar laughs forebodingly and something inside me snaps. "It was a game," I roar, slamming her balled hands into the wall. "It was all a fucking game." The engorged vein in my neck pounds violently with its own pulse. "They didn't have the right!"

Scar's expression shifts quickly to one of terror. "I know," she whispers softly. The realization of what she already knew smacking her in the face.

I collect my composure, warding off the irrational thoughts circulating in my head.

My head wavers; my mind still agonized. "I need to touch you, Scar. I have to. It's not a game or part of some diabolical plan. For my own sanity, you have to let me."

"No," she says, point-blankly.

"I have to do this. I have to erase the memories that are haunting my mind. Replace them with something else. He can't be the last one. He just can't."

I watch her neck, seeing the blotched skin rise and fall, and she swallows hard.

Moments pass that feel like an eternity.

"I can see this is torturing you, so fine. I'll let you touch me, but you have to take your clothes off, too. It's only fair. I'm naked. You have to be, too."

I've got no shame, especially in front of a girl who's seen me naked plenty of times before.

I let go of her hands and begin peeling off the layers. First my shirt, then the tee shirt beneath it. Next are my shoes and socks, followed by my pants and underwear. Until I'm standing here, completely naked, with my erection pointed right at her.

"One sec," she says, reaching behind me, through the curtain. When her arm moves back inside, she's holding a towel. I question her with raised brows.

Scar wraps the towel around her body, and screams at the top of her lungs, "Ladies! Get in here!"

"What the fuck are you doing?" I go to grab the towel from her, but she's too quick, and we both stumble outside of the shower.

"Everyone, come look at this!" she hollers even louder.

"You bitch!"

One, two, three girls hurry over. All giggling and laughing as I reach down and grab my shirt, covering myself up.

Smirking, Scar takes a step back, laughing at her own game. "Do you really think I'd ever let you touch me again?"

She disappears as more girls come to see what the fuss is all about.

"You wanna show. Here's a fucking show." I drop my shirt, spread-eagle my arms, and give everyone a look at what they've all seen before.

Four of the now five girls either sucked me off or rode my dick last year. I'll give 'em all another look at what they'll never touch again.

Once the giggles and gawking have ceased, I shoo them away and grab a towel of my own.

Snatching up my soaked clothes, I go to Scar's room in a towel that barely wraps around my body.

I don't knock. I wait, and I think.

Scar's feistiness, while annoying as fuck, is actually endearing. A pleasant escape from the girls who bend over and lift their own skirts for me.

A few minutes later, Scar emerges in her uniform that's comprised of knee-high socks, black combat boots, a plaid skirt, and the signature BCA polo. Her hair is parted on the top of her head in two messy buns and she's makeup-free, as per usual.

Her bushy black eyebrows droop when she sees me. "Haven't you had enough humiliation for a few days?"

When she goes to step around me, I throw an arm around her waist. "Not so fast, my little deviant. I came for my keys and I'm not leaving without them."

I shove her back in her room and slam the door shut behind us, turning the lock.

"Now go get them."

"Fine," she shrugs, "planned on giving them to you anyway." She reaches into the front pocket of the messenger bag crossed over her chest and pulls them out. Like the bitch she is, she chucks them over my head. "Go get 'em, towel boy."

Fuming, I cross the room to get them and allow her to leave, knowing we'll both be late for class if I don't. Another second in her presence and I might take what I want—my dick down her throat and my fingers buried in her pussy.

I tear through Scar's drawers until I find a large flannel and tie it around my waist. I'm sure to get some shit for this from the guys, especially Neo, since he's the one I'm calling to come pick my ass up.

CHAPTER
FOURTEEN
SCARLETT

"What happened to you last night? One second you were there, then you were gone," I ask Riley as she drops her books on the single desk beside me.

"It was really weird, actually. After Crew made me leave with him and Hannah, Melody found us, and he told us to all walk back to the dorms. A twenty-minute walk in the dark. It was miserable."

If Crew stayed at the hot springs...where was he?

Suddenly, it clicks. It was him watching us. I knew I saw someone in the woods, but assumed it was an animal, or maybe Crew with the girls. It never occurred to me it was Crew alone. I'm not sure why he'd hang back and watch what I let Jagger do to me. Now it makes sense why he was so worked up in the showers. He was jealous.

The possibility excites me in a deranged, masochistic sort of way. I hope it really was pure torture for him.

"Speaking of Crew," Riley begins. "Please tell me the rumors aren't true."

"Depends." I waggle my eyebrows. "Which one did you hear?"

"Oh, I don't know." She pulls out a chair. "Something that involves Crew being naked in the shower. The hushed words going around are that he tried to rape you. Tell me it's not true."

I laugh at the fallacy. "No, Crew didn't try to rape me."

"Good. Because he actually seemed sort of sweet last night when he said goodbye to us girls. There were no asshole tendencies. He was just...nice. Don't worry, I'm not into him anymore. Just saw him in a different light, I guess."

"Crew is many things, but a nice guy is not one of them."

"Maybe not. Then again, people change. Maybe there's a girl out there who can make him a better person."

I sputter, looking down at my open world history book. "If I had a nickel for every time I heard a girl say that about any of those three guys..."

She gives me this really strange look. All googly-eyed and crazy. "What? Why are you looking at me like that?"

"I dunno. I was just thinking that maybe a girl like you could—"

"Stop yourself right there." I hold a hand up. "That will never happen. I don't fall for assholes, and Crew is incapable of being a good person. Not anymore."

"But he once was, is what you're saying?"

My eyes stay on my book with a blank stare as I think back to a time when Crew was different.

"I don't care what they say, Scar. This is what I want. I want you."

"You mean that? You'd risk your friendships with Neo and Jagger just for us."

Crew pulls me down until I'm straddling his lap. His emerald eyes boring into mine, deeply and passionately. I can see the truth in

them, I see me. I see us. "Are you fucking kidding me? I'd risk it all
for you. Ya know what?" He beams all too eagerly. "Fuck it. Let's run
away together. You and me. We can get the hell out of here and
leave the Society behind."

I chuckle because I know he's joking. "You're kidding, right?"

"Do I look like I'm kidding?"

No. He really doesn't. But I wish he were because then I wouldn't
consider the possibility. "Where would we go?"

"I dunno. New York City or the beaches of Nantucket. Fuck if I
care. I'd go anywhere with you."

"We're only sixteen. We'd be crazy to run away together."

"I am crazy. You make me crazy, Scar. If I'm not with you, I
can't eat, I can't sleep. You consume my every thought."

"How about this?" I run my fingers through his messy sex-hair.
"After you graduate from BCA and I finish public school, if you still
love me, we'll go as far as you wanna go."

"If? I'll never stop loving you, Scar. You're the reason I even go
on in this fucked-up world."

The day after that conversation, Neo and Jagger busted
into the cabin and found us naked in front of the living room
fireplace.

They pulled Crew away and did or said something that
eradicated every plan we ever made.

"Yeah," I say to Riley, lifting my head to look at her. "Crew
was once a good guy."

LUNCHTIME ROLLS around much too soon. Not that it matters.
I've seen the guys in every single one of my classes today—
which I'm sure was orchestrated—so sitting beside them at
lunch shouldn't be an issue.

I'm not one to back out of a deal, even if it is with the kings of darkness and disorder.

Of all the things they could have bartered with, they agreed to give me a ride home last night as long as I ate lunch with them for the next month. We'll just be stuffing our faces in silence, so I agreed. Saved my ass from getting lost in the woods alone.

"This way," Riley nods toward a table full of girls, her tray in hand.

I look to my left and see Neo and Jagger glaring at me while Crew tips back a carton of milk with the top completely torn off. "Actually, I think I'm gonna sit over there." I angle my head toward the guys.

Riley blows out a hefty breath of laughter. "You're not serious?"

Slowly, I nod my head, lips pressed together. *I wish I wasn't.*

"Do you...want me to sit with you?"

"No. That's okay. You go ahead and sit with your friends. I'll eat fast and come join you soon."

"Look, Scarlett. If this is about last night. I'm sorry I didn't stick up for you with the guys or say goodbye before I left. It's just that I can't stand up to them, ya know?"

"No, Ry. It's not that. I don't blame you at all. I know how they are. Just please be careful with them because they know you won't stand up to them, which means they'll take advantage if you allow them to."

"Of course. Same goes for you, right?"

I'm trying. I'm really trying hard to show them I won't cower. "Yeah. I know," I say, tone tranquil.

Riley leans close and whispers, "They're not threatening you, are they?"

I look over at the guys, two of the three still watching me intently, before I return my attention to Riley. "Would it matter

142

if they were? I mean, they are the leaders of this place. Not much anyone could do about it."

Riley nods in response. "I guess you're right."

I flash her a tight smile before turning toward the guys.

Crew's shoving a forkful of gravy-smothered turkey in his mouth when his eyes lift. "What the hell is she doing here?" he asks, mouth full.

I set my tray down and pull out a chair at the round table. There are empty ones on either side of me, and the three guys are seated beside one another on the opposite side.

"She's eating with us for a while," Neo tells him.

"Why?" Crew drawls, jamming his fork into his food.

"Because we asked her to," Jagger chimes in.

My eyes roll as I poke at my salad. My appetite is suddenly gone, but I know I'll regret it later if I don't eat.

Since last night, the weight on my shoulders has been a little heavier, and it's harder to hold my head high. I feel sick about what I allowed. I'm more upset with myself than I am with them. I should've known better.

Now I'm sitting here like a little mouse while they're probably getting off again on my humiliation. Wouldn't surprise me if they were jerking each other off under the table.

I don't lift my eyes. I don't even turn my head. As they converse about the shower ordeal, I just eat and pretend they're not there.

One, two, three bites of salad before I'm reminded I'm not alone.

"So, Scar. Let's hear your side of the story," Jagger says, grinning. "What really happened in the showers today?"

Biting back a smile, I take another bite. "Ask Crew. He'll tell ya."

"He claims you threw yourself at him and dropped to your knees, begging for his dick in your mouth."

My upper lip tightens. "Really, Crew? You seriously think anyone would believe that bullshit lie?"

His mouth draws back, and he rolls his shoulders. "What can I say? I'm a catch."

Laughter spills violently from my vocal cords. "The only time your name and catch go together is when it involves a venereal disease."

"You should probably shut up before I shut you up with my cock!" Crew seethes.

Jagger laughs along with me while Neo sits there observing me, eyes narrowed, lips pursed.

He's a lion watching his prey. As if he's waiting for the opportunity to pounce and tear me to shreds.

Unwilling to dig myself a deeper hole with these guys, I resume eating. Crew has pushed his food away, likely petting his battered ego. Neo has no food, which doesn't surprise me since he doesn't eat in front of people. When we were around thirteen at a dinner party, Neo was reaching for a roll and his arm brushed against a bottle of red wine, knocking it over. Sebastian—his dad, and also a pompous asshole—went berserk. Lashed out at Neo in front of everyone, then sent him to his room for the rest of the night. At the time, I felt so bad for him. After that, I noticed he declined to eat at gatherings. I always assumed that's why, but I could be wrong.

"Might wanna touch up the double bruise on your neck a little better," Crew says, breaking another delightful moment of tranquility. "I can still see it."

"Thanks for the advice. Might I offer the same? Your black eye is looking awfully yellow. Oh," I perk up, "how's your arm?"

His nostrils flare from across the table. "Bitch."

I retort, "Asshole."

"Well, Scar," this time it's Neo's galling voice that hits my ears as he drums his fingers to the table, leaning back in his chair like a king, "you know you're gonna have to pay for that stunt you pulled earlier today with Crew. We can't have you making a mockery of the Lawless. What message would that send to the other students?"

A message that it's okay to stand up for yourself. Now there's an idea.

"What do you think, guys," Neo continues, "strip her down and cuff her to the sign in front of Vultures' Roost? I'm sure the guys in the dorm will have a good time with that?"

"Shut the fuck up!" I blurt out, now glaring at Neo. I lower my fork, not even realizing I was holding it out like a weapon.

Neo's eyes widen, stunned by my outburst. As if I'm the first person in existence to stand up to him. When I look around the dining hall, I realize everyone is watching me.

I take a deep breath, drop my head again, and resume eating. Just as I shove a forkful of lettuce in my mouth, my plate goes flying out from under me, crashing to the floor.

My eyes close softly, and when I open them, I lock my jaw, slowly turning my head to where Neo is standing over me. "Now what the hell did you do that for?"

His hand slams on the table where my plate once was. "Get up!"

I speak slowly, as if each word is its own sentence. "If...I... don't?"

He glares at me, the corded vein in his neck thumping. "Oh, you will."

My eyes travel to his balled fists at his sides. "Fine," I say, point-blankly, before pushing my chair back. The legs scrape against the marbled floor, likely drawing more attention to our table. When I stand, I cross my arms over my chest and take a stance in front of Neo.

"On your knees," he barks authoritatively.

"Oh," I snicker, breaking eye contact with him, "now that I won't do."

"I said, on your fucking knees!"

The sound of Crew's chair, as well as Jagger's, sliding back grabs my attention. With heavy steps, Crew walks toward us. "I'll handle her," he says, bumping his shoulder to Neo's as he steps in front of him.

"Sit your ass down." Neo shoves him to the side. "I've got this."

Something in Crew snaps. His hands fold together and he bends them back slowly, cracking his knuckles, chin tipped up at Neo. Then, like a bullet out of a gun, Crew shoves Neo, sending him back a few steps.

I step back, getting out of the line of fire.

Jagger rushes over, ready to step in if needed, as do a few other guys I don't know.

"What the fuck is your problem?" Neo growls, walking with a heavy hand into Crew's chest.

"You're my fucking problem." Crew puffs his chest out into Neo's, their noses brushing. "You and him." He juts a finger at Jagger.

"What's going on?" Riley asks, appearing out of nowhere. "Are you okay?"

"Yeah," I nod, watching the guys, "I'm fine."

I should go. "We should go." I grab Riley by the hand and pull her past the guys.

"Not so fast." Neo reaches out, grabbing me by my free arm. "We're not finished here."

All the blood drains from my face. This is not a situation I wanna be in. I don't interfere when it comes to friends, especially this group of friends.

"Hammond," Jagger hollers, "get your ass over here and

clean up this mess." He skims the crowd for someone else before saying, "Andy, get Scarlett a new lunch."

Andy pushes his glasses up, folds his hands together, and leans close to me. "Would that be a...chef salad, or tossed?"

"It's fine, Andy. Don't—"

I'm rudely cut off by Jagger. "Any fucking salad. Just go get it!"

Andy jolts, then scurries away while Victor Hammond picks up ranch-covered lettuce and cucumbers off the floor with his bare hands.

Neo glowers at Jagger. "What the hell are you doing?"

Jagger steps up to Neo, who is still draining the blood from my arm. "You're both making us look weak," he grinds out. "Handle this somewhere else and I'll deal with Scar's punishment."

Neo thinks for a moment, then finally drops his hold on me. "Fine. Get her out of here while I deal with this imbecile," he says, referring to Crew.

Jagger takes my hand, leading me across the hall. As we're walking, I glance over my shoulder at Crew and find him glaring at me. He's behaving like I did something wrong. He's the one who lost his mind when Neo started barking orders at me.

CHAPTER
FIFTEEN
CREW

"IN THE COURTYARD! Now!" I snap at Neo. Pushing through the crowd that's gathered around us, I head out the double doors of the dining hall to the courtyard, where a few students are eating their lunch.

As soon as the fresh air hits my face, I inhale a deep breath and pace, mentally working through the rage that's consuming me.

Neo comes out seconds later, fuming, much like I am. "Everyone, scram," he says to the students eating out here.

Most of them pack up their stuff to go, but a couple stare idly at Neo. "Now! Go eat your fucking food somewhere else." Those last ones quickly snatch up their food and hurry away.

Once we're alone, Neo's fist lands on my shoulder, not hard, but it pisses me off enough to spin around and get in his face. "Put your hands on me again, fucker. See what happens."

"Dude, chill the fuck out. What's your deal?"

"You! Him! Her! It's like I'm a fucking joke to you all." I say the words I should've said a long time ago.

"Look at the way you're behaving. *This* is a fucking joke."

"Really? This is all a joke to you because it's serious to me. You and Jagger plan all this shit behind my back. Just like last night. You sent me on my merry way, then fucked with her without even running it by me."

"Guess I missed the part where I was supposed to get your approval." The sarcasm in his tone unnerves me.

"We're a fucking team. You, me, Jagger. Lately, though, it's you and him, and I'm sitting on the sidelines. Just like that shit at the river. You were never supposed to have her pushed in. It was supposed to be a scare tactic only. You could have seriously hurt her."

"She was fine." The way he's downplaying the situation is unsettling.

"This time. What about next time?"

"Be real with me, Crew. This isn't about us leaving you out. This is about her. You don't like the idea of anyone fucking with her but you."

It's true, I don't. Scar was mine first. I saw her first, I touched her first, and I'll be damned if these guys are going to push me aside like she belongs to them now.

"You know what? Maybe I don't." I look him dead in the eye as I speak my truth. "You and Jagger made me out to be a traitor for being with Scar. You behaved as if I was betraying Maddie, but Maddie was already gone. She might still be here, but she's gone, Neo."

Neo cuts me a glare, pushing me back a few steps. "Don't you ever fucking say that again. Maddie is still here. She will always be here."

Bad choice of words, but it's still the truth.

"Did you expect me to just stay in a relationship with her forever? Am I supposed to wait for her, to what? Get better? Because she's not getting better, Neo."

"No! What I want is some respect for my twin sister. The

girl who was always at our side growing up. She was one of us until Scar began pulling her away."

Neo never liked Scar because he felt like she was always trying to take Maddie from us. Before long, he convinced us of it, too, and we followed his lead.

"I knew Maddie loved you when she was only nine years old. I didn't want to, but I accepted it. You were my best fucking friend, Crew. I approved because I knew you'd treat her right. Maybe I pushed a little too hard just to make her happy, but she's my sister. Fuck!" He grips his head, tugging at his hair. "She's my fucking sister, and she's the only person in this goddamn world I love."

"I know, man. I know. I love Maddie, too."

"Not the way she loved you. You wasted no time after her accident to shack up with her best friend—the girl who brainwashed Maddie into thinking the Blue Bloods are nothing but entitled pricks. That our rules are set forth simply to control members. Scar convinced Maddie not to attend Boulder Cove Academy and before long, she would have convinced her to leave the Blue Bloods altogether. And here you are still feeling sorry for her."

"Don't you think it's a little hypocritical for both of you to give me shit for sleeping with her when you'd crawl between her legs at the first opportunity?"

He's quiet for a second, watching me and shaking his head subtly. "There's a big difference between what we're doing and what you did."

"Oh, yeah?" I tip my chin. "What's that?"

"Feelings, Crew. You've got feelings for her. We don't." He pats my chest with his hand, then turns to walk away.

"Dammit!" I drop my head back, staring at the clouds in the sky.

I don't know what else to do. I've done everything they've asked of me, but I still don't have their trust. I've convinced myself I hate her. Even played the part. I'm just not sure how much longer I can pretend I don't care.

SIXTEEN

"YOU SURE YOU'RE NOT HUNGRY?" Jagger asks, holding up my salad in a paper bag.

I shake my head while trying to wrap my head around everything. Crew and Neo are probably killing each other in the dining hall right now, for reasons unbeknownst to me. Jagger swept me away like a knight in shining armor. But Jagger is no knight. So, why? Why is he walking casually at my side down the trail and being so nice?

"We can get this over with," I tell him. "Give me my punishment so we can go back to class."

He looks at me, a smile creeping across his face. "Actually, I have a better idea. What if we blow off the second half of classes and I take you to one of my favorite places?"

My eyebrows knit together as I glance at him from the corner of my eye. "And why would you do that?"

He shrugs a shoulder. "I dunno. With all the chaos, I guess I just thought it'd be nice to get away for a while."

I stop walking, feeling like this is some sort of setup. "What's the catch, Jagger? None of you guys do anything nice without a cost. Not to mention, your friends wouldn't be too happy if you were anything short of monstrous to me. So what are you really up to?"

His hands fly up in surrender. "No catch. No games. Just a genuine offer to escape the craziness of BCA for an afternoon."

After a moment of considering it, I shake my head and turn around to head back to the school. "I'm not buying it. If you're not going to *punish* me for standing up to Neo, then I'm going back to class."

The leaves crunch beneath my boots, but it's the only sound. When I look over my shoulder, I see Jagger still standing in the same spot I left him. "What are you doing?"

"Head back to class. If the guys ask, I made you eat your salad off the ground or something." He tosses me the bag and I catch it in midair. Jagger turns around and keeps walking up the trail, away from the main campus.

"Where are you going?" I holler at him, not sure why I care.

Jagger does a one-eighty and walks backward. His hands fly up and he says, "Told ya. One of my favorite places." He smirks, sending a flush of adrenaline through me, and I find myself smiling back.

Seconds later, he makes a sharp turn off the trail and disappears.

I'm walking back leisurely, knowing I'm already late for calculus. My arms sway with my bag in one hand as I watch my feet on the trail. The leaves are changing to a medley of colors—yellows, reds, oranges. Many have dried and fallen and now coat the trails. With all the foot traffic, they're pushed down and settled into the mix of dirt and rock. Fall has always been my favorite time of the year, and I can't help but feel giddy over the upcoming season. Crazy how it's only the first day of classes and there's already a nip in the air. Back home, school starts the week before Labor Day. At the Academy, we don't begin until a week after. I'm not complaining about that aspect of this place. A shorter school year is definitely a perk.

I still can't believe Jagger had this lunch made for me. Lifting the bag, I unfold the brown paper and peek inside to find a salad in a to-go container—as per his demands to Andy.

Beneath the container is a napkin that catches my eye. It's not the napkin that has me digging it out; it's the scribbled ink on it.

I stop walking and pull out the container, stuffing it in my arm to free my hands. When I get the napkin out, my heart drops into my stomach. Written in blood red marker are the words, *IF YOU THINK THIS IS A GAME, YOU'RE DEAD WRONG!*

Just when I thought Jagger was being civil, I'm reminded why I can't trust anything these guys do or say.

My eyes shoot up from the napkin when the sound of leaves crunching hits my ears. "Who's there?" I look left, right, then over my shoulder, finding no one in sight, but I still hear them.

"Hello," I say louder, stuffing the container and the napkin back in the bag.

The sound comes from behind me, so I spin around.

Nothing.

There's commotion to the left, so I spin again.

Still nothing.

"I know someone's there."

A familiar sound hits my ears. It's me. Or my voice, at least.

"A pact then. To never attend that abomination. We're in control of our own destiny. Fuck Boulder Cove Academy and fuck Boulder Cove University."

My stomach knots at the sound of the recording playing through the woods.

"New York City, here we come," Maddie sings chipperly.

Tears prick the corners of my eyes. *Her voice.* Her sweet, beautiful voice.

"Why are you doing this?" I shout over the static of the recording.

"How about a pinkie promise?" I continue. *"Graduate from Essex High and go to NYC to pursue our dreams."*

"Stop it!" I scream. "This isn't funny."

These guys, of all people, know how much it hurts that she's not here. That's she's stuck in that home, unable to wake up. Why would they torture me with her voice? Torture themselves?

The recording stops, but I don't. I toss the bag into the brush off the trail and my feet move as fast as they can. "Where are you, asshole? Show your damn face!"

I go around the trees, weaving in and out of them and passing trails that crisscross. I move through the woods quickly, following the sound of the crunching leaves. "Just give up already! I will find you!"

My heart is pounding and I'm on the verge of a breakdown. Of all the cruel things they could do to torment me, they have to use my best friend like that? To take a private conversation and play it aloud, to what? Hurt me? Make me feel some sort of guilt for coming here when I promised I wouldn't? This has to be Crew or Jagger. There is no way in hell Neo would use Maddie that way.

I'm deep in the woods when I slow to catch my breath, listening carefully for any sound that will tell me where they might have gone.

Bent over, I place my hands on my knees, eyes fixated on the ground.

Nothing.

I turn around to head back to the trail.

Or was it this way? I turn again.

155

Oh no.

Panic sets in as I spin multiple times, trying to figure out which way I'm supposed to go.

My heart rate excels, chest rising then dropping rapidly.

Left. I'm positive I have to go left.

I keep walking, hoping I made the right choice.

Seconds turn to minutes. Minutes turn to an hour. I'm thirsty, I'm alone, and I'm starting to get scared.

At this point, the only way I'm going to get out of here is by yelling for help and hoping someone hears me.

"Hello! Can anyone hear me?"

I scream louder. "Someone, please! I think I'm lost!"

When no one comes to save me, I drop down beside some thicket, knees bent to my chest.

"Why is this happening to me?" I cry out, tears sliding down my cheeks. I sweep them away aggressively, trying to be strong, but how can I when I feel so weak?

I sit there for what feels like an eternity when evidence of life hits my ears. My head snaps to the right. "Hello," I call out.

It's more leaves crunching. I jump up, praying it's not an animal. "Is someone there?"

"Jesus, Scar." Jagger emerges out of nowhere. "What are you doing out here?"

"I...got lost." I look at him, confused. "What are you doing out here?"

"I was heading back from Eldridge Park and heard you yelling, so I followed your voice." He crouches down beside me, still in his school uniform. "I thought you went back to class."

"Don't fuck with me, Jagger. I know it was you."

"Know it was me what?"

I press my hands to his chest and shove him, knocking him back. He catches himself with his hand to the ground. Once I stand up, he does the same. "I know you've been out here the whole time. Probably laughing your ass off. Where are the others?" I look around. "Huh? Are they here, too?"

"I don't know what you're talking about, Scar. I went to Eldridge Park right after I left you, and I was just now heading back."

"Bullshit. I don't believe a damn word you say." I step around him and begin stomping through the thicket, unsure if I'm going the right way or not.

"I'm not lying to you. I really was at the park. If you don't believe me, I'll show you." He reaches for my hand, but I jerk it away before he can even touch me.

"Don't!" I snap. "Don't touch me. Don't talk to me. Just lead me out of here, then stay the hell away from me!"

"All right," he says softly, nodding to the right, "I'll get you out of here."

With my pride in my back pocket, I follow behind him. I shouldn't trust that he's leading me in the right direction, but I have no choice, unless I want to be stuck out here all night.

We're walking in silence when I break it. "Of all the things you could do to mess with me, you just had to play that recording, didn't you?"

Jagger's head snaps around as he steps over a branch in our path. "What recording?"

"You know exactly what recording. Quit denying it and just tell me why you did it?"

"I seriously have no idea what you're talking about. Did someone do something to you out here?"

I jog up to him and grab him by the back of the shirt, stopping him from walking any farther. "You know something happened. Now tell me why?"

"Dammit, Scar!" He grabs my shoulders. "I do not know what the hell you're going on about, so if something happened then just fucking tell me."

He sounds so convincing that I almost believe him.

"In the lunch bag you gave me, there was a note. Are you telling me you really had nothing to do with it?"

He looks over my shoulder, staring into thin air as if he's pulling something from memory. "A note?" His head shakes. "I didn't leave a note. Maybe it was Andy. He's the one who got it from the cafeteria."

"Why would Andy, someone I don't even know, leave me a note that says, *If you think this is a game, you're dead wrong?*"

He tucks his chin. "It said that?"

"Yeah, it did. And right after I read it, someone played a recording out here through a speaker. A recording of me and Maddie making a promise to never come here."

Jagger looks dumbfounded, which confuses the heck out of me. "That doesn't make any sense. We never discussed anything like that."

"Well, if you are telling me the truth, it seems your friends have left you out of the loop."

"No," he bites out, "No, they wouldn't do that. Neo and I have consulted on everything, and there was nothing like that in the plan."

"What about Crew?"

"Crew's..." he trails off. "No. He wouldn't pull that shit either. Not if it involved Maddie."

"So you expect me to believe that someone else, who knows about my promise to Maddie, just came out here to fuck with me for no good reason?"

"I don't know what you should believe, because I don't know what the fuck is going on. I'll ask the guys, but I doubt it was them. Sure as hell wasn't me."

I'm biting hard on my bottom lip, observing him for any proof that he's telling the truth, but my gut still won't let me believe him. "I don't care what you say. The coincidence is uncanny. You were there, then you weren't. I was lost, and you found me. Come on, Jagger. Do you think I'm a complete idiot?"

"Actually, I don't. In fact, I think you're pretty fucking smart." He snatches my hand in an instant and squeezes as he pulls me. My feet try to keep up, but he's walking so quickly.

"Let me go!"

He doesn't stop, though, and less than a minute later, after moving through the trees, we're standing on the edge of a mountain directly in front of a Ferris wheel and an open field.

"Wow," I say, eyes on the sight in front of me, "what is this place?"

"Eldridge Park. Well, what's left of it."

Down below is a wide-open space overrun with weeds and tall grass. Only a few feet away from us is an old Ferris wheel that has tipped and is now pressing against the side of the mountain. It looks to be around fifty years old, with more than a dozen swinging cars spaced out from one another, all faded, but still showing a hint of their original pastel colors. If I reached out far enough, I could touch one of the cars.

I glance over at Jagger, who's watching me. "Is this where you were?"

He nods. "It's sort of my secret place, so don't go sharing it with anyone. My dad told me about it when I was a kid. He and my mom used to come here to escape the craziness of the Academy. Now, I like to come here to get away."

Okay. So maybe it wasn't a cosmic coincidence that he was out here. Jagger said he was going to his favorite place, which happens to be a quick walk from where I was lost. There's no way he could have known I'd try to chase the perpetrator through the woods to try and catch them.

"Come on," Jagger says, nodding toward the wheel.

"You're kidding right?"

"Do I look like I'm kidding?" He stretches his leg out so that his foot is pressed against the metal frame, while his other foot is still on solid ground.

When I don't react, he drops his shoulders, grabs a bar above him and swings onto the car.

With two hands over his head, holding on to a bar, and his feet touching down on another one, he tips his chin. "Just get on."

"You're out of your damn mind if you think I'm about to jump on that dilapidated thing."

"Suit yourself," he says, dropping into one of the cars.

It looks easy enough. The car Jagger is in is pretty close. I could probably do it without falling to my death. I'm just not sure how much faith I want to put into the stability of this thing. It's old and it obviously already tipped to be pressed so tightly to the mountain side. One of these bars could break and we'd go crashing down to the ground.

Jagger kicks his feet up and pulls a cigarette out from behind his ear. I didn't even know he smoked. It's been so long since I saw Jagger in any other capacity than him being a dick, so it's possible I never paid attention.

When the scent hits my nose, I realize it's not a cigarette, but a joint.

He draws in a hit, speaking on the exhale. "Gotta say, Scar. I never took you to be a complete chickenshit."

"Chickenshit, huh?" I take a small step forward, observing the trajectory.

"I said what I said."

I watch him with scathing eyes as he takes another drag, exhaling a cloud of smoke.

Teetering on the edge, I reach out and grab the frame.

Jagger drops his feet, stands up, and presses his hands to the sides of the car. "Nice and easy. You've got this."

"Really?" I scoff. "Seconds ago I was a chickenshit."

Stepping on, one foot at a time, I hold the bar over my head and shimmy my way to the car. One glance at the ground far beneath me has my heart pounding. "Holy shit." I blow out a breath of pent-up air.

"Atta' girl," Jagger says, cheering me on.

When I'm near the car, I grab the edge and take Jagger's hand. He pulls me in and I immediately drop onto the seat.

My head rests back and I stare up at the open sky. "I can't believe I just did that."

"I can. You're more of a badass than half the guys I know."

I narrow my eyes and exhale heavily. "Is that a compliment or an insult?"

Jagger sits down beside me, legs spread, his hand hanging between them with the joint positioned between his thumb and forefinger. "Definitely a compliment."

"Let me hit that," I tell him, regarding the joint.

"This?" He holds it up, questioning me with his eyes.

"No. Your face. Yes, that." I snatch it out of his hand, now pinching it between my fingers.

I look down at it, remembering the last time I smoked weed. I was with Maddie, Crew, and my friend, Finn, who was a member of my ski club. He also attends Essex High and hung out with Maddie and me quite a bit.

It was right before her accident. We were all lying in the snow, laughing our asses off making snow angels.

"Go easy, Maddie. This is a big hill and given your lack of skills on the slopes, you'll want a clear head," Crew says, knowing she's not an experienced boarder.

"You hush. Scar took me down Black Falls last year and I didn't even break a bone."

We all laugh. "In that case, toke it up," Finn says.

"Not breaking a bone is not something to be proud of, Mads.

You did good, though. I was impressed you only wiped out three times. That's something to be proud of."

Maddie draws in a puff, holding it in for a second before blowing out. "Tell that to my brother. He thinks I should've just stayed home."

"Neo always thinks you should just stay home," I tell her, though she already knows. "Fuck him. You're allowed to get out and have some fun. One day he's just gonna have to get over the fact that you've got a life that doesn't revolve around him."

"He just worries about me. His intentions are good."

"Yeah, right," I mumble, taking the joint that she passes my way. "He wants you under his thumb. Neo's had a stick up his ass ever since our first playdate when we were toddlers. He used to take my toys and give them to you. Push me down to get me away from you. He was so scared I was gonna steal you away from him."

"Well, you sorta did, but it's because I like hanging out with you more. Neo never lets me do anything." Maddie rolls onto her side to face me. The guys are carrying on with their own conversation about football, so we pass the joint back and forth to each other, burning it down without them even noticing.

"If anyone stole you from him, it's Crew. You and I barely even hang out since you two started dating."

"For what it's worth, I don't see Crew much either. Between school and dance, my free time is scarce."

A sorrowful look sweeps over her, and I push myself up on my elbows. "What's wrong?"

Maddie looks over her shoulder at Crew, then back at me. "I don't think Crew wants to be with me anymore."

"Why do you say that?"

"He just doesn't seem interested anymore. Do you think he's into someone else?"

My heart splinters in my chest. I know Crew is interested in someone else. I also know that someone else is me. But I don't tell

*Maddie that. No matter how Crew and I feel about each other, we
will never be together. Maddie's happiness is far more important
than my own.*

"No way, babe. Crew's very much into you."

Maddie smiles. "Yeah, I'm probably just overthinking things."

"Are you gonna hit that or just stare at it all night?"

I blink my eyes, warding off the memories. "Yeah, sorry." I
press the joint to my lips and suck in, feeling the hit go straight
to my lungs. I hold it for a few seconds then blow out before
passing it back to Jagger.

"Nah, go ahead. I've had enough."

I take a few more hits, my eyes dancing around at the
breathtaking view. It really is a sight from up here. The mountains in the distance look touchable, even though they're
hundreds of feet away.

"Hey," I say, grabbing Jagger's attention, "can I ask you
something?"

"You just did."

"I'm being serious. This is important."

"I can tell. You're puffing on a roach that's burning your
fingers."

My arm sweeps out, and I drop the joint over the side of the
car. "Did you take pictures of me a couple nights ago?"

"Pictures?" His forehead crinkles. "No. Why would I take
pictures of you?"

"Let me rephrase that." I've come to realize I have to be
detailed with my questions or I never get honest answers. "Do
you know who took pictures of me a couple of nights ago?"

"Not a damn clue. But what makes you think someone was
taking pictures at all?"

"Someone came to the girls' dorms, wearing one of those
black robes you guys wear. Whoever it was stood at the back
door, behind the steps, and took a bunch of pictures with their

phone." I turn to face him, tucking one leg under the other. "Phones are not allowed here anymore, unless you're part of the Lawless, so I doubt anyone would be dumb enough to flash it in public, except the three of you. Not to mention, the robe pretty much gives you guys away."

Jagger's eyebrows knit together, and he looks at me. "That wasn't us."

"Well, I know it wasn't Crew because he was at practice. So it only leaves you and Neo. But if you say it wasn't you, then that only leaves one person."

"Neo?" Jagger scoffs, sweeping his hand through the air. "Nah. Neo would've told me if he was doing something like that."

He might believe that, but I don't. I'm also not sure I believe Jagger. Why should I? For all I know, right now is a part of their fucked-up game. He could leave me up here on this Ferris wheel for hours...days, even.

"Is this a game?" I blurt out, my head in a fog from the weed.

"This? As in us being up here? No. Not a game."

"Then why did you bring me here? What's the catch?"

Jagger stands in front of me, holding the corner of the car roof. It rocks a little, but he holds himself steady. "You ask a lot of questions, you know that?"

"Do you blame me?"

"I just think it's best if you stop asking so many because you won't always like the answer. As for us being up here...just figured you'd want a little escape."

I bring my legs up, hugging my knees to my chest as I watch him. When I was younger, being in Jagger's presence made my legs turn to jelly. My chest felt like it was caving in and my heart would jump into a frenzy of erratic beats. He's stupid attractive, and he has this charm about him that isn't

164

apparent often. Right now, though, I see it clear as day. The apprehension in me says not to bite. Especially after what he did last night.

"I didn't think last night was a game either, yet it was." The words come out of my mouth so fast and I wish I could take them back. I don't enjoy making myself vulnerable, and saying that has put me in a position to replay the unguarded state I was in last night.

Jagger bites the corner of his lip. "I never said last night was a game."

"But...Neo—"

"Neo said it was a game. I never did."

"You laughed, though. You went along with everything he said."

"Sometimes it's best to just do what Neo wants."

It wasn't a game.

It was all Neo. He's the one who turned Crew and Jagger against me all those years ago. From the very beginning, he's manipulated them into thinking I'm this awful person, just because I was close with his sister—his sweet, precious Maddie.

Jagger drops his hand and walks across the car. He grips the edge and looks down. "We should go."

The thought has me peering over the car we're sitting in. It rocks slightly as I lean forward, getting a glimpse of the view beneath us. "Jagger," I say, still looking down, "how do we get down?"

"Same way we got on."

My arms cross over my chest as a chill ripples through the air. "I think I'll just stay here. Send food and water."

He laughs, straightening his back. "You'll be fine."

I shake my head no. "Getting on was easy. I don't think I can get off, though."

Jagger shrugs. "You're probably right. You probably can't do it." He flings a leg over the car. "Guess I'll see ya around."

"Wait," I grab his pant leg, not letting him leave me here, "are you serious?"

"Well, yeah. You say you can't do it, and I've got shit to do."

He's testing me.

"Okay. I'm coming. Just...wait for me. I need to collect my thoughts first."

With one leg tossed over the side, Jagger straddles the car, making it sway even more.

Finally, I stand up and walk over to where he's at—one leg out, one leg in. "All right. Let's do this."

Jagger drops off the side while holding on to a spindle above him, and once he's out of the way, I do the same.

Jagger is back on the mountain in seconds while I'm fighting not to look down.

I'm slogging my way over with shaky legs while he offers words of encouragement, which is odd coming from him.

Once I'm close enough to the mountain, I stretch my foot out and he gives me his hand. In one fell swoop, he lugs me onto the mountain.

I crash into his body, taking us both down to the ground. I'm lying on top of him, laughing while darting my gaze from his eyes to the mound of moss beside me.

I should get up. But when I try to, Jagger puts his hands on my hips, holding me in place. "You did good, chickenshit."

Biting back a smile, I slap his shoulder playfully. His soft, light brown eyes drink me up. No animosity, no ill-intent. Our hearts beat in sync against one another's chests, and when his eyes dart to my lips, I feel dizzy.

"Jagger...I—"

I'm not even sure what I was going to say, but I'm cut off when he rolls me off him.

"Get up, tough girl." He jabs his hand out while I lie on the ground, looking at it like it's been washed in poison. I second-guess his help, even though I was seconds away from kissing him if he'd taken the initiative. *I'm such an idiot.* It's no wonder these guys think I'm their helpless toy.

Reluctantly, I accept the offer and he pulls me up.

I brush myself off as we walk, following Jagger's lead.

We've been on the trail for a few minutes and neither of us has said anything. We just walk along in silence. Me in my thoughts, Jagger in his.

Before long, we're back at the school.

Jagger and I both stop, facing each other. He angles his head toward the building. "You've missed the second half of your classes, but at least you're out of the woods."

I bite back a smile, looking down at my feet and digging my toe into the gravel. "Yeah. If you wouldn't have found me, an animal could have eaten me alive."

"Well, we can't have that. We need you around a little longer."

Reality slaps me in the face—hard. "Right. For the games. The torture. The bullying."

"And to kick Crew's ass when he needs it."

I can't help the laugh that spills out of me. "He deserved it all."

"Oh, I know he did." His hand rests on his chest and he grins. "Trust me, I'm not telling you to stop."

Trust him. An odd choice of words.

"Listen," he continues, "the guys have a Ladder Games' event Thursday night. I don't attend the games for my own personal reasons, but I thought about watching from the rooftop of the athletic center. It gives the best view."

I chuckle. "More climbing? You really are an adrenaline junkie."

"What can I say? I like the rush. Anyway, if you're not doing anything and wanna get a glimpse of what these games entail, you're welcome to watch with me."

I'm a bit surprised at his offer. "You mean, with you?"

"Sure. Why not?"

I can think of a gazillion reasons why not, but the one reason I should—because I think I want to—fogs my logic.

"Maybe." I shrug causally.

"All right then. *Maybe* I'll see you Thursday." He spins around and heads toward the school.

Giddiness swarms in my belly, and no matter how hard I try to erase the smile on my face, it doesn't falter. A couple hours ago, I thought I'd be lost forever in those woods. Now, I think I've officially lost my mind because Jagger Cole just gave me butterflies.

CHAPTER
SEVENTEEN
CREW

"WHERE THE HELL IS SHE?" I slam the door closed, rattling the wendigo skull mask hanging on the wall. When no one answers me, I shout louder, "Where the hell is Scar?"

Jagger looks over his shoulder, phone in hand, while Neo ignores me completely. "How the hell are we supposed to know?"

"Maybe because you left from the school with her and neither of you were in any classes the rest of the day."

"I took her out of the dining hall and we parted ways. Did you check her dorm?"

"Good idea. Why didn't I think of that?" My sarcasm couldn't be more apparent. "Yes, I checked her fucking dorm. She wasn't there."

Jagger resumes tapping into his phone. "I don't know what to tell ya, man."

I reach into my pocket and pull out my keys, holding them in the air. "She stole my fucking master key. Gave the rest back, but the master is gone."

Oh, sure. Now I've got their attention.

Neo jumps up, crosses the room and grabs the keys from my hand, sorting through them like I haven't done it a dozen times already.

"My bike key, sled key, and house key are there, but the master is not."

Neo shoves them into my chest. "Well, you better fucking find it and fast."

"You think I haven't tried. It's like the girl just vanished. Jagger," I huff, "where was she headed when you left her?"

"Didn't say. She's probably off with Riley somewhere. Or that Elias guy."

"Elias? Who the fuck is Elias?"

Neo cuts in. "He's a senior. I looked him up in the database after I saw her with him in front of the library. Preppy-looking guy. Seems kinda quiet."

"And you just let him sit there and talk with her? Why the hell didn't you intervene? Or at the very least, tell us?"

"Why do you even care?" Neo asks, tone sharp.

I don't dare tell them I care because the idea of any guy hanging out with Scar, outside of our group, makes me fucking crazy. That it has for years. When she was fourteen, she had a long-distance relationship with a douchebag from the Derma Chapter and I personally tracked down a picture of him with another girl and showed Maddie, knowing she'd tell Scar. They broke up that night.

"If this guy gets in her head, he could ruin all our progress. She's about to break. I can feel it."

"Yeah," Jagger laughs, face still in his phone, "she's about to break your nose."

"Haha, asshole. I'm dead serious. She can't get close to this Eliot guy."

"It's Elias, and don't you worry your pretty little head." Neo flicks my earlobe and I swat his hand away. "I've got eyes on

170

our girl at all times." His eyes dance to Jagger and there's a moment of silence before Jagger turns around and catches his stare.

"What?" Jagger grumbles.

Neo tips his chin. Any humor he had has dissipated. "You know what."

"All right. What am I missing?"

Jagger finally sets his phone down on the couch and stands up. "Hell if I know. But if Neo has eyes on her at all times, he should know exactly where she is so you can get your key."

I've got no idea what's going on, but if these guys are withholding information again, I'm gonna lose my shit.

Still watching Jagger, Neo reaches into his back pocket and pulls out his phone. His eyes roll to his hand and he taps into something on the screen. Jagger and I watch intently as we wait for him to say something.

My impatience gets the best of me. "What are you doing?"

He swipes out of the screen and stuffs his phone back in his pocket. "She's at the library."

"Dude," Jagger says, "do you have a tracker on her?"

"Nope."

That's all he gives us. And no matter how much we pry, that's all we'll get. Because Neo does whatever the fuck Neo wants.

"All right," I tell him, "I gotta get to practice. I'll swing by the library on the way and pay our friend a little visit."

With my equipment bag on my shoulder, I head out the front door. As I close it behind me, it swings back open.

"Hey, man," Jagger says, stepping out in a tee shirt and gym shorts, "you got a sec?"

I pull out my keys, hoping this doesn't take long. Practice starts in an hour and I need to stop at the library. "Yeah, what's up?"

Jagger closes the door and steps out barefoot onto the cement slab. "What happened to you two after I left the dining hall?"

"Same old bullshit. He accused me of having feelings for Scar. Gave me shit for undermining him. You know how he is."

"Yeah. Look," Jagger says in a hushed tone, "I gotta ask you something, no questions asked. And I need you to be honest."

I nod. "Ask away."

"Were you out on the dorm trails today during school hours?"

"No. I was in all my classes today. Why?"

"No reason." He pauses. "Two nights ago, were you at Foxes' Den in a ceremonial cloak, taking pictures of Scar?"

My neck cranes, eyebrows pulled together. "What the fuck? No."

Jagger averts his gaze, rubbing his chin before looking back at me. "Was Neo?"

I shrug my shoulders. "Not that I know of."

Finally, he pats a hand on my shoulder and says, "Thanks, man. See ya after practice."

All this secrecy is getting to me. I'm starting to think that if they want to keep their own secrets, I should be able to keep mine.

MY CHEEK BRUSHES against Scar's, and I whisper, "Reading anything interesting?"

Her body jolts, and she smacks her book closed. "Jesus, Crew. You scared the hell out of me!"

Everyone in the small room looks at us scornfully before returning to whatever they're doing.

"Good. Maybe that means the devil inside you will quit

using me as a punching bag." I pull a chair out, taking a seat beside her. "What are you reading?"

"If you don't wanna be my punching bag, then quit asking me small-talk questions." She opens her book to the page where the bookmark is sticking out and says, "It's *The Handmaid's Tale*."

"Ah. Is that the one about the dolphin with the prosthetic tail?

With a pinched expression, she narrows her eyes. "No, Crew. It's not." Her head shakes in annoyance. "What do you want?"

"From you? Many things—compliance, less sass, and maybe even a blow job. But I also want my key."

"Well, you get none of those things. Now get lost. I already gave you your stupid keys."

"Shhh!" a girl sitting alone at the table to the left says. When I look at her and she realizes who she's shushing, her eyes shoot down to look at the table, and she tucks her head between her shoulders.

"No, Scar. You gave me some of my keys. My master was not on the ring and I need it back."

Scar dabs her finger to her tongue, and while she's only wetting it to turn the page, I find it quite alluring. "I don't know what to tell you. You must've lost it."

Her words, however, not so alluring.

"I definitely didn't lose it and I know for a fact that you have it."

"Oh yeah?" Her head lifts. "What fact is that? Let's hear it."

"You had my keys and one is missing. That's the fact."

"That's not a fact, Crew. That's an assumption and your assumption is wrong. I don't have your key, so please leave me alone."

She turns another page.

173

"Did you even read that whole page, or are you skimming?"

Her chest inflates as she draws in a deep breath. "Actually, I'm not even reading right now because someone is chirping in my damn ear." Her shrilling voice turns heads again, but, this time, no one says a word about it.

"Well, if you keep turning pages without reading them, you'll lose your place."

She sighs. "Why are you still here?"

"You've got five seconds, Scar. Do the right thing before you ruin study time for all these students."

She continues to ignore me, flipping another page. This time, I'm positive she didn't read it. Who reads that fast?

"Five."

Still reading—or skimming lines.

"Four."

Her head lifts.

"Three."

"Quit it, Crew. I don't have your key."

"Two."

"Don't you dare make a scene."

"One."

I stand up, and she grabs me. Her attempt to pull me back in the chair is laughable.

"Sit down!"

Peering down at her, I smirk. "Thought you wanted me to leave."

"I do," she grits out. "But I'd rather you sit and annoy me than interrupt all these other people."

I hold out my open palm, giving her one more chance. "Key. Now."

Her shoulders rise, hand stuck in between the pages of her

book. "I. Do. Not. Have. It. I swear to you. You either lost it, or someone took it."

Is she serious? I think she might be. Scar hates attention, so if she had it, she'd give it back before letting me embarrass her in front of all these people.

But I can't be too sure.

"Excuse me, everyone." I get up, grab the chair, and swing it around. As planned, I get everyone's attention, including the librarian's, who glances at me out of the corner of her eye before looking down and pretending to be oblivious to the scene I'm causing.

Scar clenches her jaw while all the color drains from her face. "Sit down, Crew."

I lift my foot, setting my boot on the chair. "This girl beside me is Scarlett Sunder. I'm sure you've all heard of her. Well, she's stolen something from me. Something really important."

Scar drops her head down on her folded arms that are pressed to the table. "I don't have your key," she hisses into the fabric of her black-and-gray flannel.

"I don't believe you," I say to her, before returning my attention to the crowd, who's hanging on my every word. "Until Scarlett returns what is mine, I need you all to make it your mission to remind her how wrong it is to disobey a member of the Lawless." I look down at Scar, who's pinning me with a glare. "Give her hell."

She winces. "Fine."

"Fine?"

"Fine. I'll give you your key."

"Situation averted. For now," I tell the crowd, "carry on."

Dropping my foot from the chair, I step behind Scar and press my hands to the table on either side of her. I bury my nose in her hair and her floral-scented shampoo fills my senses. "Well, what are you waiting for? Hand it over."

God, she smells so fucking good. What is that? Lavender? I inhale another breath, practically snorting her hair. *Jasmine, maybe?*

The next thing I know, her head is whipping around and I'm getting smacked in the face with her sweet-scented locks. "I don't have it with me. Why don't you wait here and I'll go grab it."

She must think I'm a complete idiot. I know this girl. She'll leave and never come back while I sit and wait like an obedient dog. "Nice try, Scar." I grab her bag off the table, then her book.

"What are you doing? Give me that." She grabs her bag, pulling it while I do the same. We're playing a game of tug-of-war when the strap rips off and Scar's back crushes against the edge of the table. "Ugh!" she grumbles, placing a hand on the sore spot on her back. "You're such a jerk!"

"Oh, shit."

She rubs her side beneath the oversized flannel she's wearing. "Oh shit is right."

"Looks like we're even. Now get your ass up so we can go get my key." I grab her arm, pulling her up, but she drops back down in the chair.

She scoffs. "Can't you see I'm injured?"

"Injured, my ass. You barely hit the damn table. You've got thirty seconds to lick your wounds or I'll reinstate my demands to every student in this room."

Scar sinks down in the chair, still faking her injury. It's obvious she's biding her time because she doesn't want to return my damn key. Her admission was only half the battle. The girl is as stubborn as they come, and it's really fucking annoying. Kinda turning me on, too, if I'm being honest. I'm fucked up like that.

"All right," I tell her, "time's up."

"Hear me out, Crew," she says, turning in the chair and pressing her hands on the back of it. "I need you to listen to every word I say." Her monotone voice has me dreading where this conversation is headed. "I. Do. Not. Have. Your. Key."

My head falls back and I close my eyes momentarily, willing myself not to blow up. "Cut the bullshit. You just admitted to me you had it."

"I lied because you were drawing unnecessary attention to us and telling everyone to give me hell. What did you expect me to do?"

This is getting really fucking old. I sweep my fingers through my hair, lips pressed together firmly as I tsk. "You're making it really hard to be nice right now."

She snorts. "You think you're being nice? I'd hate to see what you do when you're being mean."

"You're about to find out." I grab her arm, this time with enough pressure to yank her flimsy body out of the chair. She fusses and fights, but I don't let up as I pull her through the library, all eyes on us. "Mind your fucking business," I growl at a table of guys who look concerned for her safety.

We pass five rows of books, and when I find an empty one, out of the sight and sound of others, I drag her down it. "Ah, horror. This is fitting." I spin her around midway down the row and press her back to the shelves of books.

"Is this really necessary?" she seethes, surrendering her fight. I'm hopeful she realizes I'm not fucking around anymore.

I brace my hands on either side of her, closing in on her personal space. "Do you think this is a game?"

Her head tilts slightly to the side, a quizzical expression on her face. "What did you just say?"

"I said cut the bullshit. That key is my lifeline at this place. I need it back."

"No. After that. Repeat what you said."

"I asked if you think this is a game."

Scar licks her lips, her eyes never leaving mine. "It was you, wasn't it? All of it. The pictures, the note, the recording."

"What the hell are you talking about?"

"The jig is up. I know it was you. Might as well confess now."

"If this is some tactic to try and get me to forget about the key, it's not working."

"Fuck the key!" She literally spits, hitting me in the eye. I turn my head, seething, but hold it together the best I can. "Admit it, Crew. You came to Foxes' Den, watched me for minutes in one of those ugly robes, then took pictures of me. Earlier today, you put a threatening note in my lunch, then you had the balls to play a recording through a speaker of a private conversation between me and Maddie."

I have no idea what she's talking about. But Jagger was acting sketchy when I left the house, asking me if I was out on the trail and if I went to the girls' dorm in my ceremonial robe.

"I didn't do any of that shit. If someone really did those things, it wasn't us."

The realization hits me all at once—*someone else is fucking with her.* "Look, Scar. All bullshit aside. If that really happened, I need to know because it wasn't us and it means someone is undermining our authority and breaking every goddamn rule the Lawless has set forth."

"Oh, it happened all right. I still hear her voice in my head. The promise we made to never come to this place. Go search the trails. My lunch and the note are out there somewhere."

"Fuck." I slam my hands to the shelf behind her. *I've gotta talk to the guys.* "Wait. Did you tell Jagger about all this?" She must have, because he knew. And that motherfucker never told me when he all but accused me of doing that shit.

"I told Jagger because I thought it was him at first. So, you're really saying it wasn't you?"

I can't tell if she's being accusatory and still thinks it was, or if she's scared to death that it's not. Scar isn't afraid of me, but she might be afraid of someone else.

"I swear on Maddie's life, it was not me. And I can almost guarantee you it wasn't Jagger."

"And Neo?"

That, I can't answer. The guy is a loose cannon lately. In the past, I'd be able to answer honestly. Now, I've got no idea what he's up to.

I shrug my shoulders because telling her I know it wasn't him is a lie, but telling her it could be is a betrayal to my friend. Let's hope it is Neo for the sake of every male student at this school.

"Do you believe me?" I ask her, genuinely.

She chews on her bottom lip, something she does when she's thinking hard. Her head slowly nods before she says, "I really shouldn't, but I do. I've learned your expressions, and I think I'm starting to realize when you're lying and when you're not."

"Wish I could say the same for you. I still think you've got my key."

"I won't swear on Maddie's life because her life is too precious to be bartered with, but I will swear on everything else. I don't have it. I gave you the keys back and assumed they were all there. If they're not, it means someone stole it from my room or you lost it."

"Definitely didn't lose it."

"Then someone came into my room and stole that key and that thought freaks me the fuck out."

Dozens of scenarios play out in my mind, and each one has my blood pumping faster. Someone broke into her room. They could have watched her sleep. Followed her to the showers. Searched through her belongings. If I find out any guy in this place so much as touched a hair on her head, I will destroy them. I will watch the tears roll down their cheeks, savoring each drop as I chop off their fingers one by one.

Outside of this place, Scar isn't mine. She never was. Probably never will be. But here, at BCA, she belongs to us. We brought her here for a purpose. Our plans carefully laid out. Her body, our oyster. *Ours.* I can barely stand the thought of Jagger and Neo touching her, let alone a stranger.

"Crew," she says softly, snapping me out of my own fucked-up thoughts.

My eyes slide to hers. "No one touches you but us, Scar. If someone is out there trying to toy with you, mark my words, they will pay."

"No one touches me, period."

"Is that what you think?" I tip my chin at her. "That I can't touch you if I want to?"

I drop one hand, pressing it between her clenched thighs. "Tell me to stop, Scar."

Her nostrils flare. "Stop."

I don't. Instead, my hand moves beneath her skirt; only this time, she parts her legs slightly. "You've got a free hand now. If you want me to stop, make me."

Her tongue darts out, wetting her lips. "You know I could. I can scream. Knee you in the balls, punch you, make you bleed, and I know you wouldn't do anything to stop me. You never do."

My eyes dance across her wet, plump lips. "Maybe I like it when you hurt me."

"Good. Because after everything you did to me, I want you to feel pain." Her tone is placid, void of any emotion, which is unusual for such an expressive girl.

Moving my hand farther up, I cup her crotch, feeling the soft cotton of her damp panties. "I think you get off on hurting me, too." I smirk. "You're wet, Scar."

Humiliation be damned, she tips her head back against the bookshelf and closes her eyes. "Maybe I do."

"Mmm," I hum into the crook of her neck. "It seems so."

My mouth parts slightly, ghosting her skin, ready to feast on her like a vampire in need of a meal. "Fuck, Scar. You smell so good," I breathe out, my hot breath sending goosebumps spilling down her collarbone.

Dropping her hand that's pinned over her head, I peel back the shoulders of her flannel and it falls, hanging on the crease of her arms.

My head lifts, eyes burning into her lustful ones. "You're still not stopping me."

"I'm waiting for the right moment." Her tongue drags across her top teeth and my cock twitches.

Engulfed in silence, the only sound is Scar's heady breaths as her chest rises and falls against mine. She's enjoying this little game of cat and mouse. In fact, I think she wants me to make my move because she enjoys fighting me off. She's turned on by the war between us, much like I am.

The tips of my fingers move smoothly beneath the hem of her panties. She draws in a bumpy breath, her body quivering.

I lean closer, brushing my mouth against hers. "Make your move, baby."

Without delay, Scar clamps down on my bottom lip. Her sharp teeth digging into the layer of thin skin. I laugh menacingly while she tugs and bites. "There she is."

Like a rubber band, she lets go, wearing streaks of my blood as lipstick.

"Is that what you like, Crew? Do you crave the pain?"

Swiping two fingers across my lip, I look at the blood and

smirk. In one swift motion, I lift Scar's skirt, eyes bolted to hers as I push her panties to the side and shove the same two fingers inside her.

Her body jolts, eyes wide with shock.

Shoving deeper and harder, her body rides up the bookshelf. A whimper slips out of her perfectly parted red lips.

"I do like it, Scar. How about you? Do you like this, or does it make you want to inflict more pain on me?"

Her hands clamp down on my shoulders, fingertips pinching into my skin through my shirt. "As if you're capable of feeling anything at all."

One hand lands on her hip and I spin her around, so her back is flush to my chest. My fingers twisting inside her.

"We're in a library, Crew. You really want your ass kicked in a library?"

Still pumping my fingers inside her, I draw in a breath of her scented hair. "That's just like you—to pretend you don't want something, just because someone else is giving it to you."

When my thumb sweeps across her clit, her body quivers, and her fingers clench the shelf.

"You're wrong. Jagger did the same thing, and I fucking loved it."

Baring my teeth, my eyes go cold as I grab a fistful of her hair, jerking her head back. "Take that back."

"Never."

Tugging harder, I add another finger, flexing them and spreading her apart. She whimpers, a mix of pleasure and pain. I know this because her legs extend farther, all but welcoming what I'm giving her.

"Take it back now or I'll shove my cock in you and brutally fuck you into one of these shelves of horror novels."

In a moment of weakness, I let my guard down, and Scar slips out of my reach. She turns around, hands pushed to my chest, and she lashes out as she walks me into the shelf behind me. "I'll never take it back because, as much as I despise Jagger, it felt good. You, on the other hand, have lazy fingers. They just chill inside me like it's a warm, cozy blanket on a chilly night." She holds a hand up, grinning as she wiggles her fingers. "Work them, Crew. Make it known they're in there."

"You bitch!" I grab her by the throat in a knee-jerk reaction.

She raises a hand, slapping me hard across the face. "Asshole!"

"You're gonna regret that."

"Doubtful!" she snaps back.

My hands are still around her neck, barely squeezing, when a shadow to the left grabs my attention. Scar and I both drag our eyes toward the end of the aisle, where a petite girl with glasses is standing.

"I...umm. I'm sorry," the girl says with an armful of books.

"You should be," I say, back to dodging fists and open palms from Scar. "This is a private conversation. Now get the fuck out of here."

She hurries away, knowing better than to open her mouth about what she just saw.

I return my attention to Scar, who's now climbing my body like a spider monkey. Her flannel shirt falls off her arms, landing on the floor, as her legs wrap around my waist. A kink in my arm forces me to release my hold on her.

"Ya know. If you worked your fingers inside my pussy as well as you do around my neck, I might be coming right now."

I carry her back to where she belongs—back pressed to the shelf. "You are a dirty-talking whore, you know that?"

"Only with you."

She better fucking mean that.

My mouth crushes against hers, and I mutter, "Let's keep it that way."

Like two primal animals, we tear into each other. Bite for bite, claw for claw. Scar fists my hair, tugging my head wherever she wants it to go. I flip her skirt and slip her panties to the side again, showing her I can make her feel better than Jagger, or any guy for that matter.

I slide my fingers in, knuckle-deep. Curling and working them at just the right velocity to make her moan into the small space between us.

Her head drops back and I taste her skin, re-marking her. Showing the world that this girl is mine. Maybe not in every sense of the word, but in every sense that matters. She is not to be touched. She is not to be fucked. And she sure as hell is not to be fucked *with*.

"Tell me it feels better than last night," I demand, needing to hear the words for my own sanity.

"It feels like a stuck tampon."

"Fuck you!" I suck her neck harder, punishing her for being such a mouthy little bitch.

"No," she spits, "fuck you!"

Releasing my fingers, I push her legs down and spin her around. "Oh, I'm going to. I'm gonna fuck you until you scream my name. Everyone in this library is going to know who's doing this to you."

Holding my hand to her head, I keep her in place as I unclasp my belt, unzip my jeans, and drop them to my ankles. My cock springs free, hard and ready to stuff her full.

My knee moves up between her thighs, separating them before I push her panties to the side. Her back arches, ass out. She's not only mouthy, she's a liar, too. Scar wants this just as bad as I do, even if she won't admit it.

With one hand on my cock, I give it a few pumps, then

184

guide it into her dripping pussy. Scar slaps her hands to the shelf, pushing a few books back and causing others to crash to the floor in the next aisle over.

Her position doesn't shift, nor does mine.

I grab her hair, pulling it back again while whispering into her ear, "Say my name."

Her mouth tugs up in a grin as she says, "Jagger."

The vein in my arms pulse, the one in my neck throbbing as I deepen my voice and growl, "Say *my* fucking name."

One hand lands on her hip, and when she doesn't do as she's told, I thrust harder, with every intention of making a spectacle of her orgasm.

She cries out a muffled sound, which isn't enough for me, so I crush her ass with my pelvic bone, rattling the shelf she's holding on to. "Say my name or I'll fuck you so hard, this shelf will fall over. And when it does, I'll continue fucking you on top of it with an audience."

Her stubbornness is unnerving, but my urgency for control overpowers all my primal need. I will not come until I hear her say my name, not his.

"You won't last. I give you five minutes, tops. In case you've forgotten..." I slam into her so hard my head hits the back of hers, but she continues running her dirty mouth. "We've done this before. I know you're a quick fuck."

"And you're lying through your pretty white teeth. In case *you've forgotten*, I once fucked you until your pussy was raw."

"Oh, I remember that well. You were too lazy to even get me wet first."

Her lack of compliance has me going to extremes. I pull out of her and take her down to the ground. With her skirt bunched at her waist, I grip the hem of her panties and pull until they rip down the center. Her eyes widen and now I've got her attention. "You wanna be wet? I'll get you nice and wet."

Slipping my hands between her thighs, my fingers graze her skin, raising her hair follicles. Her legs separate, making room for me, and I part her lips with my fingers.

A guttural growl rushes out as my tongue sweeps up the length of her pussy. Scar shivers, spreading her legs wider, and a moan slips through her lips.

I lift my eyes and see her propped up on her elbows, watching me. "There's no hiding now. Anyone could come down this aisle and see you lying here with your legs spread."

The look on her face is priceless. One I've waited months to see. A glint of fear and overwhelming need.

My head drops and I suck her clit between my teeth then push two fingers inside her. She tastes so fucking good and the way she's clenching my fingers inside her tells me she's loving this just as much as I am.

Scar says I don't get her wet, but she's a fucking liar. I could drink up her juices and quench my thirst for days.

Her hips thrust upward and her moans make such beautiful sounds; ones I could listen to all day long, but as she nears ecstasy, I pull out, rubbing her arousal through the tips of my fingers.

"You're plenty wet now, baby."

She whimpers, "Please don't stop."

Her urgency is sexy as hell; it's not often Scar uses manners, so it goes straight to my head.

The corner of my lip tugs up before I reclaim my space inside her with my cock. Taking both her legs in the crease of my arm, I push them up to her head.

Fuck. It feels so good inside her. Tight, warm, wet. Like she was molded just for me. Every muscle inside me contracts. My breaths become ragged and audible.

Rolling my hips, I fuck her hard and fast. Our bodies vibrate against each other's while she slides inch by inch on the mauve-printed carpet.

Scar shivers. Her hands come up, grabbing my face and pulling it to hers. "Shut me up before I make a scene."

I slam my mouth against hers so hard our teeth clank. With a slightly tilted head, I slip my tongue between her lips and it dances with hers. Whimpers flee into my mouth. A mixture of moans and cries and silent pleas.

Sliding a hand between us, I lift her shirt, exposing her stomach.

"Fuck, Crew," she finally says my name, and it's music to my ears.

My balls tighten and I grunt, as I pull out and release, her belly button filling with beads of cum.

Scar lies flat on the ground, staring at the ceiling while I hover over her. We're both left panting through shallow breaths, and I give her a minute to collect her thoughts and pull herself together.

Using her ripped panties, I wipe up the proof of my orgasm on her stomach, then I get my clothes back on.

One glance at her and I see the regret in her eyes. Swallowing down the indignation I'm feeling about her reaction, I stuff her worn, ripped panties on the bookshelf between Stephen King's *The Dead Zone* and *Desperation*.

"Hey, Crew?" she says, adjusting her knee-high sock.

"Yeah?"

Her eyes peer up as she adjusts the other. "Who do you think is doing all that stuff to me?"

Her guess is as good as mine. I know whoever it is, though, they won't be here for long.

"No clue. But I told you I'll find out." I angle my head

toward an exit at the right end of the aisle. "Come on. If we go out this way, no one will suspect a thing."

I'm not sure why I do it, considering kindness isn't my strong suit, but I walk her out with a hand pressed to the small of her back.

CHAPTER
EIGHTEEN
SCARLETT

IT'S BEEN two days since Crew and I had the most amazing hate-sex I've ever experienced. Partially, because I've never had hate-sex, but if I had anything to compare it to, I'd say it was the most amazing. It was intense, to say the least. My body exploded with so many emotions—anger, desire, loathing, lust, and relief. Now that those emotions have been expelled, I'm left with only one. Fear.

I still don't know who my stalker is, but I know I have one. Someone is watching me, threatening me, toying with me. I've eliminated Crew and Jagger from that equation, based on my own assessment. Their words and expressions gave me every reason to believe they were telling the truth. That's not to say my guard is down with them, but in that situation, I'm sure I can trust what they're telling me.

At this point, Neo is my top suspect. He has motive and means. Neo is also the puppeteer of the Lawless, and even before taking on that leadership, he was a master manipulator when it came to his friends. Crew and Jagger have always looked up to him, and honestly, I think they feel bad for him. It's no secret that Neo's dad is the biggest asshole of the Elders. I've even heard my mom talk about how she's never liked the guy, even if they are forced to interact at social gatherings. My dad, on the other hand, is a big fan. Which also leads me to believe that Sebastian is my dad's puppeteer.

"Ready, girl? Shuttle's here."

Knotting my black-and-gray flannel around my waist, I nod and ask, "Do you know anything about the games being played tonight?"

Riley shakes her head. "No. We're not supposed to know when the games are happening. Why? Do you know something?"

I grab my messenger bag off my bed and lift the safety-pinned straps over my head, crossing them over my chest. "I didn't know I wasn't supposed to, but yeah, Jagger said the guys are doing something tonight."

"Yeah. He probably wasn't supposed to tell you that, but it seems those guys do a lot of things with you and for you that they're not supposed to do."

I laugh. "What's that supposed to mean?"

Riley walks out the door to the hall and I click the lock before closing it behind me.

"They favor you. Everyone sees it."

I glance at her, eyebrows knitted. "Favor me? More like torture me."

Riley tsks. "I dunno, Scarlett. I think they like you. Well, maybe not Neo. He's a bit intense, but maybe that's just how he flirts."

More laughter erupts. "This isn't elementary school, Ry. You don't bully someone to flirt with them. Trust me. Neo hates me."

"Why, though? I just don't get it. Did you do something back home that pissed them off?"

If only it were one thing that I could slap a Band-Aid on. Instead, it's a combination of events that watered their hatred for me.

"Neo's twin sister and I have been best friends since we were kids—"

"Whoa! Neo has a twin sister?"

"Yep. A fraternal twin. Her name is Maddie. Neo's always been insanely protective over her, but even more so when they lost their mom four years ago. His dad is in politics and never home. Neo sort of took care of her, which was generous of him, but as she got older, he kept her on a short leash. It's like he was terrified to lose her to anyone—especially me. He hated our friendship and thought I was trying to corrupt her. Being the conniver he is, he turned Crew and Jagger against me early on. The rest is history."

"So where is Maddie? Why isn't she here?"

There's a hardness in my stomach that has me wishing I'd never said anything. "She's...not coming to BCA. Not now. Not ever."

"Oh no, Scarlett. Did she pass away?"

"No!" I blurt out, before dropping my tone a few octaves. "No. She's alive." Unease gnaws in my stomach like a starving beast. "Look, can we talk about something else?"

"Yeah. Of course."

I offer her a slight smile. "Thank you." I'm grateful she didn't push because the last thing I want to do right now is relive those last days before I was left with only a shell of my best friend.

We walk out the main doors and the shuttle is waiting for us. A couple of girls get on and the driver waves a hand, calling us over. "Leaving now. If you want a ride, you better hurry."

Riley and I jog over to the door, then she gets on first. Once we're settled, we sink into a shared seat. It's only a seven-minute walk to the school, and if the weather is nice, I wouldn't mind it. Today, we've got snow in the forecast, though, and from what I hear, it won't be slowing down. This area of the state pretty much bypasses fall and goes straight to winter. It's a shame because I really love the autumn aesthetic in the mountains.

"Back to the games tonight," Riley says, and I shush her. If I'm not supposed to know, then I definitely don't want anyone knowing I know. "Oh, sorry." Her voice drops to a whisper. "What did Jagger say about them? Is it something that involves you?"

My shoulders rise. "I don't know. I hope not. He actually invited me to watch with him." I wince, knowing how terrible that sounds after everything these guys have done to me. I'd be a fool to agree. "I guess he could have invited me just to get me there."

"Doubtful." She checks me with a smirk. "He wants you."

I slap her shoulder playfully. "Stop it. He does not."

"Oh yes. He does. Need I remind you, I hopped on his bike... twice? The guy never invited me to do a damn thing. And now that I think about it, he probably only gave me a ride to make you jealous."

"Jealous?" I all but choke on the word through bouts of laughter. "Now you're definitely wrong. They all know I could care less what they do or who they do it with."

"I dunno, girl. I think you four have this thick cord of sexual tension among you and it's bound to snap eventually."

Dropping further into my seat, I fold my hands over my bag in my lap. "Not a chance."

I don't tell her that a couple days ago, I had sex with Crew in the library. And the day before that, Jagger fingered me while Neo watched. If Riley knew any of this, she'd never let go of this assumption she has about us. And I'd also look like a whore.

"Come with me tonight then," I say. "Let me prove to you that there is nothing sexual going on between Jagger and me."

Her forehead crinkles. "A third wheel? Easy pass."

An idea hits me, and it hits me hard. "What if I bring you a date? Then you won't be a third wheel. Which you wouldn't anyway since it's most definitely *not* a date for Jagger and me. What do you say?"

"I'd ask...is he hot?"

"Well, I haven't found him yet, but I'll let you know when I do."

"Good luck with that. All the guys here have boners for the Lawless."

I burst out laughing. Riley continues, "What? It's true. I swear, all their days are spent kissing their asses."

"Give me the school day and I'll find you the perfect match."

I love playing matchmaker, and I think it would be good for Riley to get her eyes off the Lawless, because as much as she denies it, I think she's got a lady boner for them. Every girl here does.

ANOTHER DAY in the miserable attendance of the Lawless. At least one of them is in each of my classes. American literature happens to have all three: one on each side of me and Crew to the left of Neo.

"Morning, Scar," Crew says with his arm draped across the table as he leans in.

Neo scoffs and scoots his chair back as if Crew and I need the space to talk.

I catch Crew gawking at me with a broad smile, and it has me returning his stare with a perplexed look.

Why does he look so happy?

Jesus Christ. If he thinks anything has changed between us since we had sex a couple days ago, he is in for a rude awakening.

My eyes roll to my textbook and I open it just so I have something to look at, other than these three.

"Still haven't found my key," he says, as if I care.

Pressing my lips together firmly, I ignore him. Talking to any of these guys in public only gets me in trouble. Sometimes I think that's what they want. To poke me until I bite back.

"It's like it just vanished into thin air," he continues.

I look over at Jagger, who's leaning into the empty chair behind him, his arm hanging over the back of the one his ass is in. "What?" I huff at him. "You think I have his key?"

Jagger lifts his shoulder. "I didn't say anything. I'm just here for the entertainment."

"Yeah. Because this is so entertaining." Turning in my chair, I shift my attention back to Crew. "We've been over this and I thought you said you believed me. I don't have your key."

"I don't believe you," Neo's gruff voice chimes in.

I match his insolence. "And I didn't ask you if you did."

"Just saying," he continues, "I think you're a manipulative bitch and you might be worming your way into Crew's and Jagger's good graces, but I still think you deserve every bit of turmoil coming to you."

The way his vile words come out so casually is a disgrace to humankind. Who talks like that to people? Who has the right to treat another person so cruelly?

"Eat a dick, Neo," I grumble, returning to my book in front of me, just so I don't have to look at him.

Neo slaps his palm on the table, hard and alarming. I flinch at the sound but do my best to remain unaffected—or at least pretend to be. I don't even look up because I know the entire class is staring.

"What did you just say to me?" His deep voice hits my ears with a heavy vibration. "Why don't you say it a little louder so everyone else can hear?"

I bite my lip, itching at the unwanted attention.

Neo presses a hand on top of my open textbook, the other on the back of my chair, cutting into my personal space. "Stand up and repeat what you said loud enough for everyone to hear or I'll have your room infested with spiders. You hate spiders, don't you, Scar?"

My skin crawls at the thought. Slowly, I turn my head to look at him, teeth grinding. "I said, eat a dick, Neo."

"They didn't quite hear you. A little louder for the ones in the front."

Drawing in a deep breath, I slide my chair back aggressively, knocking Neo's hand off.

With boiling blood in my veins, I lift my head and look at the class before saying, "I told Neo to eat a dick," I look back at him, smirking, "and he said he'd love to."

Neo's head shakes in slow and steady movements as we stare each other down. "Mr. Collins," he says, turning his head toward the teacher at the front of the class, who is pretending to ignore this confrontation. "Do we allow students to speak this way?"

"No, Mr. Saint. It's against policy to use such language."

"I agree with you. And I think you'll agree that Scarlett should be penalized for having such a dirty little mouth."

"Well…umm…what do you suggest, Mr. Saint?"

This is seriously disturbing. Since when do teachers ask students what another student's punishment should be? I'd speak up, but I worry it'll do more harm than good. I'm not one to keep my mouth shut when I have something to say. Is this what my dad meant when he said the Academy will reshape me? If so, it's working.

Neo assesses me, eyes dragging up and down my body. "After-school detention will do."

Mr. Collins nods in agreement with Neo. "Ms. Sunder, please see me after class and we'll discuss your punishment, and if you have another outburst that insults one of your classmates, I'll be notifying the headmaster."

"That won't be necessary, sir."

I drop into my chair, sulking, but glad to be out of the limelight. Neo appears to be pleased. After all, he orchestrated this, as he does with everything.

"Detention?" I grumble under my breath. "That's the best you could do?"

Neo reaches under the table and grabs my thigh, squeezing. His fingertips dig into my meaty flesh so hard it hurts, but I don't tell him so. "Detention is just the beginning." In an attempt to jerk my leg away, he tightens his hold. "What's the matter, Scar? Am I hurting you?"

His hand slides farther up my skirt, and my stomach somersaults. "No. Your touch is repulsing me." I shift again, but his reach extends.

Mr. Collins shuts off the lights and begins playing a slideshow about the birth of American poetry, but Neo's attention is solely on me. Even Crew and Jagger are watching, or at least, pretending to be. Maybe that's what Neo wants. For them to sit by idly while he slowly breaks me—afraid to stand up to him, afraid to disagree with what he's doing.

When Neo finds my panties, my heart begins racing. Leaning close, he whispers, "Be afraid, Scar. I'm thirsty for your fear." Suddenly, he's under my panties. Beads of sweat break out on my forehead and my mind is paralyzed. With two fingers, he pinches my clit. There is nothing gentle about what he's doing. He pinches so hard I have to cover my mouth out of fear I'll make a scene.

With his head bolted to the side of my head while I stare at my book, I shake my head no, knowing he senses my disdain.

With my free hand, I try to pull him out of my skirt, but we're at war when our hands hit the underside of the table.

"What are you two doing?" Crew asks.

Neo ignores him and I don't dare lift my eyes.

Jagger plays dumb, but I know he can see the shakes and shifts of my body.

I lick my lips before settling further into my seat. I'm not sure why I do it. Spite, maybe? Or it could be that I'm just plain stupid. But when Neo curls his fingers at my entrance, I fall victim. I give up my fight and let him dip inside me. He wants to get me off—make me cry out for everyone to hear. Neo loves throwing attention at me because he knows how much I hate it. But, I won't do it. I have willpower.

He's so close. His chest is practically resting against my shoulder. His watchful eyes are still on me. A glance out of my peripheral confirms it. He's watching my mouth. Waiting for a whimper to part my lips.

My chest rises then crashes as he goes deeper, while my hand grips his arm. If I remove it, he'll think I'm giving in, and we can't have that.

I can feel the dampness of my arousal sticking to my thighs, so I know he feels it, too.

"Give in to it, Scar. You know you want to." His words part my hair, whispering against my neck.

I shake my head. "Uh-uh," I groan, lips pressed together tightly.

"Jagger," Neo says in a hushed tone, "hold Scar's leg."

I look at Jagger, shaking my head no, but he reaches over and places his hand on my thigh, firmly holding me in place. He knows exactly what's going on, even if he's pretending to watch the slideshow.

Neo pushes deeper, causing me to slide down on the chair. My legs part instinctively, and I hate that I don't pull them back together.

My tongue darts out, wetting my lips, and I grab Jagger's arm. His fingertips move in slow movements, caressing the meaty flesh of my thigh.

I spread my legs farther for Neo, thankful the lights are off. But when I bump Jagger's knee, I steal his attention again. A second later, his flickered glance returns to the slideshow.

Rolling my lips together, I bite down the urge to cry out.

Right now, two things are certain: I'm going to come and Neo is going to love every second of it.

And I hate that fact.

My stomach clenches. Every muscle in my body quivers from my surging arousal. I squeeze Jagger's arm tighter. Bite down on my lip harder. I do everything I can to extinguish my dire need to cry out.

Neo is watching me. He's watching me as he brings me to this high, ready to witness me shatter into pieces when I finally fall.

A breathy moan climbs up my throat and my legs tremble as I come. In that same breath, regret overwhelms me.

Neo slides his hand out of my skirt and I straighten myself up, still unable to look at him as he whispers, "You're welcome." Then he returns to his seat.

Jagger's hand remains in place, even after I adjust my skirt.

Finally, I glance over at Neo, just to get a read on him from his expression. As I do, his eyes catch mine and his tongue slides up his middle finger. "Mmm. Sweet." Then he turns it around, flipping me off.

I hate him. But right now, I hate myself more.

CHAPTER

NINETEEN

CREW

Day four of lunch with Scar and it's still not getting any easier. I know exactly what Neo's doing. He's shoving her down my throat in hopes of watching me fall to my knees for her. That way, he can turn everything around and use it against me.

Speaking of, where the hell is she?

"Hey," I say to Jagger, "where's Scar?"

His eyes lift from his tray, dancing around the dining hall. "Not sure. But 'where's Neo?' is a better question."

"Think they're together?" Just saying the words has my stomach tightening.

"Doubtful."

"Yeah. You're probably right."

Still, something feels off. It's possible Scar is skipping lunch to avoid Neo, and he's doing the same to steer clear of her. But it's an excuse in my head rather than the real possibility that they're off together somewhere.

I stuff my mouth with a forkful of sour cream smothered burrito, trying to downplay the situation in my head.

Scar hates Neo more than she hates anyone. There's no way she's with him—not willingly, at least.

"I've been thinking," Jagger says, interrupting my thoughts.

"'Bout what?"

"Scar. Neo. Us. In class today, Scar said you believed her about the key. Do you?"

It should be a simple answer to a simple question, but nothing is simple with these guys. Telling them I believe her makes me look weak; however, I don't think she has it. My gut tells me someone else does.

"Honestly? Yeah, I think I do. Something about the whole situation told me she wasn't lying this time."

"Yeah," he nods, sticking his fork into his food and sinking back in his chair, "I believe her, too."

"Ya know, Scar said some things the other day and I went back and forth with bringing this up to you guys because I wanted to find out for myself first, but she thinks someone else has been fucking with her."

Jagger shoots up in his chair. "Yeah." He snaps his fingers, getting serious. "Some weird shit happened Monday that had me thinking the same. She accused me of playing some recording of her and Maddie in the woods and talked about one of us taking pictures of her. That's why I asked you about it."

"Yup. She told me all about it."

"Wait. Have you two been hanging out?"

"Nah. Not really. I've just been on her ass about the key. Then I realized she didn't have it and she realized it wasn't me or you doing that shit. She thinks it's Neo."

We both look at each other, neither wanting to ask the question weighing heavily on our minds.

"What do you think?" he asks, taking the initiative.

"I dunno, man. What about you?"

His head tilts to the side, staring blankly as he thinks. "I don't know either. I just don't think Neo would go behind our backs like that. We've been pretty up-front with each other about our plans."

"Yeah. You two have. Me, not so much."

He scoffs. "What do you mean?"

"You know exactly what I mean. It's the reason I got pissed the other day. You two are always changing plans or doing things that don't involve me. It's getting real fucking old."

"Truthfully, man, we haven't done much of anything without you."

"Oh yeah?" I tip my chin. "What about the night at the springs? Anything you wanna tell me?"

His eyebrows pinch together and he looks at me. I don't even have to ask. He knows exactly what I'm talking about. "How do you know?"

"I have my ways."

"For what it's worth, it wasn't planned. Neo was gonna fuck with her, but I got to her first."

I can feel the rage climbing inside me. Reaching a point of no return. My voice rises. "Doesn't matter whose fingers were inside her, just that they were."

His chin drops to his chest, weaving his fingers through his hair. "Can't believe she fucking told you."

"What's done is done." I don't tell him Scar wasn't the one who told me, or that I know because I saw it with my own eyes. "What we need to do is make sure no one outside of the Lawless has intentions with our girl. I wanna make damn sure we know it's not Neo, so we can put these assholes in their place. The question is, are you with me?"

Jagger opens his mouth to speak, but our conversation is

interrupted when Neo drops his tray on the table with a thud. "What are you two talking about?"

There's a beat of silence before I finally say, "Fuck it," dropping my fork onto the tray. "You wanna know what we're talking about, here it is. Someone's been stalking Scar and I think it's the same person who has my key. So, tell me, Neo," I turn in my chair, eyes level with his, "is it you?"

His face reddens at the question. "First of all, fucker. Why the hell would I steal your key? Second, why would I stalk Scar when I can do whatever I want with her in the light of day?"

"Because she's Scar—a handful of disobedience, who calls you out on your shit."

"You think I care what that bitch calls me out on? She called me out three hours ago in class, and two minutes later, my fingers were swimming in her pussy."

"Come again?" My brain rapid fires as I try to piece together what he's saying. I look at Jagger, who's got his head down, shaking it in slow motion. "Did you know about this?"

I expect this shit from Neo. Doesn't surprise me one bit that he'd pull something like that. He probably gave her no choice but to sit in her seat and comply. But Jagger's different. Slightly more levelheaded with a sliver of heart. Whereas, I'm not sure Neo has one at all.

The cords in Jagger's neck flex as his eyes lift. He scratches his forehead. Pokes at his food. He does everything but answer the fucking question.

"Well!" I shout, slapping the table and rattling the silverware on our trays, "did you?"

He did. Fucking A. He had every opportunity to tell me five minute ago before Neo got here, yet he said nothing.

"Why the hell do you even care?" Neo asks with his holier-than-thou attitude.

"Why do I care?" My voice rises. "Maybe I care because you

two all but disowned me for fucking Scar and now you're both dipping your fingers in her, too."

"Who's dipping what where?" Scar says, coming out of nowhere. She's empty-handed, which makes me think she ate already, which goes against the rule that she eats lunch at our table.

Her arms cross over her chest, eyes dancing from person to person. "Well? Is someone planning to tell me what you're talking about?"

Shoving my chair back, I stand up and ask the question burning in my brain. "What happened with you and Neo in class?"

Scar's face goes ghost white. It's all the answer I need, but I wanna hear the words from her mouth. She looks at Neo, then back to me. "None of your business."

I catch Neo smirking out of the corner of my eye and it's enough for me to grab him by the back of his shirt and yank him out of his chair.

"What the fuck is your problem?" He shoves my chest. "Are you really pulling this shit again?"

"Crew!" Scar stammers, trying to intervene. "Knock it off."

Why is she protecting him?

I drop my hold on Neo, who's casually smoothing his hands down his shirt like nothing happened. Just as I turn to Scar, I feel his fist fly across my face. My head whips to the left, and I bite down so hard, I catch my tongue between my teeth. Blood pools in my mouth and I spit it out on the dining hall floor.

"You son of a bitch!" I charge at him, grabbing him by the waist and taking him straight down to the ground. He's got more muscle and body weight than I do, so I know it's a losing battle, but my rage-induced adrenaline doesn't care.

"Quit it, you two." I hear Scar shouting with panic in her voice. "Jagger! Stop this!"

Through thrown punches, some that land and some that don't, Neo ends up with both my hands locked in his. He pins them over my head, gets in my face, and seethes, "You've done fucked up. You chose her over us for the last fucking time. I'm done with you. You hear me? Done!"

In an instant, he lets go, climbs off me, and takes off.

Jagger extends a hand to me and I grab it. Once I'm on my feet, I spit out another mouthful of blood.

My eyes shoot to Scar, who looks distraught. "You're unbelievable," I tell her.

I storm out of the dining hall in the same manner Neo did. Told these guys bringing Scar here was a bad idea. Then I fought them on her and these games because I knew Neo would use it to his advantage. Neo said we're done, and right now, I'm pretty fucking okay with that.

"GET your head in the game, Vance," Coach shouts at me for the fourth time since practice began an hour ago.

He's the only person at this place I take orders from and he has no problem throwing his authority at me any chance he gets.

Dexter snaps me the ball. I check Davis, motioning him to the left as the defense prowls after him.

"Throw the damn ball, Vance," Coach growls.

I hesitate, my eyes briefly skimming the field before I throw the ball to Davis, knowing he won't make the catch. Brady dives out of nowhere and intercepts the ball. His legs don't stop moving...and he scores.

Shit.

"What the hell are you doing?" Coach says, storming on the field. He grabs my face mask, pulling me toward the edge of the field. "You're damn lucky this is a scrimmage. You play like this Friday night, and I'll bench your ass."

"Sorry, Coach. Got a lot on my mind."

"Well, clear your damn mind. And get some sleep. You look like hell."

Coach calls practice and I'm dragging ass, like a sore loser, to the locker room.

Clear my mind. As if it's that easy. Doesn't anyone understand the pressure I'm under right now? Everything I'm doing is for my future, and it feels like it's all about to implode. Neo made demands when it came to Scar and I did everything he asked of me. I gave her up. I forced myself to hate her. Gave her hell. Only for both Neo and Jagger to turn around and try and take her for themselves. The difference is, they just want her body, and I've always wanted so much more than that.

At least, I did.

Fuck. I don't know what I want anymore. Once these games are done and Scar is promoted, I'm hoping we can ease up a bit and try and have a decent school year.

Who am I kidding? There's nothing normal about this place.

I'm back in the locker room, where the guys are giving me shit about that final play. I laugh it off and throw insults right back at them. Outside of the game, they know better than to give me shit at all. But I let it slide in here because it's the one place I feel a sliver of normalcy.

Once I'm changed, I grab my phone off the locker shelf and glance at it—4:20—then stuff it in the front pocket of my black jeans. Scar's got another half hour or so before she's let out of her two-hour detention so that gives me enough time to head home and shower before trying to catch up with her.

This wasn't in my plans for the evening, but she's all I've

been thinking about since lunch. I desperately need to talk to her about what happened with her and Neo earlier. I need her to tell me it meant nothing. Just the thought of anyone else touching her in general makes me crazy. Some might say it's a case of wanting what I can't have, but I think it's more about getting back what should have always been mine.

CHAPTER
TWENTY

SCARLETT

I CAN'T BELIEVE NEO. Well, I can, but I'm still in a state of disbelief that he had me put in detention. There isn't a single student here but me. How can I be the only person to get in trouble?

Of course.

The rules. The ranks. The Lawless. Everyone obeys because they're ordered to. Everyone but me.

I lick the tip of my finger and turn the page of my American lit book, not even reading the pages but skimming them in hopes that the words will somehow cling to my memory because the teacher hinted at a pop quiz tomorrow.

If I were in public school like I should have been, I wouldn't even be dealing with textbooks. We'd have Chromebooks and Wi-Fi access. For such a wealthy Society, they sure do skimp on technology.

Mrs. Evans, the detention supervisor, makes an odd grumbling sound that grabs my attention. Her arms clutch her stomach and she bends over, looking extremely uncomfortable.

208

I try to return to my book, but the sounds she's making are too painful to ignore. Maybe I should ask if she's okay. She looks like she's either gonna hurl or shit her pants.

Suddenly, she's on her feet, butt cheeks clenched and sucking in the thin pink fabric of her slacks. "Excuse me, Scarlett. I need to use the restroom." The next thing I know, she's full-on running out the door.

I'm not sure if I want to laugh or cry for her because that shit sucks—literally.

Hope everything comes out okay for her.

Okay, Scar. Study. 17th century. 13 colonies. Expressing emotions through poetry.

Ugh! I can't focus.

I slam my book shut and drum my fingers on the hardcover. I wonder how the guys are faring after their blowup today. It seems my presence—which they fought damn hard for—has caused a little rift among them. I'm not surprised Crew is going crazy. As much as we scream hate at each other, I know he hates the thought of any other guy giving me attention. Even if it is negative attention.

I'm not sure what to think of Jagger. He's actually been pretty normal and as much as I don't want to admit it to myself, I had fun with him the other day. I'm not even bothered about him holding my leg in class. It actually calmed my nerves in some twisted way.

Then there's Neo...

What the hell?

The flickering of the classroom lights pulls me out of my thoughts. I look up, noticing each panel going out, one at a time.

Sliding my chair back, I get up and cross the room to the light switch. By the time I reach it, all the lights are out. My fingers swipe up and down on the switch, but it does nothing.

That's weird.

I wonder if all the lights are out. I know we were supposed to get some snow, but I didn't expect it to be a big enough storm to knock out the power.

Confused, I grab the door handle, but it doesn't turn.

There's a rectangular glass pane on the door, so I try to look out, but the glass is too hazy to see anything.

I try the handle again to no avail.

My fist beats on the door, and I holler, "Hello."

Fear sweeps through me. It's not only dark here, due to the lights being off and the stained-glass window hiding the natural light, but I'm also stuck.

The tiny hairs on the back of my neck lift and my arms begin to quiver.

I grab the handle again and pull, shaking with one hand while pounding on the door with my other.

A glimpse of a dark shadow catches my eye through the cloudy, thick pane on the door. My body stills as I listen and wait.

When the only sound is the drumming of my heart, I say in a hushed tone, "Is someone there?"

Leaning close, I press my ear to the door and I'm not sure if I'm hoping someone is out there or terrified that there could be.

A thunderous bang on the door has me jumping back. My legs go weak, and I stumble, but catch myself, falling onto a desk behind me.

Something, or someone rather, comes closer to the glass pane. I can see his shadow. I steady myself and take a step toward the door, hoping to make out who is on the other side.

I see black. A hood? A cloak, maybe? The same robe the guys wore at the ceremony and the same robe the intruder wore at the dorms. It has to be.

Whoever it is, they're watching me. Watching the rapid rise and fall of my chest, my panic-stricken eyes, the tremble in my bottom lip. If they look closely, they'd also be able to see the pearled tears in the corners of my eyes.

Who are you? Another step takes me closer to the door—staring through it and searching for a glimmer of resemblance to someone I know.

"Neo?" I whisper, taking a step forward. But as I do, they step back. Farther and farther while I move closer and closer. I'm only a foot from the door when they disappear.

Hoping the door is unlocked now, I give it a try, but it's still locked.

"Let me out!" I shout, slamming both hands to the door repeatedly, while shouting over and over again. "Let me the fuck out!"

In one breath, something crashes into the door, shattering the glass pane and sending me flying backward on my ass. I cry out in fear, my soul leaving my body as I sit there on the floor with my hands pressed to the jagged pieces of thick glass at my sides.

I don't move. I'm too shocked to move. Too scared.

Instead, I wait, because they did this for a reason. To instill fear in me, maybe?

Be afraid, Scar. We're thirsty for your fear.

Neo said that. He's also the one who made me get detention.

All this time I was thinking it wasn't one of them, but who else would do this to me?

Mustering up the courage to face what's waiting for me on the other side of the door, I push myself up. My weak legs wobble and threaten to fail me, but I'm stronger than this. I am not a punching bag, and I refuse to be defeated. I will die before I cower to these assholes.

"Show your face, coward." My voice cracks and breaks and does little to show my resilience—even to myself.

Maybe I'm the coward. After all, I'm the one standing on the other side of this door on the verge of a mental breakdown.

It's so easy to make people believe you're strong when you cover the frail parts of yourself with brashness and crude humor. They only see what I show them. But something tells me, this person has seen it all. They know my weaknesses and have every intention of using them to their advantage.

My entire body trembles as I approach the door, stepping on broken pieces of tempered glass. Each crunch beneath my boots sends a jolt through my body that throws my heart into another frenzy of rapid beats.

It's safe to assume the door is still locked, but now there's an opening I can use to reach out and unlock it. I guess I should be grateful for that.

Whatever moment of optimism I had is shelved when I look down at my feet and see a large rock with a ribbon tied around it, holding a folded piece of paper. Not just any ribbon —it's white with black-crafted snowboarders embroidered on it and it's attached to a medal. My medal.

With a shaky hand, I pick up the rock. I don't even have to look at the medal to know which one it is. But, I do anyway. I flip over the rock, and there it is. *1st place in the 2020 Coy Mountain Snowboarding Championship.*

Curiosity has me unfolding the white paper, but when I do, another paper falls out. I bend down and pick it up, immediately noticing that it's a newspaper clipping.

A lump forms in my throat as I unfold it. The headline has me closing my eyes while tears pinch their way out.

Essex County girl, 16, in coma after tragic snowboarding accident on Coy Mountain.

"Why are you doing this?" I scream, fisting the rock in my hand before throwing it at the door. It hits hard, then drops with a thud to the ground.

I don't understand why anyone would taunt me with this information. It's nothing I don't know.

Is this about Crew? About our relationship after Maddie's fall? Neo hates what we did. So much so that he wants me to live a life of torment. Is this his way of enacting that?

In a split second, the fear inside me transforms to outrage.

Heat flushes through my body as my boots stomp heavily to the desk I was using. I drop the medal into the side pocket of my flannel, along with the crumbled paper, and snatch up my belongings, then head for the door before Mrs. Evans comes back.

There are sharp edges sticking out where the sheet of glass once was, so I take care as I reach my arm through. Bending at the wrist, I click the lock and turn the handle from the outside.

I look left, then right, and the coast is clear. Not a sound to be heard. That is until the girls' bathroom door swings open and a raunchy smell fills the air.

My hand waves across my nose, trying to stop it from swimming up my nostrils.

"Scarlett!" Mrs. Evans says. "What are you doing out of detention?"

I glance at the watch on my wrist then back to her. "It's 5 o'clock." It's a lie. It's actually only 4:45, but close enough. Once she sees the mess in her room, it won't matter much that I bolted fifteen minutes early.

Her eyes widen. "Really? That time already?"

I nod, lips pressed together firmly.

"Okay then. Enjoy the rest of your evening, and I hope I don't see you back again."

213

If it were any other teacher, that would be an odd goodbye, but considering it's detention, I hope for the same.

Before she walks away and sees the broken glass, I scurry down the hall. Just as I near the corner, I hear her holler, "Scarlett Sunder!"

Wincing, I tuck around the corner and run like hell to the door.

One way or another, I have to get myself out of this one. I'm sure she's contacting the headmaster right now and discussing my punishment. All I know is, if I'm forced to sit in detention one more day, completely engulfed in silence, my head might explode.

I knew we were getting snow, but I was not prepared for what I'm stepping out in as I exit the building. A blanket of the white fluff covers everything in view. There are fresh footprints coming and going all over the place, and I look down as I run, wondering if any of them belong to my stalker.

Once there's a good amount of distance between me and the school, I slow my steps to a brisk walk and head toward the trail with my book clutched to my chest.

My mind is racing, trying to piece together everything that has happened since I got here. I have no idea what is going on, but I have to figure out who is doing this. Unfortunately, I think there are only a couple people who can help me because I'm certain it's not them. And I really don't want to ask these people for help.

Speak of the devil.

"Hey," Crew says, appearing on the trail and walking in my direction. Before he even reaches me, his spiced sandalwood cologne hits my nostrils. His damp hair glistens in the shimmer of light casting down between the tall evergreens. It's obvious he just showered, but snowflakes also moisten the tips of his hair.

I keep on toward him, willing myself to be nice because cruelty won't get me any favors.

We meet each other halfway and stop. "Hi, Crew," I say, a bite of nervousness to my tone.

"I was actually coming to the school to find you. Did you get out early?"

I blink away the flakes falling on my long lashes and pause for a beat before telling him the truth. "No," I reach into my pocket and pull out the medal, holding it up to show him, "I was forced out."

His head tilts as he reads the engraving. "You got a medal for going to detention?"

"No," I stammer, "someone came to the detention room and threw a rock through the glass in the door with my medal wrapped around it and a news article addressing Maddie's accident. Someone is still fucking with me, Crew, and it's really starting to scare me." I'm rambling, and as I continue, anxiety rears its ugly head again. "What do they want? What do they know? It doesn't make any sense."

Crew takes the medal from my hand and looks at it like it's a foreign object that dropped down from a spaceship. With the medal still in his hand, he looks at me defensively. "It wasn't me."

"I know it wasn't you. And I know it wasn't Jagger. Look," I say, ready to make my peace, "I need you guys to help me. Starting with getting me out of trouble with Mrs. Evans. Her classroom is a mess. I know we're not friends, Crew, but you have pull here and connections. I can't be afraid someone is going to pop out around every corner."

He bites the corner of his lip. "I can talk to Jagger, but I don't think it'll fly with Neo. He's pretty hell-bent on showing how much he hates you."

"Yeah. No kidding."

"Which leads me to a question of my own." He tips his chin, eyes glued to mine. "What happened between you two in class?"

I'm taken aback at the question and really don't think it's necessary to divulge any information, but I am temporarily trying to get in his good graces. "Probably just another one of his games."

"No." He shakes his head. "That wasn't a game, but even if it was, why would you willingly participate?"

I exhale a heavy breath. "I don't know. I really don't, Crew. I guess it felt like a game to me. Neo was trying to get a rise out of me and I wanted to show him he wouldn't."

It's the truth. When it started, I had every intention of controlling the situation, but as things progressed, I lost control and Neo won.

"How'd that work out for you?"

There's nothing I hate more than the feeling of defeat, but admitting it is a very close second. I roll my lips together, eyebrows raised. "Not well."

Crew runs his hands down his face, then his fingers move to his temples and he rubs them aggressively. "Scar. Scar. Scar," he tsks, shaking his head, "what am I going to do with you?"

My shoulders rise and I force a smile. "Help me."

There's something so different about Crew right now. No aggression. No ill-intent. The more I watch him, the more I see glimpses of reform in his eyes. It's been so long since I've seen Crew carry any emotion that wasn't anger. Dare I say, he's reminding me a lot of the Crew I used to like?

He angles his head in the direction he came from. "I'll walk you back to your dorm."

I nod in response, following his lead.

We walk the trail, side by side, in silence. But the quiet is so loud in my head, and I hate this feeling inside me. Not the fear of the unknown or the wonder of who's stalking me. It's something more, something bigger. It's the pull toward Crew. All of our memories hit me full force. The smell of snow mixed with the scent of his skin. Heat flowing through my body, even when it's cold as hell. The feeling of safety and knowing I have someone in my corner when I want to cry. I missed him so much, even when I hated him. And now, he's here, and sometimes, I still miss him. It's so stupid. *I'm* so stupid.

I wish I could convince myself that everything he's done is because of Neo's hatred for me, but I felt Crew's malicious hands on me. I heard the vile words spill from his mouth. Words meant to burn me. Hands that wanted to harm me.

We reach the dorms, and Crew turns to face me. "I'll talk to Jagger, but I can't make any promises. Things are sort of rocky with the guys right now."

I nod, sorting through the scrambled emotions I'm feeling. I want to ask him why he does it—why he lets Neo control him the way he does. I need to know if he really wants to hurt me or if he just wants me to think he does. I have so many unanswered questions, but I go with the hardest of them all, because it feels like I'm asking him to choose. "Do you think it's Neo?"

If he says no, it's because his loyalty lies with him, whether wrong or right. Because the truth is, Crew shouldn't know unless it is, in fact, Neo.

If he tells me he doesn't know, I'll know exactly who I'm looking at right now. Not the stranger who's taunted me for the last year and a half. I'll be looking at Crew Vance—the guy who held me up when all I wanted to do was fall down.

Crew swallows hard, his throat bobbing. His tongue

sweeps across his lips and he wipes the melted snow from his forehead. "I really don't know, Scar." He shrugs his shoulders and walks back the way we came, with his head down.

Well, that was unexpected.

218

CHAPTER
TWENTY-ONE
CREW

SOMETIMES REALITY SLAPS you in the face and you don't feel an ounce of pain. That seems to happen to me a lot. To the point that it's barely recognizable, so I ignore it and continue on with my life.

Other times, it hits you so hard, the breath is knocked out of you. An imprint is made that won't soon fade. You're left with the constant reminder of the way things should have been.

I don't know what's real anymore. I don't know what to believe. I don't know who's got my back, who's by my side or who's walking three steps ahead of me.

Neo's my boy—my best fucking friend. We've done everything together for as long as I can remember. Neo, Jagger, and I never fought. Not like this. Neo was never one to open up about his emotions, but after Maddie's accident, he became angry and he made it known. He wants someone to blame for everything he's lost and it's not just about his sister—it's his mom and his dad, too. While his dad is still here, he's barely here. After the death of his wife, Sebastian started drinking more, which makes him unstable and unpredictable. I know Neo gets the worst of his anger, and I hate that for him.

But why should we all suffer along with him? Does it make me a bad friend for not wanting to? I tried to help Neo when he shut down. Jagger and I both did. But it didn't do any good, so eventually, we both stopped trying.

As soon as I reach the door to our house, it flies open. "Where the hell have you been?" Neo asks, anger seeping from his pores.

"Had to take care of something." I walk past him, pulling my coat off and hanging it on the coat rack. "Did you get my new key?"

I still don't know who took my key, so Neo's dad is supposed to be dropping off another one. There are only a few made because it's a risk having too many lying around. The master key opens every door at BCA, including the ones below ground.

"He never showed." Neo's empty stare is locked on the wall before he snaps out of it and returns to his typical asshole self. "What did you have to take care of?"

I sweep the air with my hand and walk toward the kitchen. "Nothing important."

Neo follows me, not letting this go. "Did it involve her?"

"She has a name."

"Just answer the damn question."

"No." I pivot around, hands pressed to the marbled kitchen counter. "I don't have to answer your questions, but how about you answer one of mine." I look him dead in the eye, not even blinking because I want him to know how serious I am. "Are you stalking her?"

A breathy laugh climbs up his throat. "No, I'm not stalking her. What kind of question is that?"

"One I've asked before and I'm certain you lied to me then and I think you're lying to me now."

Neo turns away, avoiding eye contact which raises some red flags. "You need to get over this girl before she completely ruins you."

I'm not sure I believe him, but I know one way to find out.

"If I'm ruined, it won't be Scar's doing."

His head jerks around. "What are you saying?"

"I'm saying she's not the problem."

There are two ways I could go about this, but I know Neo and he'd never agree to helping Scar if there wasn't something in it for him. If he knows he can get her under his thumb to press and squeeze whenever he wants, there's no way he'd pass up what I'm about to offer.

His hands fly to his chest. "Are you saying I'm the fucking problem?"

"No. I'm saying there's someone out there toying with Scar, using Maddie to get in her head. They're trying—"

"Whoa." He holds up a hand, shutting me up while looking at me with only one eye. "What the fuck are you talking about? What's this have to do with Maddie?"

"A couple days ago, someone followed Scar down the trail outside of the school and played a recording of her and Maddie having a private conversation. Today in detention, someone threw a rock through the door with a newspaper clipping reporting Maddie's fall."

Neo's head flinches back. "You're joking, right?"

I open my eyes wide and void of any emotion. "Do I look like I'm joking?"

"And you have the fucking balls to ask if it was me?" His voice rises. "You think I'd tarnish my sister like that? Let alone record her having a private conversation and use it to fuck with Scar?"

I don't tell him I did. But now that I see his reaction, I'm not sure I do believe it was him. "Look, I had to ask because if it wasn't one of us three, that means someone's up to something and it doesn't just stem from her attendance here. This goes years back to when Scar and Maddie were together all the time. It had to have been before Scar was kicked out of Essex High."

Neo's quiet for a minute, pacing the length of the kitchen while scratching his head, deep in thought.

"What are you thinking?" I ask, and he holds up a finger, chewing on his bottom lip.

Seconds turn to minutes and I watch as the rage climbs through him, inch by inch. Completely taking over his body. He grabs the pans that hang over the center island, whipping them around and throwing them at the wall. He clears the table, growling and cursing. I watch as Neo loses all control and I don't even flinch because I've seen it all before.

Finally, he stops, sweat breaks out on his forehead and his cheeks flush with heat. "Of all the things that little bitch has done, this one tops them all." He laughs menacingly. "She's gonna pay. Oh, is she gonna fucking pay."

My eyebrows squeeze together, confused. "What?"

He begins speaking his thoughts as if he's saying them to himself and I'm not even in the room. "Fucking bitch hones in on my sister—my family! Then she has the gall to come here and play victim. Trying to set me up and turn my fucking friends against me. She thought my fingers felt foreign inside her? Wait until she feels my cock down her throat, choking her until she admits to what a snake she is. And even then, I'll keep going until I watch her take her last breath because she doesn't even deserve to breathe the same air as Maddie."

Well, this didn't go as planned. Scar isn't faking this shit. This isn't some attempt to try and sway me and Jagger, so we turn on Neo and take her side over his.

Is it?

Has Scar been the one who's three steps ahead of us this entire time?

No. Not a chance. Absolutely not. I know Scar. She wouldn't use Maddie like that. There's just no way. She loves Maddie as much as we all do. The thing is, Neo will never see it, and I need to protect her and protect the Society at the same time.

"There's only one way to find out," I finally tell him, hoping this works.

Neo stops pacing, his shoulders pulled back. "How?"

"Easy. We play her game and she plays ours, without even knowing it."

His eyes perk up. "What do you have in mind?"

"She asked if we'd help her find out who it is, so we help her while helping ourselves at the same time."

Neo nods slowly, rubbing his chin. His eyes glimmer with mischief. "Go on."

"We need to keep a close eye on her—an extra close eye."

"As long as I'm the one who shoves the fucking knife in her back when we're done with her, then count me in."

TWENTY-TWO

"Oh, umm. Hi," Riley says, springing up from my bed and away from Elias.

My eyes travel from her to him. "Hiiii," I drag out the word, while trying to figure out exactly what's going on here. "Are you...here for me?" I ask Elias, unsure what he's doing in my room, on *my* bed.

"I am," he says, chuckling nervously.

Dropping my books down on my desk, I stay on my feet while Riley chews on her fingernails from her side of the room.

Elias continues, "I came to bring you this." He pulls a book from behind his back. Not just any book—it's *The Color Purple* by Alice Walker.

"What? Are you serious?" I snatch it from his hand, flipping it over and running my fingers down the spine. "Where did you get this? It wasn't in the library."

Elias grins. "I have my ways."

"Thank you, Elias. This is amazing."

"It's no problem, really."

224

There's an awkward moment of silence before I address the elephant in the room. "I see you've met Riley."

I look at my adorable roommate, whose cheeks are tinged pink. Normally I'd assume it's her makeup, but not this time. They're a special shade today.

"Umm. Yeah. We met." Elias nods, eyes dancing from me to Riley.

"Well," I say, hoping to alleviate their humiliation, "since you've met, you should hang out with us tonight. I heard there's something exciting happening near the athletic center at dusk."

I don't mention the games because, apparently, that's classified information, but my lack of details makes this sound anything but exciting.

"Sounds fun." Elias slaps his hands to his legs and stands up. "I can meet you outside your dorm around eight, if that works? Two pretty girls like you really shouldn't be out walking alone at night."

And now my cheeks blush as I press one to my shoulder, smiling sheepishly. "You're too kind."

"What can I say? I'm a gentleman." He and Riley share a look before he heads for the door. "See you two tonight."

I wave goodbye while Riley hides her face.

As soon as the door closes behind him, I'm on her. "Spill. Now."

"What?" She fights to avoid eye contact, so I grab her arm and spin her around. "He came here like an hour ago. Didn't know you got detention. I told him he could wait and we started talking."

"You were flirting," I tease.

"I can't help it. Did you see that guy?" she says, grinning from ear to ear. "But if he is into you and vice versa, I'll totally back off."

225

I laugh because it's laughable. "Elias is *not* into me and I'm certainly not into him. We're just friends."

She lifts a brow. "Does he know that?"

"Well, I'd say he does now. Especially since my roommate was hitting on him."

Riley's cheeks flush again. "I'm sorry. It's just been so long since a guy has even cared enough to have an in-depth conversation with me."

"Well, I for one, am glad. In fact, I think you two should continue getting to know one another. I'm just mad at myself for not realizing it sooner. But, I did say I'd find you a date tonight. So, you're welcome."

Her expression goes serious, and she places her hands on my shoulders. "Look me in the eye and promise me you're not into him."

"I. Am. Not. Into. Him."

She brings her hands together excitedly. "Thank God because he's so hot and so my type."

I open my mouth, searching for the words because I wouldn't exactly label him as hot. "He's...very attractive."

Elias *is* a nice-looking guy. Not much brawn, but I can tell has the brains. He's got this sexy nerdy look going for him and I can totally imagine them hitting it off. It's actually perfect. Now, it keeps her away from the Lawless.

There's a knock at the door that has my eyes shooting to Riley. "It's Melody," she says. "She's here to pick up my cheer uniform to get dry cleaned."

As she's getting her uniform together for Melody, I use this time to sneak my phone into my makeup bag, so I can call my mom.

When Riley opens the door, I slip out past Melody, who's giving me a snarky look. I return the gesture and stick my tongue out at her like a petulant child. "I'll be back. Need to use the bathroom," I tell Riley.

Instead of going right to the bathroom, I go to the end of the hall and onto the small balcony outside. I'm well aware that phones are not permitted here, but there was no way I could go all school year without hearing my mom's voice and checking on Maddie. After everything that's happened surrounding her accident, she's heavy on my mind, and I need to know she's doing okay.

Fully expecting a lecture from my mom, I tap in her number on the prepaid cell.

I'm not surprised she doesn't answer, due to this being an unknown number, so I leave a message, hoping she'll call me back right away.

"Hey, Mom. It's Scarlett. I know what you're thinking: *how are you calling me?* Don't worry. No one knows. I just need to talk to you. Call me back, please. Love ya. Bye."

I end the voice message, stick my phone back in my makeup bag, and I wait.

With my palms pressed to the railing, I look out at BCA property. The snow is really coming down now, but thanks to the overhead, I'm only getting hit with a few flakes.

It's so beautiful here. So peaceful when I allow it to be. If only every day could be still and silent, I might learn to love this place.

My buzzing phone quickly reminds me that silence is a rarity here. I pull it out of my pocket and answer immediately.

Before I can even say hello, my mom begins tearing into me. "Scarlett Gwyneth Sunder! Where in God's name did you get a phone to use there? You know the rules. Are you trying to get yourself kicked out?"

She doesn't even give me a chance to answer all her questions, so I listen, and I listen some more.

"If the Lawless or the headmaster catch you with that thing, do you know what they'll do? You'll be hung out to dry in front of the entire student body. I know because they've done it to me. It's not a good position to be in. Hello. Honey, are you there?"

"I'm here, Mom. It's great to hear your voice. Almost forgot how much I missed it."

"I'm serious, Scarlett. As soon as we end this call, you need to throw that thing in the river."

"Okay, Mom."

"Do you hear me, Scarlett?"

My voice rises. "I said okay, Mom!"

I hear her gulp, likely swallowing down the stress spit that pooled in her mouth from her prating.

"How are you doing, honey?" Her voice is now calm, and I'm grateful for that.

"I'm...well, Mom. I just wanted to hear your voice and make sure you've checked in on Maddie. How is she?"

"Well," she begins, and that one word has my stomach in knots, "I called to check on her, as I said I would, and apparently, they've changed her approved contacts. I'm no longer on the list. I'm sure it's part of their privacy policy and they—"

"They changed their policy? Why would they do that? It's not like she's in a hospital or a jail cell."

I've been visiting Maddie since she went to live at that private facility. My family has always been on the list.

"As I was saying," Mom continues, "I'm sure it's part of their privacy policy and they've updated it to family only. If you want any information, you might want to ask Neo. But don't mention this call. He's a member of the Lawless. Not to mention, you know how those Saint men are."

"Yes, Mom. I know." My mom despises the Saints. It's no

secret. "I doubt Neo would tell me anything. I'll just call the facility myself."

"No, Scarlett. If they have a log, her dad will be able to see it, and he knows you're at BCA now."

"Mom! I have to check on her. I need to know she's doing okay. Please talk to Dad and tell him to fix this."

"I'll see what I can do. End this call and get rid of that phone, Scarlett. You don't need to make trouble for yourself."

"Wait. Mom," I say quickly before she hangs up, "I want you to tell Dad I'm pretty upset with him for leaving my snowboard. He knows how much I didn't want that here."

She's silent for a minute before saying, "He didn't leave it. I put it back in your bedroom closet when we got home."

"What do you mean you put it in my bedroom closet? I found it under my dorm bed."

"It must be a different bag and board because I definitely carried yours in the house after we dropped you off. Now, get rid of the phone and keep yourself out of trouble. Love you, honey."

"Okay. I love you, Mom."

She ends the call. And I tap the phone to my hand.

It was definitely my bag under the bed. It had my resort tags on it. Not giving it another thought, I immediately dial the facility where Maddie is, knowing the number by heart. There's no way Sebastian would take me off her approved list. He might be an asshole, but he knows how close Maddie and me are and how much I worry about her.

"Heartland Home. This is Tammy. How can I help you?"

"Hi, Tammy. It's Scarlett Sunder."

"Oh, hey, hun. How are you doing?"

"I'm good, thanks for asking. I was hoping to get an update on Maddie. How has she been?"

"I'm so sorry, Scarlett. Unfortunately, Maddie's dad has

removed everyone from her authorized list aside from her brother. I wish I could give you more information."

"You can't be serious? Maddie's my best friend. Why would he do that?"

"He didn't say and I really can't tell you much more. I suggest reaching out to Mr. Saint."

There's no sense in arguing this with Tammy because I know it's not her fault, but I will definitely be arguing with someone about it.

I end the call with a heavy heart. No matter how much Neo hates me or how much my mom hates Sebastian, they know how close Maddie and me are. Not to mention, my dad and Sebastian are like brothers.

It just doesn't make any sense, but I'm certainly going to make sure someone explains what the hell is going on.

"You do realize it's forty degrees and snowing out," I say to Riley as she buttons her jean skirt.

She bends over and comes back up with a pair of white leggings in her hand. "That's why I have these. They match the snow." She bunches a leg of the fabric and steps one foot in, then the other, pulling them up beneath her skirt.

"Well, at least you'll match nature." The sarcasm in my voice is apparent as I pull a black oversized garbage band hoodie over my head. It hangs down, touching the thigh rip in my blue jeans.

Riley adds the finishing touch of a black leather jacket over her white-cropped turtleneck. She looks cute as hell with her hair in double French braids while I'm going for the all-down frizzy look. She puts on a pair of knee-high leather boots while I opt for black canvas shoes. We really are polar opposites, but it works well for us. Riley has been such a saving grace at this place, and I never thought I'd be grateful she was chosen as my roommate, but I am.

We leave the room and Riley locks up. As he said he would be, Elias is waiting outside for us. I never mentioned to Jagger that I was bringing friends, so hopefully he doesn't mind. I still can't wrap my head around the fact that I'm doing anything with Jagger that doesn't involve me giving him lip.

"Look at you two beautiful ladies." Elias beams as we come down the steps toward him.

Riley blushes. "You're so sweet, Elias."

I'm terrible with compliments, but I add, "Yes. So sweet."

The snow has really accumulated over the last couple hours, but there's a shoveled path, which is good, considering I'm wearing shoes and not boots.

The roar of a motor, or maybe a couple motors, has me looking around the area. I can't imagine the guys are on their dirt bikes in this weather. "Snowplows?" I ask Elias when he catches my darting gaze.

"That, and snowmobiles. The Lawless broke out their sleds, and they've been tearing up the trails."

Oh joy. More means of transportation for them. If we could all be so lucky. Instead, we'll trek through the frigid temperatures on foot, just to get where we want to go.

Elias reaches into the hood of his hefty winter jacket and pulls out a pint of liquor. He unscrews the top, tips it back, and takes a swig. His mouth draws back as he swallows it down in one gulp.

When he passes it to Riley, she takes a shot, then it comes to me. I really should keep a level head tonight, but what the hell. The stench of cinnamon burns my nostrils, and I hold my breath as I press it to my lips and take a small amount. It burns going down, but the feeling quickly subsides. "Not bad,"

I say, handing it back to Elias. "Where'd you get that anyways?"

"There's a student here who outsources from locals, and she can get us pretty much anything we want."

"Ah, Melody?"

"Yep. That's her name."

"Do you know her well?"

It's hard to imagine Melody and Elias having anything in common, other than booze and blunts. Not that I ever saw him smoke, but I take him to be a closet pothead. One who gets stoned and reads books in the dark with a flashlight. Actually, that used to be me. But Elias and I have so much in common, it wouldn't surprise me.

"Not at all, actually. I was talking to this guy who knew a guy who banged her and he hooked me up with a few bottles."

"Neo?" I laugh, knowing that Melody is obsessed with Neo.

"Nah. I don't think so. Neo Saint wouldn't help anyone if there wasn't something in it for him."

This is true.

We come off the trail and the athletic center is in view. I immediately look at the rooftop, where Jagger said he'd be, but it's too dark to see much of anything outside of the bright lights on the field and the lampposts on the sidewalk.

"Who'd you say we're meeting here?" Elias asks.

Unsure if he's talking to me or Riley, I answer, "Jagger."

"Jagger Cole?" He huffs in surprise.

"Yeah. Is that a problem?"

His lips press together and his head draws back. "Just a little shocked you'd even talk to any of those guys, after what they're doing to you."

I'm not sure how much he knows, but it's not like my encounters with the guys have been made public knowledge.

Sure, the students here know I'm participating in the games, but they don't know what went down with all of us. Unless there's something I don't know.

"Why do you say that?"

"My buddy Steven—"

I stop walking. "Did you say Steven?"

"Yeah. He's the one who hooked me up with the booze."

"Oh, hell no!" I kick up a chunk of snow, immediately regretting it as it rides up my pant leg. "You're friends with that asshole? He's one of the guys who kidnapped me."

My chest caves in as I consider the possibility that Elias was also one of them. He's a senior, though. He couldn't have been, could he?

Riley steps to my side, looking at Elias with her hands pressed to her hips. "Did you know about this?"

Like a deer in headlights, Elias's eyes widen. "I mean, I heard what happened, but I didn't know until after the fact. It was a game, though. Games *she* signed up for."

There's so much I want to say to defend myself, but I can't because, the truth is, I did sign up for this. I can't be mad at the boys who took me there; they're just trying to get through this the same way I am.

"It's fine," I finally say. "Elias is right. It was a game." I start walking again, but each step has the memories of that night flooding my mind. The feeling of being in that water, unable to see or speak. It could have ended so badly and it worries me for future participants in these games. Now I can see how some have gone missing or ended up dead. One small mistake can change the course of their fate.

"Scarlett," Riley says, jogging to catch up with me, "I don't think he meant it like that."

"I know he didn't, and I'm not upset."

"Are you sure?"

"Yes, Riley." I chuckle. "I'm not mad. It's a game. A game that will be over soon."

She nods in response as we step onto the snow-dusted sidewalk. A gust of wind ripples through, and I hug my arms to my chest. "Damn. I wish they'd do this inside where it's warm."

"Where exactly did you say we were meeting Jagger?"

I look up at the building. "Up there."

Elias winces. "Like all the way up?"

"Mhmm. I'm just not sure how we get to the top."

Elias angles his head toward the side of the building. "This way. I think there's a ladder on the backside."

"You didn't mention we'd be on a rooftop," Riley says, hesitation in her tone.

"It'll be fine. It's just a little climb." We round the building, and sure enough, there's a ladder attached to the building.

"Nope," Riley says, "no way." Her head shakes. "I don't do heights and I certainly don't climb ladders."

"Seriously, Ry? It's not that far up."

"It's off the ground and that's far enough for me to bow out gracefully with all my bones intact."

Elias lifts his shoulder. "Riley and I can watch from the ground. If that's cool with you?"

I look at her, seeing if that's what she wants, and she gives me a subtle nod. "Yeah. That's totally cool. Just don't leave Ry alone, okay?"

"Of course not." He places a hand around her waist, and I know she's in good hands.

"Be safe," Riley says to me as I ascend the ladder.

"You, too."

I reach the top and stand tall. I'm able to see Riley and Elias walking closely together, and it makes me smile. Riley deserves those butterflies I know she's feeling.

Jagger comes out of nowhere, startling me. "You made it."

He looks warm in a pair of straight-legged black jeans, combat boots, and a navy blue BCA hoodie. His brunet hair is sprinkled with flakes of snow that glimmer as he comes closer.

With a slow swag and some swaying, he continues toward me.

"Yeah. Decided to see if the guys have to endure as much torment as I do."

"Baby," he says, sweeping an arm around my waist, "you ain't seen nothing yet." He pulls me close, and I immediately smell the liquor seeping from his pores.

I give him a gentle nudge back, so I can look at his eyes. They're bloodshot and glossed over. "Are you drunk?"

"Little bit. You?"

"No. I had a small sip on the way over, but it did nothing for me," I say, placing a hand on his back, leading him away from the edge. "We should sit down."

Jagger laughs boisterously as if I'm being funny. He pulls away from my touch and stands directly in front of me. His fingers sweep through my hair, and he tucks it behind my ear. "How did such a pretty girl like you end up on our bad side?" His body sways some more, but he's sturdy enough to stay on his feet.

"You're definitely drunk and you really should sit down."

"I'm serious, Scar. Why couldn't you just stay away all these years? Maybe then Neo wouldn't want you here so badly just to fuck with you."

He's talking too much, but his drunk words could actually prove to be beneficial—if I can keep him from falling off the side of the building, that is.

"We can talk about this all you want, if you'll please just come sit down."

"Fine," he bellows, grabbing my hand and pulling me

across the rooftop. Our fingers tangle together and my heart gallops.

We step around a wind turbine and a couple box vents on our quest to get to the other side.

Once we're there, I spot a plaid BCA-colored blanket near the edge, facing the football field, and on top of it is a half-empty bottle of whiskey.

"Did you drink all that yourself?"

Jagger grins. "Yep. Want some?" He bends at the waist, still holding my hand, and picks it up.

"Maybe later," I say to appease him. Truth is, I will not be drinking this far off the ground, and he shouldn't be either. It's an accident waiting to happen.

Releasing his hand, I kneel down on the blanket, hoping he'll come down, too. "It's a nice view."

"The field's empty now, but wait until you see what they're about to do out there."

Finally, he drops down beside me. Well, it's more of a flop onto his side. His head is near the edge of the building and his legs are stacked beside me. With a hand pressed to his head, he looks at me. "Oh, Scar," he tsks.

Grinning, I mock him. "Oh, Jagger."

He cackles. "You're something else, you know that? Always giving us a hard time."

I don't even humor him with a response.

His hand rests on my thigh and he fidgets with the tear in my jeans. "I think that's why we like it. You don't roll over for anyone. You keep things interesting."

"Yeah? Is that why Neo likes it, too?"

"Nooo," he drawls, his mouth forming an O, "Neo does not like that. Neo wants you to roll over and he'd love nothing more than to keep rolling you over until you're on the down-side of a mountain."

"Wow. Thanks for the detailed explanation."

His shoulders rise and fall. "Sorry, but it's true."

"It's cool. It's nothing I don't already know." I turn my head slightly, still eyeing him. "But what I don't know is why you and Crew are suddenly being kind to me."

"Oh, how naïve you are, Scar. Don't mistake anyone's kindness for weakness. There isn't a student at BCA who isn't painting a beautiful picture for everyone to see while using another person's blood on their canvas."

I'm not sure if that's drunk talk or brutal honesty because if what he's saying is true, he and Crew are both using me as their own personal stencil.

"Maybe I should go then." I shift my legs, acting like I'm about to get up and leave. "If you only invited me here as some diabolical tactic to get in my good graces, I should've never come."

Jagger clamps a hand on my thigh, holding me in place. "That's not what I said. Tonight, you can trust me."

"And tomorrow?"

His head drops back and he looks up at the sky. "Why worry about tomorrow when we've got today?"

My hand rests over his. "Because I have to look out for myself. No one else here is going to do it. I asked Crew for help from you guys, and it's obvious that was a mistake." I peel his fingers off me one by one, then take his hand and rest it on the blanket.

"What do you mean you asked Crew for help?"

I watch intently as he balls the blanket into his fist. "I was convinced it was someone outside of the Lawless who's been stalking me, but now I'm not so sure."

"And you asked Crew if we'd help you?"

I nod.

"He never mentioned that. Not to me, anyways."

"Hmm. Seems you three aren't as tight as you want everyone to believe you are."

He bites his bottom lip, staring blankly at the bottle beside me. "Seems you're right." He scoots closer, hand back on my leg. "Maybe it's time I stop worrying about what Neo and Crew want and I take what I've wanted all along."

His free hand glides across my cheek before grasping it and pulling me down. My mouth meets his, but this time, I don't give in. I gave in to all three of these guys at one point or another, and look where it got me.

"No," I tell him, pulling away from his touch.

He blows out a heavy breath and lies back on the blanket. "What do you want from me, Scar? You want my help finding this guy who's been fucking with you?"

"Yes," I say point-blankly, "that's exactly what I want. And one more thing. A bonus, if you will."

His eyes lift to mine, neck straining. "And what are you gonna do for me?"

"You help me and I'll do whatever you want. But you can't fake it. I want you to seriously find this guy because, whoever he is, he's been watching me for a while and it really creeps me out."

"And the bonus?"

"Find out how Maddie's doing for me. I can't exactly check in on her."

I leave out the part where I tried and was denied information because they'll know I called.

Jagger shifts his body and sits up, legs bent at the knee and arms draped over them. "All right. I'll ask Neo and let you know."

"So you'll help me find out who's stalking me?"

"I'll talk to the guys, how about that?"

Of course. He can't do anything without their approval.

"Well, Crew is already supposed to be talking to you and Neo about it, so I guess we'll wait and see what the master says." My eyes roll while Jagger picks up the bottle and takes a swig.

"The master?" He laughs. "Maybe I'm the master and Crew and Neo do what I say."

"Doubtful."

He winks at me, sending a wave of flutters through my stomach. "Like you said, we'll wait and see."

The next thing I know, around a dozen guys are running out onto the field. I gasp and giggle, watching them prance onto the field in adult diapers with navy and teal pacifiers in their mouths and baby bottles in their hands.

Jagger's eyes follow my line of sight, and he grins along with me. "Told ya this would be fun."

"Half-naked men dressed like babies? Definitely worth the climb up here."

A guy in a black cloak with an air horn comes out on the field; I'm not sure if it's Neo or Crew. "Here's how this goes. You're split into two teams—navy and teal. The losing team attends tomorrow's party at the Ruins in exactly what you're wearing now—that means no changing, and if you shit your pants, you wear that shitty diaper. Any drinks you have tomorrow will only be permitted from the bottles in your hand. The winning team gets the night off and is free to drink whatever the fuck they want while enjoying the party."

"So what is this? A game of football?"

"Sort of. It's like flag football, but you steal the pacifier from the player instead of a flag. If they drop their bottle, they're automatically out."

"This is the most fucked-up thing I've ever seen."

"Right," he laughs, "my money is on the navy team, what about you?"

"I guess for the sake of disagreeing with you, I'll go with teal."

Jagger looks at me, brows raised. "Care to make a wager?"

"Depends. What are the stakes?"

"If navy wins, I get that kiss."

"And if teal wins?"

"Your choice."

I tap my index finger to my chin, thinking because, if I have a choice, it has to be something good.

I could ask for their help again, but that's not something Jagger alone can give me. I need all three of them. Maybe I could tell him I want to be released from my duty to sit with them at lunch, but then again, that was Neo's bargaining chip.

"I don't know. How about if I get to bank my win?"

His shoulders dance. "Works for me. You're going down anyway."

We watch the guys hauling ass and making passes on the field, laughing our asses off in the process. It's freeing after spending so many minutes in the day, worrying and wondering what is going to happen to me next.

In the end, there's only one winner. And that's the navy team, which also means I lost to Jagger.

"There's something refreshing about a win. Ya know?" he teases. "Well, you don't. Because you lost." He takes another swig of his whiskey. Once he's got the top back on, he sets it back down, gets on his knees, and leans into me. "Now to cash in."

"You really wanna kiss me? Of all the things you could've won, you chose a kiss?"

"I really do. Come on, Scar. Just a kiss. I showed you my secret place. I invited you here for your company. I'm being as nice as I can be."

"And now you're using your simple gestures to manipulate me into kissing you."

"No, I'm cashing in on my win." His lips ghost my mouth. "But you want it, too, don't you?" Softly, he sweeps his lips across mine, noses brushing.

The intoxicating scent of whiskey and his cologne entices me. If he weren't so damn sexy, I'd have more willpower, but I'm weak to his beauty. It masks his malevolence and sucks me in.

Jagger cradles my head in the palm of his hand, slowly guiding my mouth to his. "Just fucking kiss me, Scar."

So I do. Because Jagger won and I'm a girl of my word. I grab his shoulders and force the kiss deeper. It's abrasive and rough, nothing sweet about it. Years of anguish spill into his mouth while he reciprocates the gesture.

The bitter taste of aged whiskey soaks my tongue as it laps at his.

He grips my hair and digs into my scalp, knotting it around his fingers. My body falls back and he covers my chest with his. "Fuck, Scar. You have no idea how long I've wanted you."

His words hit my ears like a drum, the vibration shooting between my thighs. I'll never admit it out loud, but I've dreamt of what it would be like to have all three of them, individually and at the same time.

A win on his part has suddenly become a win on mine, and there isn't a part of me that feels an ounce of regret.

"What the hell is going on here?"

Until now.

I shove Jagger off me and he rolls onto his back. My body shoots up. "Crew?"

The betrayal in his eyes slices through me, and it's a feeling I won't soon forget.

Without another word, Crew spins around, leaving as fast as he came.

"Crew, wait." I sit up, tugging my sweatshirt down.

Jagger tries to pull me back down on the blanket, but I don't give in this time. "Let him go. He's fine. Everything is fine."

No. Everything is not fine. If it were, I wouldn't feel like I betrayed Crew in some way. Earlier on the trail, things felt different. Like old times. I'd hate to ruin the progress we made. Even if it wasn't real on Crew's part, it was on mine.

"I'm sorry." I stand up, sweeping bits of snow off my pants. "I have to go."

"Wait a damn minute." Jagger gets up, too, bringing the bottle with him. "I'll come with you."

I nod. "Okay." He really should have someone around when he goes down that ladder. I'd hate to be responsible if something happens and I'm the last person who could've helped him.

We're slow moving due to Jagger's sluggish pace. When we do get to the ladder, I let him go first because, as much as I don't want to see his brains splatter at the bottom, I don't want him taking me down with him either.

"Here," I reach for the bottle, "give me that so you can use both hands."

He huffs and puffs. "I've got it. I've got it." And he tucks it under his arm. Facing me, he steps down and he seems to be doing all right.

"Slow," I tell him.

"Would you quit worrying so damn much?" His body disappears and all I see is his head when he says, with a lopsided grin, "You still owe me a kiss since that one was interrupted."

Jesus. What more can one get from a kiss? It was pretty fucking intense.

"I think you've been paid in full."

"We'll see about that."

His head goes down, and the next thing I know, the loud thud of the shattering bottle rings in my ears. "Dammit, Jagger!" I blow out a breath as I step off the edge.

I look down and see him stopped on the ladder while staring up at me. "Oops."

"Just go."

He keeps moving and so do I, hoping that Crew isn't too far away.

As soon as my feet hit the ground, I see him. Face to face with Jagger; his fists clenched at his sides.

He doesn't even look at me, just raises his fist in the air and lays it right across Jagger's cheek.

"Crew! No!"

CHAPTER
TWENTY-THREE
CREW

I LOSE ALL CONTROL. Over my mind, my body. Words fly out of my mouth as my fists whale, but I can't stop. "Who the fuck do you think you are touching her like that?"

Another one lands, this time on the back of his head. If Jagger weren't three sheets to the wind, I'd be the one with my back pressed to the ground.

"Get off him, Crew."

Her voice is there, but I don't hear her. Everything she's throwing out slips through my ears as empty words.

We're rolling in broken pieces of glass, and I can feel them splintering my hands, but the pain doesn't stop me.

It isn't until Scar puts her arms between us that I finally get a grip. I grit my teeth in warning. "Get the hell away from me."

I can see the turmoil in her eyes with just those few words.

In a moment of weakness, Jagger shoves me off him and I fall backward, catching myself with my hands to the ground.

"What the hell is your problem? She doesn't belong to you. Never has and never will," Jagger shouts, kicking up glass with the toe of his boot.

"She doesn't belong to you either."

"Hello," Scar raises her voice, "I'm right here. Quit acting like I'm not."

We both look at her, but she only looks at him. "Jagger. Can you give us a minute? Please."

A sense of relief washes over me and I get off the ground, dusting my hands off while rubbing streaks of blood into my palms.

Jagger doesn't say anything as he huffs and walks away.

Scar shoves me back a few steps. "What is the matter with you?"

"You kissed him!"

Her hands fly in the air as she shouts back at me, "So what?"

"Are you fucking stupid, Scar? Didn't you learn your lesson last time you let that fucker touch you? It's a game to him. It's all a game!"

"It's a game to you, too. Isn't that what this week is about? A bunch of stupid games that hurt everyone?"

"No!" I shake my head, hoping she hears the truth in my words, "it's not a game to me. Not this time."

Her shoulders slouch, and she tilts her head. "What are you saying?"

"I'm saying I want to help you. Find out who this asshole is who's fucking with you. I was coming up there to talk to Jagger about it since Neo agreed, then I saw you sucking his face."

She crosses her arms over her chest, popping her hip up. "What's the catch?"

She's not gonna like this, but if she wants our help, she has to abide by our rules, and we all know how much Scar hates rules.

"The catch is, you stick with us at all times. You can't be alone, unless we're using you as bait to draw him out."

"All times?"

"All times. You're moving into the Lawless house."

She laughs, as if this is some sort of joke. "Yeah, right."

"I'm serious, Scar. If someone's trying to get to you, it's not safe for you to stay at the dorms. There's no cameras, no protection. It has to be this way."

"So let me get this straight. You freak the fuck out when you see me kissing Jagger and you lose your mind over Neo touching me in class. But you want me to move in with those guys?"

"Well, I'll be there, too."

Her weight shifts from one foot to the other. "And that makes it better?"

"Maybe not for you, but it does for me."

Scar goes quiet, which isn't like her, and it leads me to believe she's actually considering it. That is until she spits out, "Nope. Not happening."

Trekking past me through the snow, she doesn't stop. Just keeps walking away.

I turn around and shout, "Where are you going?"

"Home!"

Without her knowledge, I follow closely behind, because Scar has a problem with listening. Even after I just told her she's to be with us at all times, she still wanders off like there isn't quite possibly a crazy person waiting for her in the woods.

My steps are quiet while her sounds are thunderous, due to her heavy breathing as she huffs and puffs her way back to the dorm.

I'm about ten feet away when someone else appears on the trail. Someone that has her stopping. I step behind a tree and listen to them.

"Where's Riley?" she asks the guy.

"Just brought her back to your room. Apparently, she

246

regretted her choice of clothes tonight and was freezing her ass off."

Scar chuckles and says, "I tried to tell her."

"I'm headed back out for snacks. Care to join me?"

Who the hell is this guy and why are they acting like old friends?

"Actually, I'm pretty tired. I'm gonna head to my room and call it a night."

"All right. I'll be outside the library for a while if you wanna talk."

"Thanks, Elias."

Elias? Why does that name sound so familiar?

This is the guy Neo said Scar's been hanging out with. He must be a friend of Riley's, too, if he walked her back to her dorm.

Scar continues walking while *Elias* heads my way. Just as he passes the tree I'm behind, I reach out and grab him by the collar of his coat.

"Whoa. Whoa. Whoa," he says, hands up in surrender.

I spin him around and push him up against the tree. "Who the fuck are you?"

His eyes are wide with terror as he slowly lowers his hands. "Elias. Elias Stanton."

"How do you know Scar?"

"I...I met her when she arrived at the Academy," he sputters. "Saw her at the party. We're just friends."

"No, you're not. Scar doesn't have any guy friends. Stay the fuck away from her unless you want a year of hell."

He nods, though skeptically. "Okay. Yeah. No problem."

"Mark my words. If I see you near her again, I will fucking destroy you." His throat bobs as he swallows, and I give him a forceful shove into the snow. "Get your ass up and go back to your dorm. You won't be getting any snacks tonight."

Elias gets up and veers off the trail, headed in the direction

RACHEL LEIGH

of Vultures' Roost, so it's safe to assume that's where he's staying. I keep walking to Scar's dorm, and once I'm there, I make
myself comfortable on the ground by a tree where there's no
snow. I sit. I watch. And I wait. I'm not sure what I'm waiting
for. Maybe to see if anyone suspicious comes by. Maybe for
Scar to fall asleep.

After a good hour has passed and I've tortured my mind
thinking about what could have been and what could still be, I
see the lights go out in Scar's room. On a whim, I put in a call
to Neo to send a Rook over with a key to her room.

"Why do you need it?" he asks.

"That doesn't concern you. Quit questioning everything I
do."

"Fine. I'll send our demoted Ace, Victor, over. But don't you
fuck this up by getting attached to that girl."

"Don't worry about me. How about you worry about
Jagger? He's the one who was making out with her fifteen
minutes ago."

"Jagger's back here, and he's drunk. He had an excuse."

"Of course he did. Because he wouldn't do it sober. So if I
take a few shots, I can fuck her and tell her I love her and all is
forgiven?"

There's a beat of silence before Neo says, "Do you love her,
Crew?"

"No, I don't fucking love her. I'm trying to prove a point."

"Point proven. I'll talk to Jagger. You both need to quit
fucking around because you're making us all look weak as fuck.
We need her in the right headspace for tomorrow."

Tomorrow. Fuck. I almost forgot about what's going down
tomorrow.

"About that," I begin, "I don't think she's ready. The river
and the riddle was one thing, but this is a new level of
torment."

"Torment she deserves. It's happening, so I suggest while you're in her room, you break her down piece by piece, so we can all watch her completely fall apart."

"Whatever," I tell him, knowing this conversation is futile, "just send the key."

Twenty minutes later, I'm heading up.

I don't bother knocking, knowing I'll wake up Riley. If that happens, I'll have to force her out of the room, and I don't really feel like playing the part of the asshole right now. My mind is exhausted and all I want to do is talk to Scar. I can't stay away anymore. I'm drawn to this girl like a moth to a flame and I think one day she could be drawn to me again, too.

With the key in the hole, I turn it, hearing the lock click. Slowly, I twist the handle and pull the key out, pushing the door open at the same time.

As soon as I see her in her bed through the dimness of her bedside nightlight, my heart jumps a beat. She's on her side with her eyes closed; a mouthy demon when she's awake, but a dark-haired angel when she's asleep.

I close the door gently behind me until it latches, then I drop the key in the pocket of my jeans.

Hushed steps lead me over to her bed and I sit down on the edge, taking care not to wake her—not yet.

Until I'm ready, I watch her, and I think back to a time when we were good. A time before chaos was unleashed, and I became one of the big bad wolves.

"You're watching me, aren't you?" One eye opens, then the other.

I sweep the wispy strands of hair from her face, some stick to the sweat on her forehead. "Maybe."

She cracks a smile, throwing an arm around me with her cheek smooshed in the pillow. "What time is it?"

"Almost noon."

Her body flies up and her eyebrows hit her forehead. "Noon! We have to go. The Aarons family is using the cabin this weekend."

"Calm down, Sleeping Beauty. I took care of it."

She lifts a brow, grinning. "What do you mean you took care of it?"

I slide down the headboard, lying on my side to face her. "Put in a call and told them the sewer was backed up. The cabin's ours for the whole weekend."

Her lips press together and her head shakes against the pillow. "No, Crew. I can't stay all weekend. I have to go see Maddie at the hospital. You should visit, too."

My chest tightens at the thought of seeing Maddie lying in that hospital bed hooked up to all those machines. I haven't gone to see her yet. Don't think I can. I'm afraid once I do, the guilt I feel will become a burden I can't handle.

"Not yet," I tell Scar.

She props herself up on her elbow, her face hovering over mine. "Then when?"

I shrug my shoulders. "One day."

"Look, Crew. I know how you're feeling. I feel it, too. We both love Maddie, but as wrong as this is, I think she'd want us to be happy."

I huff. "Try telling her brother that. He'd never agree."

"Then we keep our secret. It's ours and no one else's. One day, when things have calmed down, we can tell everyone."

My lips press to her soft warm ones. "If only the world could see what we feel and feel what we see."

"They don't have to," she whispers into my mouth. "If my only chance of having you is by having you in secret, then this secret I will keep."

We can have our secret again if she'll let us. I know we can.

"Oh my god, Crew!" Scar springs up, bringing the light sheet to her chest. "What the hell are you doing in my room?"

"Shh," I press my finger to her lips, "you'll wake Riley."

Her willful breaths slow down, and she takes my hand, moving my finger from her mouth. "What are you doing?" she asks, now whispering, "How'd you even get in?"

"I got a key. I had to see you."

"You shouldn't be here, Crew. You need to leave."

"Come live with us, Scar. For your safety. For my sanity."

"You broke into my room at midnight to convince me to move in with you? Have you lost your damn mind?"

"Maybe I have." I drop my head, running my fingers through my hair. "Fuck. I don't know. I feel crazy lately. Every time I see you with Neo or Jagger. Every time they push you around or pull you in. I can't fucking take it. I know they're here and I know you've got something going on with Jagger, but seeing it just makes me crazy."

"I don't know what to tell you, Crew. Jagger and I have nothing going on, but if that's what you want to think, I guess you need to get over it, because I'm not yours and I never will be. Not after everything you did to me."

"But you'll be his? You'll kiss Jagger? What's next? Are you planning to fuck him? You already let him stick his fingers inside you."

Her hand flies across my face. "I deserved that."

"You deserve so much more," she seethes. "Now quit judging me and get out of my room."

"I know you still feel it." I grab her hands, holding them down while I close in on her. She leans back, but I eat up the space by leaning forward. Her shaky breaths cause her chest to rise and fall.

Her gaze darts to my mouth, then quickly moves back up to my eyes. "What do you want from me, Crew?"

"Everything."

251

"It's too late," she says with contempt in her tone. "You lost Maddie and you've lost me, too."

Her words slice through me, depriving me of oxygen. "I only ever wanted you. It's always been you."

She swallows hard, her eyelids fluttering. "You hurt me."

"I know I did and I'm so fucking sorry. I wish I could make you understand what it's like being on this side of things. It'll never make sense so all I can do is ask you to trust me."

Her head moves slowly before escalating to quick shakes. "I don't think I can ever trust you again. Not when your loyalty is tied to Neo. And your loyalty will *always* belong to him. Has since you were a kid."

"Just give me a chance."

Her posture slumps and all she says is, "I can't."

Hope diminishes in that instant. I can't pretend I don't see the emptiness in her eyes. They no longer hold the wonder and lust for me they once did.

I've lost her. But I won't give up trying to get her back.

"Okay," I tell her with slow nods, "I'll go, but nothing's changed, Scar. If you want us to help you, you have to do what we ask. Pack your things this weekend, so you can be in the house Sunday night."

TWENTY-FOUR

I woke up this morning to a note beside the door addressed to me. I've been pacing the room, convincing myself not to open it, while curiosity about what it says eats away at my stomach. Or maybe my stomach is eating my intestines because I'm so fucking hungry.

"Just open it," Riley says from her vanity where she's applying her makeup.

"It's seven in the morning. Who does this shit this early?"

"The Lawless. That's who. You're playing their game, remember?"

Yeah. I remember. And I've only got thirty-six hours to go until I'm free. But will I ever truly be free? I've been asked to move into their house, and while I haven't decided, I also haven't told Riley. If I accept, it means protection, but it also means I leave her behind. If I decline, it means I'll have to try to catch this person myself. Which seems almost impossible since they've been ahead of me long before I arrived.

"Okay. I'm just gonna open it and get this over with. It's just a note. No big deal."

"No big deal?" Riley chuckles. "Anything from them is a big deal."

I snarl at her. "You're not helping."

"Just open it!"

My finger slides under the flap. It's the same envelope, addressed to me the same way as the one that was at the river, so there's no doubt it's from the guys.

I pull out the letter and read it silently.

The end zone is near. Just a couple more plays and you score a new rank.

Unfortunately, when one wins, another loses.

Go to the laundry room at the athletic center and pick up the cheerleaders' uniforms. Your instructions will be waiting for you.

You have thirty minutes.

My heart sinks into my stomach as I quickly fold the letter up and stuff it back in the envelope.

"Well, what did it say?"

Shit. Shit. Shit. I stomp my foot on the ground. *What the hell are they up to?*

"Umm. Nothing. I'll see you at school. I'm walking today."

I snatch my bag off my bed and head for the door, hoping Riley doesn't press for more information.

"Wait. Scarlett—"

I open the door and slam it shut before she can ask any other questions.

With the letter in hand, I tap it to my palm.

I'm not sure what's waiting for me at the athletic center, but this note has Crew's name written all over it. Figuratively. Not literally. It actually has my name, but I'm certain he left it.

He came to my room last night, tried seducing me—which almost worked—then he left and dropped the note by the door.

I'm hauling ass down the trail, feeling snow fall into my shoes, and I wish like hell I'd opted for boots this time. There's no time to waste, so overthinking this isn't an option.

Soon, it'll all be over.

I make it to the center in record time, with twenty minutes to spare. I can only hope my next task doesn't delve into that time because class starts in thirty.

Where's the laundry room? I look left, then right.

I know students have laundry rooms in the dorms, but I have no idea where the one inside this building is.

"Hello," I say to a janitor, who's pushing a mop across the floor, "do you know where the laundry area is?"

"End of the hall on the right."

"Thank you," I holler as I hurry down the slippery marble floor, trying not to fall on my ass.

A sign above the door at the end says *Laundry*, so I push it open. It smells like sea breeze and clear water, if that's even a scent. If not, it's what I'd describe this smell as.

My eyes skim the room and I spot the uniforms immediately. They're hanging over a bin, all individually covered in plastic.

As I near them, I see another note that sends my pulse into a frenzy.

My head drops, and I sigh. *I really don't want to open it.*

I glance at my watch. *Sixteen minutes.*

Pulling down the note that's taped to...a bottle of lighter fluid, I immediately notice it's holding more than paper. I quickly rip open the envelope, this time not taking care to leave it intact.

A box of matches falls out, but I catch them before they hit the ground. Holding them in one hand, I read the note.

Burn them.
If you fail your mission, it's your ass that will burn.
You have five minutes.

Five minutes! What the hell, I was supposed to have thirty in total.

Fuck it! I tear down all the uniforms, bunching them in my arms—there's about ten total—and I grab the lighter fluid.

This is another one of the most fucked-up things I've ever had to do, but it beats being thrown in the river.

If Riley ever finds out what I'm doing, she's going to be so pissed at me. Then again, she said so herself that it's *all just part of the games.*

As soon as I'm back outside, I drop the uniforms to the ground. The note didn't say where to burn them, just to burn them. It also didn't say anything about how much of them has to burn. There's enough snow out here that they should extinguish fairly quick. People pass by, some giving me weird looks, others not paying me any attention at all.

With shaky hands, I twist off the top of the lighter fluid, waiting until more people pass. Once they do, I begin dousing the plastic.

Before I realize it, the whole damn bottle is empty.

My eyes dance around the area, making sure the coast is clear before I slide the box of matches open and pull one out.

"Sorry, girls. It's just a game." I strike the match and toss it on the pile of plastic-wrapped uniforms. In a matter of seconds, they all ignite and flames dance in the air while slowly eating away at the plastic.

I quickly toss the box of matches in, causing the fire to grow more rapidly, then I haul ass out of there.

"Fuck off," I tell Neo and Jagger as I drop my tray down on the table. They haven't even said anything and I'm not sure if they're planning to, but it feels fitting given my morning. I've been sweating balls all day, waiting for a cheerleader to pop me in the jaw.

"Hello to you, too," Jagger says, barely able to lift his head off the table. "And next time, could you set your tray down a little more gently?"

He's hungover. That's cute.

I lift my tray up, inches from the table, then slam it down again.

His head shoots up, and I say, "Sorry," in my best little girl voice.

"What did you do to Crew?" Neo asks, pegging me with a stare.

"I didn't do anything to him. Maybe you should ask what he did to me, considering he broke into my room last night."

Now that they mention it, Crew hasn't been in any classes. I assumed he was ditching, which still could be true.

Jagger rubs his temples aggressively, staring down at his untouched burger. "He never came home last night."

"He didn't?" I pick up a fry, dunking it in ketchup. "Where would he have stayed?" I pop the fry in my mouth, watching the two of them and waiting for an answer.

"He always comes home," Neo says, leaning across the

table with a hardened expression. "So tell me, Scar. What did you do to him?"

"Back to what I said when I first arrived... Fuck off."

I'm trying to ignore their unwanted stares as I eat, but it's hard, considering Neo looks like he wants to eat me. Maybe if he'd fill his belly once in a while, he wouldn't be so damn grumpy.

"You bitch," hits my ears, and my head immediately snaps around.

"Excuse me?" I say to Melody, who has a girl gang standing behind her, including Riley.

Oh fuck.

"You burned our uniforms and you're gonna pay!" Melody hisses the threat with her hands pressed on her hips.

Ignoring her, I look at Riley. "It was a game. I had to."

Riley shakes her head, her disappointment in me apparent, then she whips her head around and walks away.

"Sit your asses down and don't come to our table without an invitation again." I look across the table and see Jagger with his hands pressed firmly to it as he stares Melody down.

"But she—"

This time, it's Neo who cuts in. "I don't care what she did. You do not approach Scar or speak to her again unless she speaks to you first."

I'm speechless. I don't even know how to react to what he just said. Is Neo defending me?

Melody shoots me a glare before spinning on her heels and walking away with her posse.

"Why'd you do that?" I ask immediately, not beating around the bush.

"Are you moving into our house?" Neo asks.

"I...don't know. I haven't decided."

"Well," he draws in a breath, expression stoic, "if you do,

you'll be under our protection. If you don't, may the Lord have mercy on Melody Higgins's soul."

"Why would she need mercy?"

Jagger chuckles. "Because she'll be coming for you and you'll tear her to shreds."

I look down, biting my lip and trying not to smile. That almost sounded like a compliment.

We finish eating and I leave well enough alone. Neo was semi-normal today and while I don't trust his intentions, I'll take a win when I get one.

The rest of the day goes by fairly quickly, but as more time passes, the more I start to wonder about Crew.

Wherever he is, I hope he's okay.

"I THINK I OWE YOU A THANK-YOU," Riley says as we walk down the trail to the Ruins. "Had you not set our uniforms on fire, we would have frozen our asses off tonight. Thanks to you, we got to wear our warm-ups."

I want to laugh, but I still feel so bad about that. "I'm glad you're not mad. Those guys come up with the most awful games. If you even call them *games*. It feels more like hazing to me."

"It's almost over, babe."

"Yeah. Almost," I say quietly.

Riley reads my expression and I know it's obvious my thoughts are getting the best of me. "Still worried about Crew?" she asks.

"Something just isn't right. It's not like Crew to miss a game. Back at Essex, he never even missed a practice."

"Maybe so, but is it really our problem?"

She doesn't get it, and I'm not surprised. I've kept Riley in the dark about so much. Maybe it's time to give her a little insight into my relationship with the guys.

"There's something I have to tell you, Ry."

Her head turns, eyes snapped to me as we keep walking. "This sounds serious."

"It is. Well, sort of. Not really."

She chuckles. "It is, or it isn't'?"

"It is. You see," I begin, "I lied when I said things with the guys were good back home. My problem with them is not just the games I'm forced to play. It goes beyond that."

"Whoa. Hold up," she says, stopping me while scoping out our surroundings. Her voice drops to a near whisper. "You have bad blood with them?"

"Why are we whispering?" I whisper back. "It's not like the whole school hasn't seen how they treat me."

"True. Go on."

"Yeah. There's bad blood," I continue. "Do you remember me telling you about Neo's sister, Maddie?"

"I remember."

"Maddie and I were best friends. Maddie was also Crew's girlfriend."

Riley gasps. "She was?"

I can't help but laugh at her dramatics. "Yeah, she was. Maddie had a crush on Crew for as long as I can remember. I also had a crush on Crew, but I never told anyone. Well, Maddie had this horrific accident that I won't go into detail about, but it left her in a coma."

"Oh my god, Scarlett. I'm so sorry. So what happened to her and Crew?"

"Obviously, Crew moved on. The thing is, he moved on fast. Like, a few days later," I pinch my eyes shut as I say, "with me."

I go on to tell her how Crew and I were into each other for

years—long before he and Maddie started dating. That he was only with Maddie to appease Neo, because *everything* he does is to appease Neo. Then I tell her how Neo and Jagger caught us together at one of the Aima Chapter cabins and Neo turned Crew against me not even a day later.

"But how? I mean, I understand why Neo would be upset because it was his sister's boyfriend, but how does Neo have such a strong hold over these guys?"

"I've been trying to figure that out my entire life. I guess it comes down to superiority. The Saint family is powerful and master manipulators. I can honestly see Neo Saint as the future President of the United States."

"Totally." Riley chuckles. "Really, though, Scarlett. That's just awful about your friend. I can understand why you'd feel guilty, but we can't help who we fall for. The Blue Bloods are no exception."

"Only, as a Blue Blood, we aren't given the choice of following our hearts, which is really sad because one member's soul mate might be an outsider, and they'll never get a chance to feel that love due to the rules."

"Hey," she whispers, pulling me off to the side of the trail, "wanna hear a secret?"

"You know I do."

"I heard a rumor that a member once had a relationship here at BCA and when the Lawless found out, they killed the guy."

"Come on," I sweep the air with my hand, "you can't believe everything you hear. Sure, all the Lawless, then and now, are pricks, but they aren't actual murderers." Even if it wasn't long ago, I assumed they were all capable. Funny how things change.

Her shoulders rise and she clicks her tongue. "I dunno. I think you'd be surprised."

Our moment of secrecy and gossip is interrupted when three guys, wearing diapers, come strolling down the trail carrying baby bottles.

Riley and I both bust out in laughter while the guys, totally embarrassed, fight to avoid eye contact.

I snort. "Those fucking games."

Once the show is over on the trail, we head to the party, where the real fun is waiting. After the hell I've been through, I'm ready to enjoy myself and have a few drinks.

As soon as I spot Elias by the large bonfire, Riley nudges me. "I'll catch up with you in a few, 'kay?"

"Yeah. Go. Have fun."

I watch as she skips to Elias's side, all the while, he's watching me over her shoulder. His eyes don't leave mine until I offer him a glint of a smile and turn away. I've gotten the feeling, on more than one occasion, that Elias is into me, and it may be a bit pompous to assume so, but now I feel it more than ever.

Brushing away the feelings, I skim the area in search of a drink. There's a crowd gathered around in the same spot where the keg was at the last party, so I head toward it, and wouldn't you know, Victor is front and center holding the nozzle.

This Rook is about to find out what it's like to be someone's beer-filling bitch for the night. I opt to wait in line this time, but when Victor spots me, he waves me to the front.

"To the side, everyone. Let my friend Scarlett in."

"Friend?" I laugh, while moving through the close-knit bodies. "We're not friends."

"Tell that to the Lawless. They've made it clear to everyone that you're to be treated like the queen you are."

"They did not!"

"Oh yes. They did." He hands me a cup, already filled to the brim.

I'm not sure if I should be flattered or humiliated, because those assholes know how much I hate attention.

I accept the offering and take a sip before saying, "Thanks. I think."

"Hey," Victor announces, "if anyone spots Scarlett with an empty hand, or an empty cup, you get her a damn drink." He looks back at me and winks. "I've got you, girl."

Last I knew, Victor was still a Rook, so it's pretty ballsy of him to be barking orders at anyone. Must be in his nature to take control. Either that, or he was instructed to do so.

I'm blowing out heavy breaths when I begin my search for my dear Lawless friends. They're up to something; I can feel it in my bones.

Standing six feet away, leaning against a rock half his size, is Jagger. His ankles crossed in front of him. Arms folded at his chest. His eyes on me.

My body flushes with heat and I give him a small wave while bringing my drink to my lips. *Why the hell did I wave?*

Jagger pushes himself off the rock and stalks toward me with slow steps. He nods toward my half-empty cup. "How's the drink?"

"Cold, crisp, and refreshing."

"Glad to hear."

"Hey," I say, a bit of seriousness to my tone, "have you heard from Crew?"

"Nope. I was just about to ask you the same thing. What happened with you two last night?"

I lick the excess beer from my lips, thinking about all the events of last night. "He was upset when he saw us kissing. Gave me hell then I went back to my room. An hour or so later, I woke up and he was in my room."

"Did he say why he came there?"

I shake my head no. I'm not really sure I should tell him

263

about the conversation we had at the risk of getting Crew in trouble with Jagger and Neo.

"It's so fucking weird. He must've been pretty pissed to just vanish like this without telling anyone."

"You don't think something happened to him, do you?"

"I don't know, but..." His words trail off as his phone starts vibrating in his pocket. Reaching in, he pulls it out and his eyes lift to mine. "It's Crew."

I should've known he was fine. He probably just needed some space to lick his wounds and figure out how he was going to live with me and keep me out of Jagger's and Neo's reach at the same time.

"Dude. Calm the fuck down so I can understand you. You keep breaking up."

My heart jumps, and I step closer to Jagger in an attempt to hear Crew through the phone.

"All right. Stay put. I'm coming." Jagger ends the call, still gripping his phone. "I've gotta go." His feet move quickly, but I move just as fast to keep up with him.

"Wait. Is he okay?"

"Physically, he's fine. Mentally, he's prepared to murder someone. He's locked in the tunnels."

"Oh my god. Who would do that?"

Ignoring me completely, Jagger taps into his phone. After a few seconds, he curses and ends the call.

"Trying to call Neo?" I ask, and he nods.

"Son of a bitch. How the hell did Crew get himself locked down there?"

"Well, it's Crew. So there's a good chance he did it to himself, considering he doesn't have a master key anymore." Jagger looks at me skeptically. "What?" I huff. "I don't have it."

"I know you don't. Go find Riley and stick with her for the night. If you see Neo, let him know what's up."

"Um. No way in hell," I huff, "I'm coming with you."

Jagger shakes his head. "Like hell you are. We don't know what's waiting down there."

His pace has picked up and I'm trying not to spill my drink while walking and talking at the same time. "Since when are you worried about my safety? In case you've forgotten, you guys had me dumped in the river and sent a mob of cheerleaders in my direction. Why'd you do that, anyways, if you planned to tell them to back off?"

"To make a point."

"Well," I drawl, "I personally missed that point, so if you wouldn't mind telling me—"

"You sure do like to talk, don't you? I don't remember that about you from our childhood. You were always so quiet. What happened?"

"And you always deflect when I ask a question. But if you must have an answer, you three happened. You guys made me what I am today."

"You should be thanking us for the backbone then."

"Thanks. Now answer my question. What was the point with the cheerleaders?"

We've reached the Ruins and Jagger hasn't forced me away yet, so it's safe to assume I'm going down with him. Not that he could stop me anyway.

Crouched down, he sticks a key in a padlock and flips it open, before lifting the one side of the metal hatch, then the other.

"How far down do you think he is?"

"No fucking clue."

Jagger's feet go in first, and once he's halfway down, I lower myself, too.

It's well lit, and for that I'm grateful. It still has the same smell, same look, same feel. Only something about being down here again feels eerie, like someone is watching us.

We're traveling down the familiar passageway when Jagger finally answers my question about the uniforms. "We had to make sure they knew you were off-limits. Melody's a bitch and once she caught wind that you were moving into the Lawless house, she would've fucked with you."

"And that's a problem?"

"It is now."

Right. Because I am *moving in with them.* I never even agreed to this and they're already making plans like it's happening. I still don't understand why it needs to happen or what their sudden interest in protecting me is. Sure, I asked Crew for his help, but I didn't think Neo, of all people, would agree. Jagger, maybe. He's been decent to me the last couple days. But Neo? Not a chance.

We keep walking and then spot Crew, about ten feet in front of us, heading our way. He's shaking his head, covered in dirt, and beyond irate.

"I'm gonna kill someone. Whoever did this shit is fucking dead!" His tone is chilling, even I'm nervous for the offender. "What is she doing here?"

"I came to make sure you were okay."

"She followed me down," Jagger says, answering for me, even though I just answered for myself.

"Why?"

"I don't know." I shrug my shoulders. "I guess I was worried. Maybe a little nosey."

Crew walks past me, bumping my shoulder with his, while Jagger walks next to him. "All right. Start from the beginning. What the hell happened?"

"I don't even know. I was leaving Foxes' Den when I was

hit over the head. Next thing I know, I'm waking up down here with this." He hands Jagger a note.

"Wait," I cut in, "that's the same envelope I was getting for my orders with the games. Is that just a coincidence?"

Jagger opens the envelope while Crew talks. "Definitely not a coincidence. Neo ordered this stationary online and had it delivered here."

This has Neo written all over it, but I don't say that because I know these guys will defend him.

Jagger reads the note out loud. "Blood is thicker than water." He looks at Crew, eyebrows raised. "What's that even supposed to mean?"

"I've been trying to figure that out for the last twenty hours while strolling through the tunnels, looking for a signal, and beating on doors, hoping somehow, someone would hear me."

We reach the ladder again and they gesture for me to go first. If the vibe right now wasn't so fucked, I'd assume it's so they could look at my ass. Not this time, though. These guys are on a mission, and for once, it doesn't involve me.

"Come with me," Crew says, taking my hand.

I look down at it, then to Jagger, and finally back to Crew. "Why?"

"Because I'm not leaving you alone. There's a good chance whoever knocked me out is the same person fucking with you. I told you, Scar. If you want our help, you will be with us at all times. I never even should have left you last night."

I laugh grimly. "I was fine. It seems you're the one who needs protection."

Crew draws in a deep breath, still pulling my hand. "Let's go."

A glance over my shoulder shows Jagger shrugging his shoulders at me. I guess I'm going.

TWENTY-FIVE

"You're sure Riley got the message from Victor?"

"Positive. She said she's fine and she'll see you later today." Crew picks up his phone, types something, then slams it down. "I've gotta go knock some sense into Neo. Stay here," he says, referring to his room.

I'm sitting cross-legged on Crew's bed, wearing his tee shirt. Which is where I woke up this morning because no matter how hard I verbally fought, Crew wouldn't let me leave. This time, I didn't resort to physical fighting because he was being far too nice to harm. I did make him sleep on the floor, though.

It's surreal being here. Like I don't belong. But, I won't pretend I don't feel safe, because I do. As much as I hate what these guys have done to me, I feel safe with all of them, even Neo. For some reason, they want to scare me, but I don't think they want to hurt me.

A knock at the open door has me straightening my back. "Hey," I say to Jagger, who's poking his head in.

"Where's Crew?"

"I guess he went to *knock some sense into Neo?*"

Jagger crosses the room with jerky steps while rubbing his inked arm up and down. He's shirtless, wearing only a pair of gray gym shorts. His hair is messy, and if I wasn't so tense right now, I'd probably be drooling.

Half of his ass cheek plants on the bed beside me. "Wanted to let you know, I talked to Neo and he said Maddie's doing good. Her blood pressure has been stable. No change, but I suppose that's a good thing, right?"

His words are like music to my ears. "That's great. I've been so worried about her." I place a hand over his. "Thank you, Jagger."

A smile lifts his lips. "Sleep okay?"

I'm not sure when we went from threats and insults to small talk, but the abrupt shift in the atmosphere that surrounds us is giving me whiplash.

"Yeah. Slept great. You?" It's a lie because, as much as I'd love to push the past away while engaging in small talk with Jagger, or any of the guys, I still get the feeling this is forced. Therefore, opening up about how I didn't sleep at all is pointless.

"Not a wink. There's so much going on, ya know?"

I nod. "Yeah. But you expected all of this."

"The games? Yes. This other shit? Not so much."

"Well," I say, ready to be the optimist in a situation I should be bitching about, "today's the last day of the games, so hopefully, things calm down after the Gathering."

He nods in slow movements, biting his lip. "Yeah, I don't think that's happening."

I don't either. Something tells me things are going to get worse before they get better. Much, much worse.

His hand rests on my leg, and he squeezes it gently. "Be safe today, okay?"

269

"Okay?" I grimace. "I'm always safe."

"Today's gonna be different. Just keep your head up. It's almost over." He gets off the bed, leaving my thoughts clouded.

"What's that even mean?"

Stopping in the doorway, he looks over his shoulder. "You'll see."

Once he's gone, I rest my head back and stare at the ceiling.

I'm not sure how much more of this I can take. For someone who is a control freak, I sure do feel like I've lost all control.

Throwing my legs over the bed, I get up and go to the en-suite bathroom. I don't have a toothbrush, so I squirt some toothpaste on my finger and do my best to clean my teeth. After I've splashed some water on my face, I put on my clothes from last night and leave the room with my shoes in my hand.

It was late when we got in last night, and Crew brought me straight to his room, so I'm not familiar with the layout of this place.

It's an old house, but the upkeep is spectacular. Everything's fresh and new. The paint, the floors, the furniture.

I'm walking down the long stretch of hallway, passing closed doors, when something outside the window at the end of the hall catches my eye.

My bare feet pad quickly across the hardwood floor, and I stop before fully reaching the window, so the people outside don't hear me.

It's not just any *people*, though. It's Neo and his dad, Sebastian Saint.

What is he doing here?

I fail at an attempt to open the window, so I quickly go down the stairs. When I reach the end, I look to the left and see a set of open French doors. On my tiptoes, I creep over and hide on the side of the door, so I can listen.

"Do you think I care about your little games and your idiot friends?" Sebastian shouts authoritatively. "This Society is what matters and you will protect it at all costs. You have to let this thing with your sister go. We've taken care of it. It's over. Do I make myself clear?"

I peek out, seeing Neo with his hands folded in front of him and his eyes down. The only person I've ever seen intimidate Neo is his dad. I used to think it was out of respect, but as time has passed, I've realized it's out of fear.

"Yes, sir," Neo says, avoiding eye contact with his dad.

"Don't make me come back here or there will be hell to pay." Sebastian hands Neo something and growls, "If he loses another key, he's shit out of luck." Then he gets behind the wheel of his UTV.

With a shaky hand, I slip one of my shoes on my barefoot—unsure where my socks went—then the other.

"Wait," I holler, running out the door while trying to adjust my foot in my shoe. Neo and Sebastian both look at me.

My feet sink into the snow as I hurry toward them.

Neo hurries to my side and grits in my ear, "What are you doing?"

I hold up a finger to Sebastian. "Don't go yet. Please. I need to talk to you."

Sebastian pins Neo with a hard glare. "What the hell is she doing here?"

Neo's too stunned to speak, which is unlike him, so I answer for him, "I'm here with Crew."

"Shut up, Scar," Neo seethes, while staring at his footprints in the snow.

Sebastian starts the ATV and the sound has my heart pounding.

"Wait. Please don't go. I need to know why you took me off Maddie's call list." My voice cracks and shakes as the words fly out. "My mom and my dad, too. Why can't we check on her anymore?"

"Get her out of here and get this school back in order." Sebastian's voice rises to a spine-chilling shout. "Now!"

He takes off, not giving me the answer I so desperately need. "Why?" I scream over the roaring engine, but it's no use. He's gone.

The next thing I know, Neo is walking his chest into mine, fuming. "You fucking bitch!"

"I need to know, Neo!"

"How do you know? That's my question. Who gave you a fucking phone to call from here? Was it Crew?"

"No," I shake my head, "Crew didn't give me a phone. I...it doesn't matter. Tell me why, dammit!" I shove him, but he eats the space back up.

"Why?" He laughs devilishly. "You wanna know why?" He's so close, I can smell his toothpaste and feel the heat of his rage spilling down my shivering body. "Because you don't deserve her. I don't buy into your act like they do, Scar. I know the real you. We might protect you from those outside of the Lawless, but it's only because we want all your tears. *I* want to be the one who wakes you from your dreams and turns your days into nightmares."

"Neo," I say, tone soft, "I...don't get it. Why do you hate me so much? Why do you want to keep me from her?"

"Because she's my sister! *Mine!*" His eyes glimmer with mischief as his lips twitch. "It's your fault she's lying in that fucking hospital bed."

My eyes are wide with panic. "My fault? Why would you even say that?"

"You know exactly what you did and I won't let you get

272

away with it!" With a shove to my chest, I'm pushed down. Snow creeps up the sleeves of my sweatshirt and tears threaten to fall down my cold cheeks.

"You're wrong," I shout as he walks away, "I'd never hurt Maddie. Never!"

I look at the doors as Neo stalks toward them, and I see Crew and Jagger standing there idly watching, without saying a word.

As Neo steps inside, so do they. The doors close and I'm left alone out here in the snow, wondering what the hell just happened.

CHAPTER
TWENTY-SIX
SCARLETT

AFTER DRAGGING my frozen feet through the snow in only a pair of thin canvas shoes, I came back to my dorm and haven't left my bed all day. Riley is having dinner with Elias and while I was invited, I'm just not in the mood to be around people.

I've laid here, wide awake, replaying my conversation with Neo, and I still can't make sense of it.

It's your fault she's lying in that hospital bed.

I don't even know what to think. I'm not sure what's real anymore. Neo blames me for Maddie's accident, but it was just that, an accident.

Wasn't it?

Could I be wrong? Could we all be wrong?

Someone knocks at the door and I don't even flinch. If it's important, whoever it is can come back later.

The knocks grow louder.

And louder.

Until finally, I throw the blanket off me and stomp my way to the door.

I tear it open and huff, "What?"

My head pokes out the door and I look both ways, but no one's there.

When I look down, I see a note, and rage ripples through me. "Seriously?" I grumble, bending down to pick it up. Of all the fucking days they could have done this, they choose today. A day when I can barely muster the strength to get out of bed.

I'm still in the doorway as I open the envelope and pull out the note.

Be at the top of Eldridge Mountain in one hour.

If you don't show, you don't move up.

"What the fuck!?" I throw the note into the hall and slam the door shut.

Knowing I'm in a time crunch, I pull myself together and dress warmly in my black snow bibs, winter coat, and a pair of snow boots. I throw a beanie over my messy, unwashed hair and head out the door.

I'm taken aback when I see a snowmobile with a rider sitting out front. As I come down the steps, Jagger gets off his sled and pulls his helmet over his head and hands me a spare one.

Feeling numb at this point, I don't even have the strength to argue when Jagger sits back down on his sled and says, "Get on."

I could fight him and make the hike, but I'd never make it in time.

"You've got some fucking nerve." I pull the helmet on and slide my legs around him.

"It's nothing personal, Scar."

"Everything about this is personal. For example, why did Neo accuse me of hurting Maddie? Is that what you all think?"

"It doesn't matter what we think." He accelerates the sled and takes off.

Nothing is said during the ride because it's too loud and

275

too cold to even speak. We come to a stop at the backside of the mountain, near the river, and Jagger removes his helmet and gets off, offering me his hand as he stands.

I tear the helmet off my head and throw it in the snow at his feet, not accepting his offer of help.

"I actually started to believe you and Crew were sincere. It was all lies, though, wasn't it?"

"No, it wasn't. I meant what I said, Scar. It's not all games for me and I'm certain it's not for Crew either."

"Why allow it then? Why let Neo control your lives like this?"

"You don't know what it's like. You'd never understand."

My chest feels like it's caving in. I can't do this anymore. "Tell me, Jagger. I need to know." Tears prick at my eyes and my words catch in my throat. "Does he think I hurt Maddie?"

Jagger sits down on his sled, fidgeting with his helmet. "Yeah. I mean, I know he blames you."

"You think I did something to her?" I shout. "You think I hurt her?"

"No! Fuck, Scar," he runs his fingers through his hair, "I don't know what to believe. The more time we spend together, I start to think that maybe he is just overreacting. His demands are out of control. His anger intensified."

"He *is* overreacting, Jagger. Neo always overreacts."

"You could be right. Neo's never liked you and I think he just wants someone to blame. You're an easy target."

"Well, make him understand. He has to. This isn't right!"

"We've tried, but he won't listen. I think the only one who can make him understand at all is you." His shoulders slump and his voice softens. "Finish the games, Scar. Move into the house and let us handle whatever the hell is going on out there. Show him you're not who he thinks you are. But don't push too hard, it'll just make things worse."

I drop to my knees in the snow and no matter how hard I try, I can't stop the tears from falling. "I miss her so much."

"We all do," he says, flinging a leg over the seat. "It's a good ten-minute walk up the backside. If you go now, you can make it in time."

I look up at the mountain, red flags waving in my head. "I have to go up there?"

He nods. "Your instructions are waiting."

"No. No! I can't go up there."

He slips the helmet over his head and says, "You can do this."

Before I can grab him, yell at him, or jump on the back of his sled, he's gone.

Getting to my feet in this heavy snow is a struggle, but I manage. I'm breathless before I even get to the top, but I make it.

My heart is pounding, my entire body has broken out in a sweat beneath the layers I'm wearing, and my breath has escaped me.

"I'm here assholes," I shout into the night sky. "Are you happy now?"

Anxiety rears its ugly face when I see my snowboard bag with a note on it.

My throat opens up and I scream at the top of my lungs, "No!"

I pace for what feels like minutes in front of the bag, before finally grabbing the note and reading it.

Go down.

Heat rushes through my body, starting at my toes and working its way up, until my head feels like an inflated balloon. *I can't do this.*

All the memories I've repressed hit me all at once. Like a wave crashing on the shore, they break and scatter, and I can only hope they will disappear. Because I don't want to remember.

"Where's Maddie?" Crew asks, walking toward me from the backside of the hill. His slow swagger and the smirk playing on the corner of his mouth has my heart skipping beats, so I quickly turn around.

"Maddie is taking a piss and Finn went down already."

"That fucker. He was supposed to wait for me."

I can feel his presence drawing nearer. His warm breath trickling down my exposed neck. "You nervous?" he asks.

"Not even a little bit. Besides, I'm too stoned to be nervous."

"True."

He's close. Really close.

I spin around and we're face to face. "What are you doing?" I ask him, warranting another sly smile.

"Just waiting."

I quirk a brow. "For my best friend? Your girlfriend?" It's more of a statement than a question to remind Crew that he's dating my best friend.

"I'm breaking up with her tonight."

"No, Crew!" I gasp. "You can't do that. You'll break her heart."

"I've thought about it for a while and I have to. Her heart will heal, but I need to follow mine. I don't love her, Scar. Not like I should."

"You're only sixteen, Crew. You're not expected to love anyone in any certain way."

"I do, though."

My heart swells at his words because I know what he's getting at. Crew's told me many times that he has feelings for me. And I've told him just as many times that regardless of how either of us feels, we can't act on it."

Before I can even react, Crew grabs my face and pulls my mouth to his. The harder I try to fight him off, the deeper he kisses me.

Once I break free, my fist lands on his face. "Why the hell did you do that?" I hiss, wiping his kiss from my lips.

"Scar!" Maddie snaps. "Did you just hit him?"

She didn't see the kiss. Thank God, she didn't see the kiss.

"I...umm. He tried to steal my board." I bend down and pick it up as if it hasn't been lying at my feet the entire time."

"So you hit him over it?" She slides up to Crew, who's cupping his nose. "Crew! You're bleeding!"

I look down and notice drops of red blood falling into the snow, painting it like a cherry snow cone. Maybe I went too far, but he can't just kiss me like that. I'm just glad Maddie didn't see it.

"I'm sorry, Crew," I say.

"I'm fine," Crew tells her. "Let's just go down."

"You go down. Scar and I need to talk."

When Maddie gives Crew her back, he mouths the words, "I'm sorry."

A minute later, once his feet are on his board, he asks me to help her down the mountain. Knowing she's an amateur, I nod, and he disappears down the steep slope.

Maddie gives me a look of sheer evil. "You wanna explain to me what that was all about?"

"It was a misunderstanding and not a big deal. I'm too high and too anxious to go down to deal with any of this. Can we talk about it later?"

"No! We're talking about it now. I know you don't like Crew, or Jagger, or my brother, but do you really have to be so cold to them all the time?"

"Me?" I laugh. "Your brother hates me, Maddie. As for Crew and Jagger, they only like me when he's not around."

"You know, all this time, I thought maybe they were the problem. Now I'm starting to realize it's been you all along. Crew is my boyfriend and he's going to be around, whether you like it or not. If you can't deal with it, you can just..."

Her words trail off, but I don't need her to finish her sentence. "Okay," I nod subtly, "you choose him. Fine." I go to the edge of the cliff and stick my shoes in the board, bending down to fasten the straps. "Enjoy your ride down the fucking hill."

Maddie can keep living in the clouds while I keep my feet on the ground. Tonight, when Crew breaks her heart, I won't be there to pick up the pieces.

"Scar! Wait. Don't leave me. You know I can't go down this mountain by myself."

Tears slide recklessly down my cheeks, one after another. I swallow hard, forcing down the ball in my throat.

I left her. I left her on one of the steepest and most dangerous hills in the state, knowing she was scared to go down. All this time, I wouldn't let myself go there. I covered up the guilt, replacing it with something new—my relationship with Crew.

When I got to the bottom and Finn and Crew were waiting, Maddie never came. We waited for close to an hour before Crew went back up for her and even then, it was another hour before we got the news.

A skier found Maddie unconscious, not far down the mountain. It wasn't until the med copter touched down that we knew something wasn't right. Crew sped through traffic, so we could meet her at the hospital, but she was rushed right into surgery to stop the bleeding on her brain. When she came out, she never woke up.

Maybe Neo's right in thinking it's my fault. I might not have pushed Maddie, but I might as well have.

Pulling myself together, I unzip my bag and look down at my board—it's just like I remember. A mountain landscape with the Burton logo down the center. I run my fingers over it and close my eyes, pinching out tears.

280

Finally, I pull out my board and place it in the snow. Next, I grab my goggles and slide them over my head.

With shaky knees, I step into the shoes that are still adjusted to my fit.

I scoot closer to the edge and whisper into the wind, "I'm so sorry, Maddie."

"She knows." My head snaps to the left, following the gruff sound of Crew's voice. "Are you ready to do this?"

"Why are you here?" I ask him as my board teeters on the edge. He's wearing the same ski outfit he's always had. His goggles are resting on his forehead and his board is tucked under his arm.

"Didn't think you should do this alone. Don't tell the guys, though. They'll probably abolish me from the whole damn Society."

"Your secret's safe with me."

Those feelings of safety I get from Crew return and just having him here makes everything better. It shouldn't—not after everything he's done to me—but it does. No one gives me whiplash the way Crew does. And no one else can make me want more of it but him.

"Now answer my question. Are you ready to do this?"

I shake my head no. "I don't think I can."

After Maddie's accident, I vowed to never go down a mountain again. Just the thought of it brings back all the turmoil I felt during the days that followed. If it weren't for Crew, I'm not sure how I would have survived it. There were so many times I considered ending the pain permanently. He saved me, and in some ways, I think I saved him, too. Our grief brought us together, but it's also our grief that tore us apart.

"You're stronger than you think, Scar." He reaches his gloved hand out. "Take my hand."

Curling my fingers in my glove, I slowly reach out and take his hand. "Thanks, Crew."

He cracks a smile. "Let's do this."

We crouch down, come up, and lean forward at the same time. As we take off, we're forced to part ways, but Crew sticks close by. The wind hits my face and I roar back at it, hooting and hollering as a smile grows on my face. One of the things I've always loved about this sport is the feeling of your soul leaving your body. It's like it's trailing behind you and fighting to keep up, but you're faster. For a short period, you're free... free from it all.

I'm riding into the orange glow of the sunset as I put my weight on the left side to go around a tree. Shifting right, I dodge a large rock. It's a bumpy terrain, and the snow is unpacked, but that makes it all the more thrilling.

"I've gotta go," Crew shouts. "You can do this."

The next thing I know, he's shifting to the left and taking a different path while I keep straight.

I'm alone in my thoughts, and while on a typical day, that's scary, right now, it's exactly what I need.

Neo hates me, that much I know for sure. After recollecting that day, I can't say I blame him. Doesn't mean I'll cower, it just means I need to make things right.

Crew still loves me, I also know that for sure. He wanted to hate me and blame me because it's what Neo wanted, but I can see it. I can feel it. His feelings haven't changed.

Jagger is trying. He's stuck in the muddled mess of what's right and wrong. Then again, I think we all are.

When I reach the end of this mountain, I have to make a choice. I can keep on pretending nothing ever happened. I can go back to my dorm, live with Riley, and try to survive all this on my own.

Or, I can move into that house, show Neo how far I can

bend before I break, and prove to him I'm not the monster he wants me to be. In doing so, I'll also earn their help in finding out who's trying to hurt me.

The sun has dipped farther and there's only a sliver of light left as I near the bottom. Bent over, I take a sharp turn to the right and go around a large evergreen. As I come out in front of it, I see someone.

It's not Crew, but someone else. Just standing there in a trench coat with a hood pulled over his head. No board, no skis. Shivers skate down my spine, and as I pass him, I look over my shoulder, noticing he's turned to keep watching me go down.

My balance gets shaky and I lean back, trying to steady myself. When I lean too far, I come forward.

Shit.

I see the fall coming before it happens, so I flex my legs, tuck my arms inward, and fall back.

I'm on my ass when I look behind and see that the person is gone. This wasn't a case of a stranger being on the mountain. No. Whoever that is knew I'd be here. And the only person I can think of is Neo.

I get myself back up, and it's slow moving at first, but a minute later, I'm flying again.

By the time I reach the bottom, the sun has completely set, but it doesn't matter. Standing at the bottom of the hill is a large crowd, probably half the student body. There's a large fire, people around it, drinking and having a good time.

Before I come to a complete stop, Neo steps in front of me, and I lift my feet, spraying him with snow from under my board.

"Knew that was coming," he says, brushing off his chest and wiping his face.

"You deserve it." I drop my board and pick it up, stuffing it under my arm. "Are you happy now?"

"I have to say, I didn't think you'd do it."

"Your first mistake would be doubting me. Your second would be thinking you know me at all." I step past him and lift my goggles to my forehead.

I spot Jagger by the fire and he raises his cup, smiling at me.

Riley comes running at me and throws herself into my arms. "I can't believe you went down that big-ass hill." She has no idea of some of the mountains I've conquered in my lifetime. I'd invite her to go along for a ride, but I'm not sure I'll ever bring an amateur back on the slopes.

I'm standing alone, taking it all in, when I spot Crew alongside Neo. He's no longer in his ski clothes and doesn't have his board, which leads me to believe no one else knows he went down with me.

Neo is talking, but Crew is paying him little attention as he watches me over his shoulder. I lift a smile while he does the same. Neo is mid-sentence when Crew pats him on the shoulder and walks toward me.

"How'd it feel?" he asks, still grinning from ear to ear.

"Really good, actually. Ya know, you guys really need to step up your games if you wanna totally break someone."

It's a joke, and Crew knows it. Had it not been for him, I may not have gone down.

"I'll let the guys know." He lifts his chin. "You need a ride back to your room to change?"

"Uh. Yeah. That'd be great. Hey," I say, "someone was on the slope after you veered off. A guy, maybe?"

Eyebrows raised, he says, "Maybe just a local?"

I shake my head. "I don't think so. I think it was *him*. Whoever he is."

"All right," he rests a hand on my back, leading me, "let us handle this. You'll be fine."

Crew leads me to his snowmobile, which is in line with Jagger's and Neo's. We're walking side by side when we pass the fire and my eyes catch Jagger's soft ones. My feet keep moving, but my eyes fight to keep up as I watch him watching me. He takes a sip of his drink, peering at me over the rim of the glass.

"You coming?" Crew asks, and I realize I've stopped walking, his hand still on my back.

My head jerks around and I start walking again. "Yeah."

One more glance at Jagger and he's now engaged in a conversation with Hannah, who seems to be flirting with him.

Jealousy brews inside me and my stomach hardens. I don't like this. Not one bit.

CHAPTER
TWENTY-SEVEN
CREW

SCAR GETS off the sled as I lift my helmet over my head. Holding it in my lap, I take a deep breath. "It's been quite a night."

"And it seems it's just begun." She shoots a thumb over her shoulder. "I'm gonna get changed and I guess I'll see you back at the party?"

"Not so fast." I swing my legs over and get up. "We had a deal. You're not to be alone. I'll come up with you and you'll ride with me."

"Still barking orders, I see."

"One day you'll thank me."

"We'll see about that."

Her attitude makes me laugh while making me fucking crazy at the same time. "Just get your ass up those stairs so you can get ready."

Once we're in her room, I close the door and press my back to it, watching her while she takes off her coat and steps out of her snow bibs.

"What?" she asks, pulling her hoodie over her head and exposing the thin tank top underneath.

286

"Nothing. Just looking."

She snorts. "Well, stop it."

"How'd we get here, Scar? From friends, to enemies, to tormentors, to this?"

Her lips roll together and she sits down on her bed, hands pressed behind her. "This?"

Sluggish steps close the space between us and I sit down beside her. "Yes. This."

"Well. I wouldn't say we're friends, but I am grateful for your help today and I'll admit, when you were missing yesterday, I was pretty worried."

I tuck a damp piece of hair behind her ear. It's a mixture of sweat that rims her forehead from her hat and moisture from the cold. The back of my hand runs over her flushed cheek. "Things are changing from here on out. It's time I take back control of my life. Be it on the field, or with the guys."

"I'll believe it when I see it."

"If I was lying, would I do this?" I take her chilled cheeks in my hands, pulling her mouth to mine.

"The party? My promotion?" she says softly into my mouth.

"Congratulations, you've been promoted. We're skipping the party."

"But Neo will—"

"Fuck Neo. Now kiss me."

Our lips brush, slow and steady, and I inhale each shaky breath she exhales. My mouth parts slightly and I drag my tongue across her lower lip. "Let me show you how sorry I am."

Scar nods and her hands rest on the back of my head.

My pulse quickens as our mouths connect. Every inch of my body is thrust into the kiss as I gently lay Scar down on her back. My body rests on hers like a warm blanket. Running one hand up her thigh, I squeeze when I reach the crease where her leg ends.

A whimper slips through the crack of her mouth, spilling into mine, and I swallow it down.

I've kissed Scar since she got here, but it was nothing like this. Those moments were empty of emotion, but this one has me bursting at the seams, ready to give her all of me—my mind, my body, and my soul.

My cock digs into her hipbone as I slide up and down her body, feigning for pressure. Wanting her more than I've ever wanted anything in my life.

She wraps her arms around my head, cradling it while digging her fingers into my hair. Her hips flex upward and she grumbles, "Fuck me, Crew."

Her words are like music to my ears. My nose grazes her cheek, and I inhale her scent. "Are you sure?"

She pulls back. "Did you ask permission in the library?"

"Things were different then. We're different."

Slipping a hand between us, she pops the buttons on her jeans, eyes filled with lust. "You have my permission."

I sit up, bringing her into my lap. Her legs wrap tightly around me, caging me in. Running my fingers along the bottom of her tank top, I lift it. Her arms rise and I slip it over her head, tossing it on the floor.

My chest expands as I take in the sight of her cleavage peeking out of her bra. I lick my lips before pushing down her right cup. Powdering her breasts with open-mouthed kisses, I work my way to her nipple, sucking it between my teeth. Her back arches, and I move to the next breast. My hands run up her sides, to her back, and beneath her bra strap. One click of my fingers against the clasp has it falling to her waist.

With her breasts in my hands, I look at her eager eyes. "You're so fucking sexy."

We dive into a passionate kiss. One that's abrasive but not forced at all. It's like our mouths were molded for this kiss alone. Scar's hands run up the back of my shirt, nails grazing my skin, leaving a trail of goosebumps. Her arms keep rising, and when she removes my shirt, I break the kiss. Only to return my mouth to hers once I'm free of it.

I move to her neck, savoring every taste. Her head tilts to the side and I fall into her as her back hits the bed. Positioned between her legs, I unzip her already unbuttoned jeans and remove them.

My chest smooths down her body until my head is enveloped by her legs.

When she brings them together, I growl and nibble at the sensitive skin on her inner thigh. "Spread 'em."

She does as she's told, dropping them wide open. My tongue runs over my lips when I see a damp spot on her white cotton panties. My cock reacts with a twitch.

"Thought I didn't make you wet," I grumble as I pull them down, pressing my thumb to her stained arousal.

She bucks her hips, bringing her pussy up to my face. "Just shut up and do something."

Tossing the panties, I kiss her clit. "You're so sexy when you're demanding."

Her legs close in on me again as her body writhes, so I punish her with another bite to her thigh and she spreads them again.

I push two fingers inside her, watching as they seamlessly glide in and out. Her juices coating my digits. *Such a little liar.* Scar knows damn well I make her wetter than any dream ever has.

Bringing my mouth to her clit, I graze my teeth over the sensitive nub, drawing a moan from her. It's a sound I could listen to all day and I work tirelessly to hear it again.

My fingers dig deeper, until all that's visible is my raised knuckles pressed against her sex.

"Crew," she mutters in ecstasy, and that, too, is a sound I'd like to record and replay all hours of the day.

Everything about Scar is perfect. Every sound, whether a whimper or a shout. Every touch, be it a slap or pull on my cock.

I look up, catching her lustful stare. Her mouth parts slightly, and she pants a breath. "Don't stop," she grumbles, fisting my hair and forcing my mouth to her.

Humming, I suck her in while working my fingers inside her. I breathe in the scent of her arousal and pocket it to memory, so I can jerk off to that aroma and this view on a rainy day.

"Oh god," she cries out, fisting the sheets on either side of her. She lifts and pulls and her body seizes. I dart my tongue out, flicking endlessly at her clit. Faster and faster while my fingers delve deeper and deeper. "Fuck, Crew."

Her walls clench around me, and when they relax, I slow my pace until I slide my fingers out completely.

Wasting no time, I tear off my pants, ridding myself of my boxers, and I pounce on her like a feral animal.

My cock slides right inside her like it's home. She welcomes me with raised hips and a kiss. And my God, she feels so fucking good.

I scoop my hands behind her and levitate her back off the bed. Tugging her bottom lip between my teeth, I repay the favor from when she bit me the other day, and I clamp down. Her whimpers of pain only entice me further and I stretch her bottom lip out until I can see it with a downward glance. Only then do I let go, a little pissed at myself for not drawing blood like she did to mine.

My mouth moves to her neck, sucking on the same spot

where I branded her over Jagger's blemish. I suck hard, wanting to show everyone here that she's spoken for, that's she mine.

I'm granted another cry of pain, mixed with pleasure, and the sound has my balls tightening.

I glide up and down, watching the way her tits bounce. My face nuzzles between them, and when I turn my head, I nibble at the side of her breast.

I hum into her breastbone. "Let me live inside you, Scar."

My words bring a reaction I wasn't expecting, when she grabs my head and forces it up. She doesn't kiss me or do much of anything, just stares into my eyes and says, "Watch me while I come."

As if she couldn't turn me on any more, her love language has done it again. I'm on the brink of explosion, wanting to fill her up, but knowing I can't. Her mouth falls open and she moans. Her breaths ragged while my chest heaves in sync with hers.

Right before I come, I lift my chest, pull out, and stroke myself as I release all over her milky smooth stomach. Even as we're both coming down, our eyes never stray from each other's.

I kiss her lips softly, still lost in her gaze. There are meaningful words on the tip of my tongue, but I keep them to myself —for now.

TWENTY-EIGHT

CREW GRABS his shirt and cleans me up, then slides his naked body up mine. This moment is everything I wanted for so long, until I didn't want it at all. Now that it's here again, I want it to last forever.

I run my finger over a tattoo on his collarbone. It's some words in a different language that I don't understand and it's inked over a scar. "What's this tattoo mean?"

Crew bends his neck to see which one I'm referring to. There are several different ones that flow together, so I press on the one I'm talking about.

"Remember when we were twelve and racing bikes in the alley behind Aima Hall and I crashed into that fence, flipped over it and got a nasty cut?" I nod, and he continues, "Everyone laughed but you ran in and got a first aid kit and helped me clean it up. When it healed, I had a nasty scar there. Last year, I had it covered."

My fingers float over the letters, tracing each one. "What's it say?"

"It's Latin for, *with you, I am me.*"

My heart doubles in size, and in a knee-jerk reaction, I pull his mouth to mine. "What am I going to do with you, Crew Vance?"

His head lifts, fingers trailing down my arm. "Let me be me, because you're the only one I can be myself with."

"Then be yourself. Quit trying to please Neo because, in the end, he'll never be happy, no matter what choices you make."

"I need you to be honest with me about something," he says, and I straighten my back, ready for a serious conversation.

"Okay," I drag out the word, "I'll try my best."

"What's up with you and Jagger? And don't say it's none of my business. I need to know what to expect with you moving into the house."

I blow out a heavy breath, and his eyes widen. "Is it that hard of a question?"

When I avert my gaze, he presses further. "Come on, Scar. Just answer me."

"Well," I say, knowing there's no easy way to answer this, because truthfully, I don't know the answer. "Jagger took me by surprise." My shoulders shrug against the crinkled sheets. "He's nothing like I thought he was, much like you. I came to realize you were both brainwashed by Neo, and I can't fault you for being manipulated by that asshole. Hell, Neo manipulates everyone."

"You're avoiding the question."

"I guess it's because I don't know. Am I drawn to him? A little. Am I going to jump into bed with him, like this? No."

I can tell that's not what he wanted to hear. To know that I could possibly be catching feelings for someone else, when he's made it clear that just the thought of me being with anyone else tortures his mind.

"Look, Scar. You know where I stand with you. I'm here, if

and when, you're ever ready. Just be careful. Even living at the house, you can't let your guard down. Okay?"

"I know."

We lie there for a while, letting time pass. Crew's phone has rung at least a dozen times, but he's ignored it. I know once we get off this bed, reality, in the form of Neo, will be waiting for us.

As much as I try to ignore the giddy feelings in my stomach, I can't.

Am I really falling for him again?

I think I am.

It's like Crew transformed into this monster temporarily, and since I've arrived, we tore into each other like hungry beasts, but now, that monster is gone and he's back. He is sweet, attentive, and kind, and my God, he's sexy as hell.

Over the last couple days, I started seeing him in that light again, but on the top of the mountain, I really saw him.

But I see Jagger, too. My heart and my body are torn between two men. Crew is comfortable. He's what I know. Jagger is new and exciting, and the way he looks at me brings warmth to every inch of my body. I don't know what I'm going to do, but I'm in no position to make any decisions right now.

But there's still something I don't understand.

"Hey, Crew," I ask him, still naked and tangled in his arms. "How'd you guys get my snowboard from my room back home? That's a long drive for something so mundane."

His arm twitches as he draws back to look at me. "We didn't bring your snowboard here."

"Umm. Yes, you did. My mom brought it home with her and put it in my closet." I shut myself up quickly before blurting, "Don't ask me how I know that." I'm always putting my damn foot in my mouth.

"Noooo. I saw it under your bed the first day you got here, when I came into your room to snoop."

"It was you!" I slap his chest. "I knew it."

"I didn't take anything. Just looked around a little bit. Anyways, it was definitely there. A few days ago, we sent a Rook into the room to get it."

"If my dad didn't leave it, and my mom brought it into the house, then how the hell did it get here?"

"You're sure she brought *your* bag into the house?"

"That's what she said."

"If it was here on day one, that means it likely came up with your other bags. Who brought your bags up?"

"Elias. It was the first time I met him."

"Elias?" He drags out his name like he's referencing Satan himself. "That's how you met that dumbass?"

"He's not a dumbass. He's a really nice guy and Riley happens to like him a lot, so back off."

"Don't be so sure. People aren't always what they seem. I mean, looking at you, I'd think you're a sweet girl. Deep down, you're a feisty thing with the mouth of a sailor."

I chuckle at his description of me. "Very funny. But seriously. Leave Elias alone."

"I will. For now. But I'm gonna be keeping my eyes on him."

I don't argue with that. Moving forward, I have no doubt Crew will be keeping his eyes on anyone I associate with.

When Crew's phone starts buzzing again, he decides to take it, so I use the time to get dressed.

As I gather up my clothes for the bathroom, I glance over my shoulder to make sure he's not looking.

"No, fuck you. It's about time we do things my way and if you don't like it, you can step down and me and Jagger will run the show."

My neck tips back as I breathe out a laugh. He's so sexy when he stands up for himself.

Knowing he's occupied, I reach into the pocket of my makeup bag where my phone is.

When I don't feel it, I tense up. Peeling the pocket open with two hands, I see a piece of paper inside with the three pieces of makeup I own.

I pull it out—it's the same paper as the game notes, but there's no envelope.

"What is that?" Crew asks over my shoulder, startling me.

"I don't know." I unfold the note and read it out loud.

"The games have just begun."

"Did you know about this?" With the note pinched in my fingers, held straight out in front of us, I look up at Crew, who seems just as stunned as I am.

He pegs me with a look, then snags the note from my hand. "No. This isn't the Lawless's doing."

I swallow hard, re-entering this nightmare. My bottom lip trembles. "I thought the games were over."

Crew wraps his arms around me from behind. "It seems with this person, they've only just begun." His lips press to the back of my head. "Don't worry, baby. We'll find them and when we do, we'll fucking destroy them."

EPILOGUE
CREW

One Week Later

"You're sure it was this way?" Jagger asks with his flashlight pointed in front of us.

"Positive."

When I spent some time down in the tunnels after some shithead knocked me unconscious, I came across a door that was different from the others; it was newer. Nothing like the originals that are custom-built from heavy wood planks. Even if I'd had a master key on me at the time, it wouldn't have done any good. The door was equipped with a combination lock, as opposed to a standard keyhole.

"This is fucking stupid. So what if the door was different? Some drunk students probably busted through it and broke it down, so they replaced it."

We're deep in the tunnels, and while the guys and I have explored them many times, I only ventured this far that one night.

"No," I tell him, "whoever put that door up, did it with the

297

intention of keeping people out." I lift my chin, eyeing the door in front of us. "There it is."

Jagger walks closer, flashlight held out in front of us, illuminating the modern-day door. It's stainless steel and resembles a door to a vault, or a safe. "Damn. That is different."

"Right? I get the feeling this isn't the work of any maintenance employee."

He looks at me, eyebrows raised. "The Elders?"

My shoulders rise. "Maybe. But why?"

We both move closer, inch by inch, as if we're approaching a detonated bomb.

"I don't think my pick is gonna get us in this one," Jagger says, and I nod in agreement. "Get Neo on the phone. Tell him to bring Evan Marshall down here. His dad's a locksmith. And I don't just mean your typical locksmith. He can crack just about any lock and Evan's done some work with him in the past."

My forehead crinkles. "How do you even know that?"

"Evan's the one who hot-wired Scar's car to get it over to her principal's house during the fire."

Oh, right. Another plan they left me out of. It wasn't until after the fact that I even knew what the guys were up to that night. Scar doesn't know that, though.

I pull my phone out of my pocket, holding it over my head while assessing the signal strength. "I'll try, but service is sketchy down here. Hence me being stuck for hours last time."

"Use my phone," he tosses it at me, and I catch it in midair, "I get a signal pretty much anywhere."

I click the side button, turning it on, and sure as shit—four bars. "Could've really used this last week," I mumble as I tap Neo's name to call him.

He picks up on the second ring, sounding like the asshole he is. "What d'ya want? I'm in the middle of something."

"Glad to hear you haven't changed in the last three hours."

"You seem to have missed the part where I told you I'm in the middle of something."

"Right. We need you to get Eli Marsh—"

"Evan. You dipshit," Jagger hisses as he fucks with the combination.

"Sorry. Evan Marshall. Bring him down to the tunnels. We've got a little bit of a situation."

"What kind of situation?" he asks, growly and annoyed.

"Remember that door I told you about last week? Well, Jagger and I came down here and he thought he could pick the lock, but he can't. So we need Evan, since he's worked with his dad on this stuff. We're pretty far down. Go past the Vultures' Roost door. Take a left. All the way at the end, you'll take another left, and we're way the fuck down. I'm talking a good mile."

"Are you shitting me? You two had to do this tonight?"

"Ya know, we'd like to get out of here at some point tonight, so we can have a little fun ourselves. So are you coming or not?"

Neo must've pulled the phone away from his mouth because his voice is strained. "Bend over. We need to make this quick." He returns and says, "Give me five minutes and I'll grab him and head down." Then he ends the call.

"Well," I say, handing Jagger his phone, "he's coming. In more ways than one."

"Get comfortable. It's gonna take him at least an hour to get Evan and get down here."

I slide down the wall and drop to my ass, knees bent in front of me. "What do you think it is?"

"If I had to guess," he says, kicking the door out of frustration. "I'd say it's a secret room for the Elders. I'm sure we're not the first to find it, but we're likely the first to try and get in."

299

"Yeah. You're probably right. Either way, curiosity's got the best of me and I'm not leaving here until I know."

It's over an hour before Neo shows his face. "About fucking time," I say, getting off the cement floor and dusting off my pants.

"You're lucky I came at all." Neo gives Evan a shove in our direction. "Here's what you asked for. Now if you don't mind, I've got two more chicks waiting on me back at the house. If they're gone when I get back, because you assholes dragged me down here, I'll just have Scar take their place."

My veins flex in my forearms as my fists clench at my sides. "Leave her the fuck alone."

"Ohhh," he singsongs, "did I hit a nerve? Is someone finally admitting their feelings?"

"Fuck off."

Neo knows damn well that Scar and I have been getting closer. We haven't given ourselves a label but we're well on our way. I told both Neo and Jagger that if I had to choose, I'd choose her. Jagger shrugged his shoulders then handed me a beer, while Neo asked if I planned to share—not with him, but with Jagger. Seems I missed a lot and she and Jagger got closer than I thought. I'm not sure how I feel about it, but time will tell. All bullshit aside, we all have one mission now and that's protecting our girl. Neo is still being an ass, but I'm hopeful that, over time, he'll come around.

Jagger and Evan are working on the lock while I watch intently. Neo is still here for whatever reason, and I'm glad. He needs to see what's on the other side of the door, too. Whatever it is, it involves all of us. We're family in the eyes of the Society. All for one and one for all.

Once the door opens, we all hoot and holler and breathe out heavy sighs of relief. It didn't take as long as I thought it would.

Neo grabs Evan by the back of his collared shirt. "You. Get lost."

"But I don't know how—"

"Do I look like I care?" He shoves him away, and Evan leaves with his tail between his legs.

I'm sure we'll catch up with him on the way out, in which case, we'll silence him with threats that we'll make good on, if necessary. No one can know about this door until we know what's behind it.

"You guys ready?" Jagger asks, his hand on the U-shaped metal handle.

"No," Neo says, sarcasm dripping from his mouth, "thought maybe we'd tell a few jokes. Maybe a ghost story or two first." His voice jumps a few octaves. "Yes, we're fucking ready."

Jagger clicks on his flashlight, while I do the same, and he pulls the door open.

My heart is racing like a motherfucker. I'm not sure why. It's just a door—just a room. Something in my gut tells me it's so much more than that, though.

"Fuck!" Jagger bellows, while at the same time I see why. "Another damn door."

I push past him, heading straight for it. When I turn the handle, I lift a smile over my shoulder. "Not locked."

"Well, open it," Neo says, bored with this entire situation.

I pull it open, and nothing could prepare me for what looks back at me. "What the actual fuck?" I drag out each syllable, while my eyes scan the room.

"Dude," Jagger says, "this is unreal."

"This definitely isn't a Blue Blood," Neo chimes in, picking up article after article, picture after picture.

Pointing my flashlight in front of me, I take in the collage of pictures, newspaper clippings, and notes that covers two entire walls. They date back to the early 1900s, hung in sequential order, all the way up to...

I pull down a note dated from last week and read it out loud:

They promoted Scarlett Sunder to an Ace because of her inside affiliation with the Lawless. She doesn't deserve it. All she deserves is a six-foot hole in the ground, and that's even generous for a dirty Blue Blood.

"Holy shit," Neo says, grabbing my attention. I fold the note up and stuff it in my pocket, then follow his voice to where he went. "You guys have to fucking see this."

With my light held out, I follow his line of sight inside the large closet—or small room—he entered.

I gasp when I look inside. Every bone in my body aches, intending to break someone else's. My heart pounds. My jaw tics.

"Son of a bitch!"

Jagger and Neo scope out the room while I tear down more than a dozen pictures of Scar, one by one.

"Whoever this is, they are fucking obsessed with our girl," Jagger says, walking along the walls and taking it all in.

"Obsessed doesn't even begin to describe this shrine. This creep has been watching her for years. Two, maybe three?" Neo stops at a picture of Scar and Maddie, he swipes it, and I turn my head, using my peripheral vision to see that he quickly stuffs it in the pocket of his BCA jacket.

"Who in the hell would do this?" Jagger asks, shaking his head in the same state of disbelief I'm in.

"I don't know. But we're gonna fucking find out," I tell him. "And when we do, he'll get his own six-foot hole, if we decide to even do him that service."

The End.

Book Two, Vicious Lies is available now!

ALSO BY RACHEL LEIGH

Bastards of Boulder Cove

Book One: Savage Games

Book Two: Vicious Lies

Book Three: Twisted Secrets

Wicked Boys of BCU (Coming March 2023)

Book One: We Will Reign

Book Two: You Will Bow

Book Three: They Will Fall

Redwood Rebels Series

Book One: Striker

Book Two: Heathen

Book Three: Vandal

Book Four: Reaper

Redwood High Series

Book One: Like Gravity

Book Two: Like You

Book Three: Like Hate

Fallen Kingdom Duet

His Hollow Heart & Her Broken Pieces

Black Heart Duet

Four & Five

Standalones

Guarded

Ruthless Rookie

Devil Heir

All The Little Things

Claim your FREE copy of Her Undoing!

About the Author

Rachel Leigh is a USA Today bestselling author of new adult and contemporary romance with a twist. You can expect bad boys, strong heroines, and an HEA.

Rachel lives in leggings, overuses emojis, and survives on books and coffee. Writing is her passion. Her goal is to take readers on an adventure with her words, while showing them that even on the darkest days, love conquers all.

www.rachelleighauthor.com
Rachel's Ramblers Readers Group

ACKNOWLEDGMENTS

Thank you for reading Savage Games. I hope you enjoyed the beginning of the series. I want to give a big thank you to everyone who helped me along the way. My alpha reader, Amanda and my beta readers, Erica and Brittni. Candi Kane PR, thank you for all you've done to help me promote and get the word out. My amazing PA, Carolina for all you do. Thanks to Rebecca at Rebecca's Fairest Reviews and Editing for another amazing edit and proofread, as well as Rumi for proofreading. To my street team, the Rebel Readers, I love you all so much and I'm so grateful for all you do. Thanks to The Pretty Little Design Co. for this amazing cover! And to all my Ramblers, thanks for being on this journey with me. xoxo-Rachel

Printed in Great Britain
by Amazon

19042632R00185